A Lady's Unexpected Chı

A Clean Regency Romance Novel

Amanda Stones

Copyright © 2024 by Amanda Stones
All Rights Reserved.
This book may not be reproduced or transmitted in any form without the written permission of the publisher. In no way is it legal to reproduce, duplicate, or transmit any part of this document in either electronic means or in printed format. Recording of this publication is strictly prohibited and any storage of this document is not allowed unless with written permission from the publisher.

Table of Contents

Prologue 4
Chapter 1 7
Chapter 2 14
Chapter 3 20
Chapter 4 27
Chapter 5 34
Chapter 6 44
Chapter 7 52
Chapter 8 59
Chapter 9 65
Chapter 10 73
Chapter 11 80
Chapter 12 87
Chapter 13 92
Chapter 14 99
Chapter 15 107
Chapter 16 114
Chapter 17 121
Chapter 18 128
Chapter 19 135
Chapter 20 143
Chapter 21 149
Chapter 22 152
Chapter 23 159

Chapter 24	165
Chapter 25	171
Epilogue	178
EXTENDED EPILOGUE	181

Prologue

Summer, 1810

Addy Fawcett barely managed to suppress a laugh as she focused on her target across the lawn, tightly clutching the slingshot she'd borrowed from James. He was none the wiser of course, just as oblivious as Alistair Dowden, the prig her brother called his best friend.

The two of them stood chatting together by the fountain in the garden of Fairfield Manor. They were evidently trying to hide from her, but they could try all they liked. She'd found them, and now, she'd enact her revenge.

And what better target than Alistair, with his priggish starched shirts and breeches, his perfectly coiffed hair, his spotless hose? A giggle rose in Addy's throat as she crouched in the brambles, which provided the perfect concealment. She could be a soldier in the king's guard—she was meant to, Addy was certain. She'd perfected her silent walk, and loved to blend in, especially when she needed to steal a biscuit from Cook, or spy on her brother and his misdoings.

She grasped the slingshot, lifting it and peering through the twin prongs to ensure she'd hit her target. And James thought she'd be a poor shot. No, she could shoot as well as any man. And she'd prove it now. Biting her lip, she closed one eye, holding her breath as she took aim. The cherry lodged in the sling would make the perfectly round. And what pleasure it would give her to see priggish Alistair Dowden with a blood-red stain upon his crisp white shirtfront. His mama would have fit.

Addy released the slingshot and watched, delighted as it sailed through the air and hit its mark. Alistair let out a cry of dismay and whirled towards her, his blue eyes flashing into her brown ones. *Oh heavens, he's seen me!*

"Addy!" he roared. "You little—you little hellion!"

Addy shot to her feet, heart pounding. She'd not been as well-hidden as she hoped. She needed to run, fast.

Luckily, she was the fastest girl in the countryside. She leapt to her feet and sprinted across the lawn, hoping to reach the main path leading back to the house and find a good hiding spot. But Alistair caught up to her in no time at all. Of course, he had the advantage of long, grasshopper-like legs. And it didn't help that her foot caught on a root in the grass and she toppled to the ground.

"James, you ought to control your sister," Alistair shouted over his shoulder, looming over her.

James' laughter floated to them across the lawn. "You know as well as I do that to do so would be an impossibility."

Alistair had never looked so angry before, though the sternness written across his features was nothing new. He always looked so stern and serious. Stiff. His face was as red as the cherry juice on his clothes.

Addy could not stifle the explosion of laughter that tore from her throat as she stared at the vivid cherry juice that stained his shirtfront.

"When will you learn to behave like a proper young lady, Adelaide?" he demanded, glaring. His words stung her, though she'd die before she let him see that.

"I shall do so when you learn how to stop being a stuffy old bore." She lifted her chin defiantly and watched as Alistair's face darkened.

"If by old you mean *mature*, then I will not argue that. There is nothing *dull* about wisdom," he told her, narrowing his eyes.

"Ha!" Addy rolled her eyes, scrambling to her feet. "An old history book would be more riveting than you."

Something like hurt flashed across Alistair's eyes, and for a moment, Addy wondered if she'd gone too far. But then, his lip curled into a sneer. "At least I'm more refined than a stable hand. I couldn't say the same for you."

Addy's mouth fell open and she balled her hands into fists. Yes, that was it. Tonight, she'd leave some cherries on his seat at dinner and watch as he *sat* on them. With relish.

But before she could voice this threat, James stepped behind Alistair, clamping a hand on his shoulder. "Don't pay her any mind. She's but a silly little goose. And stop tormenting our guest, Addy. Or Mother will be sure to hear of it."

"You wouldn't!" Addy shrieked.

"If you continue to torment Alistair, then perhaps I will."

"He makes it so wonderfully easy," Addy muttered, folding her arms and glaring at the both of them.

Alistair began to fuss over the growing stain on his starched shirt. "I pity the gentleman who will be forced to tame you, Adelaide Fawcett."

Addy's heart began to pound, anger rushing through her veins. She was probably red now as well. She couldn't help but shout. "And *I* pity the lady who must endure your company." Alistair's eyes went wide at her outburst and James flashed her an exasperated look.

"Come, you can change into one of my shirts," he told Alistair.

As they together started walking towards the large double doors that led from the gardens into Fairfield Manor, Addy stared after them, her vision blurring with unbidden tears. She could leave some cherries on his seat at dinner, but then Mother would be furious with her. At least she'd succeeded in today's ambush.

Yet…why wasn't it giving her the rush of triumph she'd hoped for? She'd forced that stuffy Alistair to notice her, after all. She ought to be rejoicing, but instead, she couldn't shake the sense of regret that gnawed in the pit of her stomach. He'd certainly noticed her, but his words echoed through her head in a constant stream. *I pity the gentleman who will be forced to tame you, Adelaide Fawcett.*

She straightened her shoulders, clenching her jaw. *Nobody shall ever tame me, Alistair Dowden.* Least of all, *someone like you. No matter how lovely your blue eyes are, or how handsome your absurd face is.*

Chapter 1

1818
Fairfield Manor

Addy was flying. Yes, flying. At least, it seemed like that each and every time she rode her beloved Ares, the most beautiful horse east of London. Father would have a conniption, but Adelaide released her reins and stretched out her arms, closing her eyes. She trusted Ares wholeheartedly, that she would guide her across the meadows on hooves that scarcely touched the ground, that she would be perfectly safe without keeping hold of the reins.

And now, Addy soared. At least, she pretended she was. Like the sparrows across the sky overhead, like the falcons swooping over a glassy sea.

Her lungs seemed as though they might burst with exhilaration, her heart thudding heavy in her ears, as she relished the way the wind rushed through her dark curly hair. The cold air stung her face, but she didn't mind.

At last, she opened her eyes as Ares slowed, tossing his head, silky chestnut-brown mane flowing out. A more majestic horse didn't exist.

Ares' sides heaved as he slowed to a trot across the remainder of the meadow, and Addy lifted her eyes to the treetops, over which a plume of smoke rose from Fairfield Manor's chimneys.

She didn't want to exhaust Ares though. Slipping out early this morning, she had gone for a ride before Mother awoke and tried to intervene—or, at the very least, insist she ride side-saddle. Mother would likely be displeased that Addy had been out riding for so long. It was a wonder she hadn't sent a servant to fetch her. Addy, however, usually chose different routes to avoid just that.

She stroked Ares' lathered side, murmuring to him that he was the best horse in all of England. She told him this after every ride, for he was in fact the best. She believed it wholeheartedly.

Addy guided him down the woodland path towards Fairfield Manor until she at last reached the clearing where the Fawcett plot began. Guiding Ares to the stable, she dismounted and began to unsaddle him, handing the bridle, reins and saddle to a stable hand before starting to brush him down.

He drank water and munched on oats as Addy ran the brush over his sweaty coat.

This had to be one of her favourite parts of the day, a moment of calm before returning to her mother, to the crush of societal expectations that some days made Addy feel as though she were being smothered.

A stable handled Ares back to his stall, with promises to Addy that he'd feed the horse several apples as a treat. And just like that, her favourite time of the day ended. Addy paused at the pond in the gardens to check her appearance.

She wasn't surprised to see how much of a mess her curly hair had become, and with a small sigh, she realised that someone in the family was bound to see her. After all, the house had to be up by now. She took pains to comb her fingers through her hair to somehow tame her hair. Her cheeks needed no pinching, rosy from the biting air. It would just have to do. She straightened and turned. Her heart dropped when she spotted the familiar figure of her mother on the terrace, obviously watching her, a frown creasing her forehead.

Addy sighed and hurried across the lawn to the stone steps. Mother was a sight to behold, certainly. Her displeasure was carved across her features indisputably, and she did not return the sheepish smile Addy gave.

Pinching the bridge of her nose, Lady Fairfield made an exasperated sound. "Adelaide, I do not know what I am meant to do with you. God," she raised her eyes to the heavens, "Grant me the patience to manage this daughter *you've* given me."

Addy sailed forward, but her mother snatched her wrist before she could slip indoors. "Your hair is a *horror*, Adelaide." She still refused to call her Addy. Even after all these years. No matter if Addy hated her given name. It was so pretentious.

"Good morning, Mother," she called over her shoulder, rolling her eyes to the ceiling.

"Why was I granted such a daughter," Mother whispered, loudly. She'd wanted Addy to hear that. They hurried into the drawing room as Mother droned on. "You've been neglecting your embroidery and pianoforte abominably. Why on earth did your father purchase a pianoforte if you never meant to use it."

"I did not ask for it," Addy replied, flinging herself upon the sofa. "And Ares needed his daily exercise."

Mother held up a finger, wagging it. "I never said that you were not to ride. I simply cannot abide how you do so without a *thought* for appearances."

"Are you distressing our mother again, Addy?" James' voice rang out just then, and distracted Mother from her lecture, thankfully. James and Father entered the drawing room, James casting Addy a critical look that she didn't miss.

"She is distressing herself." Addy sat up, combing her fingers through her unruly hair.

"Myself!" Mother's eyes went wide, her voice pitching up shrilly. "Says the young woman who cares nothing for the nerves of her mother and father."

James and Father exchanged glances, as if to say, "Ah! Here we go again!"

"May!" Mother called for their housekeeper. "Tea!"

Addy stared out the window gloomily. Perhaps she should have just kept riding and never returned.

"Richard writes that Agatha has requested to rent their neighborhood staff for their Christmas party this year. I'm afraid they're going to outdo themselves," Father declared, packing snuff into his pipe by the mantle.

"You know Agatha. She is most eager to see her Eloise married. The poor girl is as shy as a mouse." Mother cast Addy a pointed look. "But at least she does not shame her family by flying about the countryside like some sort of barbarian on horseback."

"Ares needed to be exercised," Addy retorted, leaping off the settee. She walked over to the window to stare out at the lawn. A storm threatened, the sky overhead heavy with rain—or snow. She hoped for snow. Perhaps she could convince James to have a snow fight with her, like in old times. Though it would send Mother into a conniption.

"You know, your aunt writes that she has someone who she thinks would suit you very well Adelaide," Mother called to her as she rose to fetch her embroidery hoop.

Addy grimaced at the window pane. "Oh, joy."

"There is no need for that sardonic tone, my dear. You are twenty years of age, and it is high time you settle down with a respectable gentleman and begin a family of your own. You are in great danger of becoming a spinster, I fear."

Addy stiffened. Her mother would never let a year go by without warning her of the horrors of spinsterhood. She tried to ignore these remonstrances, but all the same, her chest tightened with apprehension.

But she would not marry simply for the sake of marrying. It would be an affront to everything, to her ideals, and the deep-seated resolve to marry for nothing less than love. To marry for anything else would be a horror.

"Addy," Father's gentle voice caught her attention, and some of her irritation melted. "Your aunt tells me that the young man in question is a remarkable fellow. She is certain that the two of you may enjoy one another's company greatly. He is a great rider, I've heard."

He's just trying to placate me. He does detest when Mother and I quarrel.

She cast him a weak smile, before turning back to watch a pair of sparrows soar through the sky, twirling about each other midair before plummeting ground-ward.

It was exhilarating to watch, and for a moment, she imagined herself and a young man riding together, soaring across fields and heather in tandem. To find someone who matched her heart, who shared her love of adventure...that would be a wonder beyond words.

"I believe his name is Lord Sebastian Badley. Agatha declares in her letter that he is a most remarkable fellow, and seeks to make a name for himself in London, in Parliament."

"Parliament?" Addy raised an eyebrow, watching as the sparrows vanished into the forest. *A politician?* She tried to picture what it would mean, to be wed to a politician. Perhaps exciting, exhilarating.

If he enjoyed travel, then even better. But she wouldn't give Mother the satisfaction of interest in Aunt Agatha's matchmaking schemes. She'd tried before, twice, with the blandest men in all of England. And as much as she detested bringing Father any pain or worry, she would not let herself be entrapped in marriage for anything less than love.

"Well," James rose, joining his father at the fireplace. "I pity whoever is brave enough to marry our Adelaide. She is a force to be reckoned with."

Mother huffed out a laugh at that, and Addy turned to shoot her brother a glare. He grinned at her, affection in his gaze, and she fought a grin of her own. Somehow, she could never stay cross with him, despite his teasing. "This Badley will never know a moment's peace with Addy as his bride."

"I could say the same about the young lady who wins your affections," she retorted, leaving the window to return to the settee.

But that evening, she was restless and considered sneaking out to the stable to go on another ride in the icy moonlight. She would catch her death if she did and send Mother into a fit. So she stayed put in her bedroom, wearing invisible trails into her floor as she paced back and forth before the blazing fire in her hearth.

Perhaps, she could convince Father to give her a year to travel, just as he'd given James. Of course, when she'd asked before, Mother had convinced Father to decline the request. "When she is wed, her husband may take her travelling anywhere she likes. But we would merely be rewarding her for her tomfoolery."

Perhaps this Lord Badley enjoyed travel as much as Addy did. She would find out soon enough.

At last weary, she sank down into the armchair in front of her bedroom's fireplace, just as the door flew open and her maid, Gemma, hastened. On her heels, Cushing, one of the footmen, carried Addy's trunk.

After Cushing set down the trunk for Gemma, the young maid began to go through her wardrobe to begin packing for the annual trip to Aunt Agatha and Uncle Richard's for their famous Christmas party. They were about half a day away by carriage.

Addy roused from her chair and crossed the room to perch on the edge of the bed, watching as Gemma chose dresses likely selected by Mother. She watched glumly, leaning her head against the bedpost.

Mother had chosen all of Addy's most fetching gowns, notably her red silk that complemented Addy's dark hair and eyes, as well as her rosy cheeks. "Did Mother say when we would be leaving?" she inquired of Gemma.

"Tomorrow morning, ma'am," Gemma replied, eyeing her with a touch of sympathy. She was no stranger to Addy's grievances or her conflict with her mother.

Someone knocked on the bedroom door and Gemma hurried over to open it. James strolled in, sipping a glass of brandy. "Well, sister. Are you ready to be endlessly paraded before eligible bachelors by our aunt?"

Addy flopped back onto her bed with a loud sigh. "I do hope you know that you are *not* safe from Aunt Agatha's machinations."

"You know, one thing I have learned in my five and twenty years is that sometimes, the path of least resistance is simple compliance. Humor our mother and aunt, and they'll leave you be. The more you baulk, the more they'll push."

"Ah, what a grand fortune it is to be granted a sage for a brother."

"Sneer all you like. But I've found it's a proverb to live by, Addy. Let them think they're having their way, and you won't be under scrutiny."

"You wouldn't understand what it's like," Addy told him, sitting up and folding her arms. "You are a man. You have the freedom, the luxury of waiting 'till your five and *thirty* to wed, and nobody will bat an eye. But should I do the same, I will be declared a spinster, and be shunned by all of society."

"It is wonderful to see that you have not lost your flair of dramatics." James sat next to her on the edge of the bed, ignoring her scoff.

"It is true!" she cried, as Gemma continued to pack in silence behind them. "Scorn by society is always weighing over me, should I decide not to wed. I will be labeled all sorts of things if I choose to not take a husband. And—and it is not that I don't want to marry. I am merely certain that there is hardly any chance I will meet a gentleman of the right estate and title who will also be my soul's match."

"Ah, I see you've been indulging in those novels again. They fill young ladies' heads with notions of passion, mysterious strangers, and forbidden love in dark castles on windswept moors.

"You sound precisely like Vicar Moreland," Addy sniffed. "And no, I am not so foolish as to imagine that love and marriage ought to be like something out of a novel." Under her breath, she couldn't help but add, "Though, it wouldn't be such a dreadful thing."

"Ah! I knew it! You've got this notion that you are meant to find your true love in some monastery."

"I *knew* you took my copy of *The Monk*," Addy cried, leaping to her feet.

"Of course I didn't," James retorted, though the corner of his mouth twitched.

"You did! And you left it out in plain sight, and Mother burned it in the hearth the moment she discovered it."

"Fine. I did borrow it. Several fellows at Oxford were speaking of it, and I was…I was intrigued."

There was another knock on the door, and Mother poked her head in. "Children, we depart for Worthington Manor bright and early tomorrow morn. At half past eight. Do *not* oversleep."

"We shan't, Mother," James called sweetly.

Addy flopped back again onto the goose-feather mattress, closing her eyes and groaning. Dread cinched tight in her chest.

Chapter 2

Dowden Manor

Alistair Dowden pressed his aching head into his palm as he studied the estate ledgers. Running his finger down the page, he calculated in his head the amount it cost to pay the staff at Dowden Manor. A hefty sum, though necessary. Next line…he ran his forefinger down the page, before reaching over to bring the taper a little closer to the book. It was already well past nightfall, and he had no idea how long he'd been in here, poring over these pages. But if he didn't do it, who would? And he couldn't let Dowden Manor fall into disarray.

Tomorrow, he'd have a word with his father's estate manager, and ask him if anything could be done to reduce expenses. If he hoped to keep Dowden Manor in good standing, he would need to focus on keeping a close eye on these ledgers.

Perhaps it was excessive, to take such measures, but Alistair would not forgive himself if the estate came to ruin on account of his own lack of care. He would not live in the shadow of a legacy clouded by unmet expectations. And the thought of Father, watching him fail…it turned Alistair's stomach.

A light knock on the door pulled his attention from the book in front of him, to find his mother, Rosalind, hovering in the doorway, her slate-blue eyes filled with concern. "Have you slept at all, my dear?" she inquired, advancing across the room to stand beside his desk.

"Not yet, Mamma," he replied, managing a slight smile.

"You will make yourself ill," she sighed, shaking her head.

"Someone needs to tend to these ledgers." Alistair leaned back in his chair as his mother patted his shoulder. "But I'll end for the night soon. What time is it?"

"Nearly midnight," Rosalind murmured. "What did I do to deserve such a son as you?" she caressed his cheek gently, shaking her head. "You must know your father would be most proud of you."

Alistair let out a humorless laugh. "Our villagers turned a smaller crop this year than last. The ledgers say it all." He tossed his quill down on the book, rubbing the bridge of his nose again, before removing his spectacles and placing them on the desk. If he kept up nights like this, he'd need to wear them all the time.

"We are to leave for Worthington Manor in but a few days' time. Do you think you can tear yourself away from all of this for Lord and Lady Worthington's Christmas party?"

Alistair swallowed down a groan at the sight of his mother's hopeful expression. She'd been looking forward to this party for the past several months since receiving the invitation back in October. She'd been especially lonely as of late since Belinda married and moved several counties over. Her spirits had been low over the past few months, and he despised the idea of disappointing her.

She could scarcely keep the excitement from her tone. He took a deep breath and nodded.

"But of course, Mother. I wouldn't think of missing it," he told her.

She beamed, clasping her hand and pecking him on the cheek. "I shall tell Carson to set about packing your trunk then. And I have a special something for you. Consider it an early Christmas present."

Alistair made a show of flipping through the ledgers. "I suppose I should make a line in here for Christmas presents, then."

Rosalind laughed, shaking her head. "Don't worry, you shall be able to make good use of it in a few days' time. I will have it packed away in your trunk."

He picked up his quill to resume his work, but Rosalind brought him up short when she said, "Do you remember the Fawcetts? You were very good friends with their boy—James? They will be in attendance at the party, I am told. They are relations of the Worthingtons."

Alistair's smile flagged, but he could not be faulted for it. Truly.

In his mind's eye, he glimpsed a younger version of himself, in the gardens at Fairfield estate. And Adelaide stood before him, hands on her hips, her dark curls untamed, her eyes flashing. Her eyes had always flashed, with defiance, with fury, with something wild that always lurked just beneath the surface.

They'd always been arguing about something, but in this particular memory, he recalled how they'd been quarreling about whether it was better to maintain decorum, or to freely speak one's mind. Of course, Adelaide had declared she should be able to speak freely if it was called for, never mind decorum. Alistair might have conceded if it weren't for the fact that it was *Adelaide* espousing this position. Her mocking voice had needled him, and his irritation flared. There was no chance he'd concede to her.

And of course, there was James, trying to keep the peace. He'd always sought to intervene when Alistair and Adelaide—*Addy*—quarreled about this and that. And yes, they'd always been going at it. Of course, he'd valued his friendship with James, but Adelaide had always seemed intent upon tormenting him, getting a rise out of him. She usually succeeded, if he were to be honest.

But that was years ago. He'd been a boy, she'd been a girl. He hoped she had given up being such a disruptive young lady, but he doubted it. It was as ingrained in her nature as was his tendency for…priggishness. She'd loved calling him a prig, he recalled. Just the memory stirred renewed irritation towards her.

"Ah, well, it will be quite nice to see James again." *I can hardly say the same about that sister of his.*

"Speaking of the party," Rosalind's expression into something almost sheepish. "The Ashworths shall be in attendance as well."

"The Ashworths?" Alistair nearly sighed but swallowed it at his mother's eager expression.

"That Cordelia Ashworth is a delightful girl. Do you remember her? We met them in town this summer."

"Ah. Indeed, I do recall." Though, he truly didn't—at least not much. The last several months blurred together. *Is it really December already?*

"She is a beauty, and quite accomplished. Her parents, the Baron and Baroness of Ashford, are highly admired in society."

Alistair kept his smile pasted on, twisting his quill between his fingers as apprehension sent his stomach churning. Rosalind had only somewhat subtly persisted in bringing up Cordelia Ashworth in conversation since they'd first met her in the summer. She might be a sweet girl, but he could not say he was particularly intrigued or attracted. And now, his mother hoped to play the matchmaker between him and the girl.

Of course, Cordelia was everything a young lady ought to be. Decorous, modest, gentle. Yet…something lacked. It was not her fault whatsoever, but his own. He told himself it was simply the strain of managing the estate—how Father managed it all those years so effortlessly was beyond him.

Rosalind pecked a kiss on his cheek and hurried out, reminding him over her shoulder to get some rest.

Alistair did sleep, eventually. But at his desk. When he woke, he was stiff and groaned as he rose and stretched before walking over to the commode and splashing water into the porcelain bowl. Early morning sunlight glowed into the study.

He washed his face and gazed out the window as a falcon soared across the pale sky, and he caught his breath. A ride would do him good this morning, or at the very least, he would welcome the solace he found in tending his stallion, Apollo.

After drying his face, he slipped out of the study, the entirety of Dowden Manor quiet, still. But faintly, he could hear the servants stirring downstairs in the kitchens.

He strode out a side door that opened upon a path leading to the stables and could not help but sigh with relief as he reached them. He entered Apollo's stall and began to brush him, stroking the beast's neck and giving its muzzle a pat. Pulling an apple from his pocket, he let Apollo eat it from his palm and tried to forget the pressures of running his father's legacy. It was easier said than done, of course.

"What do you say to a ride about the country," he murmured to Apollo.

Instead of calling one of the hands, he saddled the horse himself, sliding on the bridle and securing the girth-strap. Then, he was ready for a ride. But the morning was bitterly cold, the chill biting deeper now that December had settled in. He sent a hand in for his coat as he finished up readying Apollo, his face stinging from the winter chill.

Once he'd received his coat and donned it, he pulled himself up into the saddle and set off on his ride through the frost-covered heather. The rising sunlight set everything a-sparkle, and he caught his breath as he took in the beauty of it all. A guilty thought stole through his mind—what he wouldn't give for a chance to steal away from the duty of running the estate, just for a time—just for a chance to travel, perhaps. See the Alps or Mont Blanc. Or he could visit Spain, even. He would welcome the reprieve.

Heaving a sigh, he chastised himself inwardly. Even if the opportunity did present itself, he could not in good conscience simply abandon his duty to his father's estate. Duty, after all, was his father's motto, if mottos could be but one word. It was something he'd instilled in Alistair's very being, that one's duty was paramount to all else.

Patting Apollo's neck, he urged the horse into a canter down the dirt road and off onto a quieter side road that wound through the countryside. It was lined by poplars and beeches, and it was wonderful to escape the confines of the office, stretch his muscles and feel the wind against his face.

These rides alone were his solace. Guilt pricked in him again as he gave Apollo a tap against his sides to urge him on faster. At last, he reached his favourite place, a giant oak that spread its boughs far and wide on a slight crest. He was afforded a good look at the country, at his father's land, from the Dowdenshire village to the manor itself.

Once he tied Apollo's reins to a low-hanging branch, he walked to the tree trunk and leaned against it, pulling his pipe from his pocket and lighting it. The plume of smoke lit in the silver-and-gold light of dawn, and he exhaled it in a long breath, grateful for the tobacco's calming effect.

If he had to name his vices, he would say smoking his pipe, and perhaps his inflexibility. He did not need Adelaide Fawcett to point the latter out, certainly. He was more than aware of it. Would he be so fortunate to endure her cutting mockery this Christmas? He prayed not. Perhaps she would be wed by now, off gallivanting with her husband, and he could enjoy a peaceful holiday, catching up with James and reminiscing about old times.

Alistair drew again on his pipe, closing his eyes as the tobacco smoke burned through his lungs. Of course, there would be Cordelia Ashworth. There was no doubt that Rosalind Dowden would attempt to pair him with the girl. And who knew how many other matrons would attempt to foist their daughters upon him?

Another memory flickered through his head, of his visit years ago to Fairfield, the country parties, the cricket games on the lawn. Adelaide's cutting wit might tickle other gentlemen, but for whatever reason, she'd always counted Alistair as her special target.

Grimacing, he snuffed out his pipe and pushed it into his pocket, grasping Apollo's reins to remount him. Giving him a light nudge, he urged the horse into a gallop and flew across the meadow. On his way back to Dowden Manor, he rode through the village, with its bustling inhabitants already stirring for the day.

From the rectory to the pub, everything was under his management, and it pleased him to see the townspeople of Dowdenshire flourishing, despite the poor crops this year. Children raced each other about the streets, and many waved to him, greeting him blithely.

Already, wreaths and ribbons decorated the village, lending a festive air to the place, and carolers stood before the church, warbling merrily like a flock of songbirds. The vicar and his wife greeted Alistair as he rode into the churchyard.

"Well, well, if it isn't our young Lord Dowden," said Vicar Kent with a smile, lifting his hat for Alistair.

"We hear from your mother that you are departing for Christmas. For Worthington Manor. Their Christmas parties are quite illustrious, so I've heard," Mrs. Kent remarked.

"Indeed. My mother is most eager to attend."

"Mayhap we shall hear of a new Lady Dowden when the new year comes around?" Mrs. Kent beamed.

"Mayhap," Alistair forced a grin, and Vicar Kent let out a hearty chuckle, slapping Alistair's leg so hard he nearly winced.

Wheezing, the portly vicar shook his head. "No doubt of it! You are a capital young man, exactly like your father. The very spitting image, isn't that so, my dear?"

"Oh, without question," Mrs. Kent clasped her hands. "The very likeness of the late Lord of Dowdenshire."

"When do you and your mother depart?" Vicar Kent inquired.

"In two days' time. We shall be away but a fortnight. Upon our return, it would please my mother and me greatly to host you both for dinner at Dowden Manor in the new year."

"But certainly," Mrs. Kent cried. "We should be delighted."

Alistair tipped his hat to them and rode on, up the winding road back towards Dowden Manor. He would endure this party and the solicitations by his mother and likely the other mothers and aunts and busybodies who would endeavour to match him with a prospective bride. He would endure it, if only to bring a smile back to his mother's face.

Chapter 3

Addy stared up at the majestic edifice that was Worthington Manor, an almost gothic structure, situated beside a glassy pond so still, it seemed almost mirror-like, with lily pads decorating its surface. It had been a year since her last visit for her aunt and uncle's annual Christmas party. And already, she missed Ares terribly.

She was permitted to ride one of her uncle's horses, certainly, but here, Mother kept a close eye on her, as if fearing that Adelaide would do or say something to mortify her in front of Aunt Agatha. Mother was always worried about being embarrassed in front of Aunt Agatha.

And Addy couldn't count on her hands the number of times she'd done or said something to send Aunt Agatha into a conniption, to Mother's horror.

Uncle Richard and Aunt Agatha might already have a daughter of their own, but still, they seemed intent upon acting as secondary parents to Addy and James. They did not shy from sharing their opinions on how Addy and James lived, their education, their debut seasons, and now, their marriage partners.

Aunt Agatha had tried tirelessly to arrange matches between various people she thought would suit Addy and James, both as far as station and prestige. James had even nearly been betrothed to one girl whom Aunt Agatha selected for him. The girl was handpicked, nearly, from one of England's finest finishing schools, until the girl ended up disgracing herself with a soldier in Bath.

For a time, Aunt Agatha had been cowed by this travesty, but she did not let it dampen her ambitions as a matchmaker for long.

As was evident this year.

During the carriage ride, Mother had heralded James and Addy with details about the individuals their aunt had found for them on her travels. Of course, there was Lord Badley for Addy. Mother's eyes gleamed when she mentioned him.

And for James, a Miss Scott of London. She came from a prestigious family, one of the oldest in London. Her great-grandfather, Duke Simeon Scott, who was also a respected member of the House of Commons, was a figure of great distinction in London society.

Addy couldn't resist giving James a playful kick beneath the carriage seat. She fought a grin as, from the corner of her eye, she watched his jaw clench.

"Do you suppose we are the first guests to arrive?" Mother murmured anxiously as she peered out the carriage window at her sister's manor. She fluttered her hands with excitement, and for a moment, Addy could almost believe the old bat had once been a fun-loving girl. Not a grim biddy who lambasted her daughter with antiquated ideals about propriety this and that.

Father patted Mother on the arm, casting Addy a knowing smile. "Now, now, my dear. Settle...the party is not going to start without you."

Mother huffed. "Of course, it isn't. It wouldn't." With that, she sailed out of the carriage to greet her sister and brother-in-law, and their daughter Eloise, on the steps.

Addy followed reluctantly, dragging her feet a little, and braced for the inevitable barbed comment that Aunt Agatha would send her way. Something about her hair, perhaps, or her dress being rather light for her complexion. Something along those lines.

When she paused in front of Aunt Agatha and Uncle Richard, she forced a bright smile and curtseyed.

"Well, Adelaide. I do not know if your mother has told you, but we have found a marvellous suitor for you."

"She had certainly told me," Addy kept her smile pasted on, but couldn't help glancing towards Eloise Wortham, her rather shy cousin, who hovered behind Uncle Richard.

Eloise fought a smile as well, lifting her eyebrows in a silent apology.

Addy pecked kisses on both her aunt's cheeks and then moved forward to greet her uncle. Richard Wortham barely smiled ever, but he gave Addy a wry smile. If it weren't for Aunt Agatha and her scheming, Addy might actually enjoy her visits to Worthington. She and Eloise got along well, and Uncle Richard always had a joke up his sleeve.

Eloise pulled her into a tight hug once Addy had finished greeting Uncle Richard. Though she spoke little, Eloise still managed to say a great deal with her large hazel eyes. She and Addy dissolved into giggles, inexplainable but warming just the same. Together, they entered the house arm-in-arm, sharing commiserating looks. "Come, I know you are dying to run to the stables. To check on Pippin, your pony," Eloise whispered. "If I weren't mistaken, you are far more eager to see Pippin than any of us."

She steered Addy towards the stables, where they stopped before the old pony's stall. Addy covered her mouth, letting out a squeal that would have caused her mother to glare if she were around to hear.

"I can't believe he's still alive and kicking," Addy exclaimed, covering her mouth. "He's rather grey around the muzzle, isn't he?"

Eloise smiled, leaning against the stall post nearby. "He is. I can swear he waits for you some days. He misses you dearly."

"I miss him, too. And you of course," Addy grinned.

Eloise laughed again, and Addy laughed with her, spirit lifting. One thing she prided herself upon was being one of the few people—aside from James—to break past Eloise's usually strong reserve. She was certainly one of the quietest people Addy had met, especially around those not within her family. But with Addy and James, she was practically a different person.

"I thought the two of you would run out here," James' voice made them both turn to greet him as he strode up the path from the house.

"I was just greeting Pippin. He's gotten so fat, hasn't he?"

"Indeed he has," James raised his eyebrows as he inspected Pippin, chewing on hay nearby. "Now, what's this I hear about a Captain Crawford coming to visit? Is he truly the very same Crawford as the one at Waterloo? Uncle Richard and Father already scurried off to hunt, and our mother and yours are chattering about the lot of guests coming this year."

"He is one and the same as the hero of Waterloo. This summer, Father and I travelled to Brighton, and there we met Captain Crawford. Father and he were instant friends, and he accepted Father's invitation to our Christmas party. He would have come sooner if not for an assignment in the West Indies."

James shook his head, eyes wide with awe. "Well, then! This whole Christmas party is looking up after all. Now, I'm going to find Father and Uncle Richard and do a bit of hunting myself."

He left them to have a horse saddled and readied, and together, Eloise and Addy returned to the house.

"Come, I'm sure your things are in your room by now. You're just across the hall from me," Eloise told her. It didn't take long to reach upstairs, where Eloise led Addy to her designated bedroom. In past years, she'd been relegated to another room down the hall, but at last, Eloise had managed to orchestrate it so that they would be neighbours. This would allow for more late-night chats without disturbing the rest of the house.

Gemma had already laid out Addy's dinner clothes, which she changed into behind a paper room divider. Eloise perched on her bed and informed her of who else would be attending this year. "The Scotts are to be in attendance," she began. "Mother is quite pleased to have secured their acceptance. As you know, they are the Viscount and Viscountess of Scotfell. Naturally, she has turned her thoughts to their daughter, Miss Serena Scott, as a match for James."

"So, I've heard." Addy emerged from behind the divider, now clothed in her evening gown. She took a seat at the vanity, where Gemma began to arrange her hair, crimping the locks around her face as was the fashion.

"The Baron of Ashford and his wife and daughter shall join us, the Ashworths. Cordelia Ashworth is very sweet, very kindly and pleasant."

"Well, I am eager to make her acquaintance," Addy said, smiling at her cousin in the mirror. After a moment's pause, she asked, "Can you tell me more of this Lord Badley?"

"Well, he is very handsome. Tall. Formidable. He comes from a long line of parliament members, and I understand that he shares the same ambitions as his forebearers."

"Don't you think one can be rather too ambitious?"

"I suppose if one were less handsome and of noble blood, it would be less of a virtue. But Badley has taken London by storm, so I hear. And yet, he is very careful about whom he intends to wed. He has courted half-a-dozen ladies, and yet none have come to an understanding. Mother hopes he will court either you or me."

"Ah, so we are to be rivals," Addy laughed. "Does she mean for us to duel to the death for Badley's hand?"

"Oh, Addy, how I've missed you. Your wit is as sharp as ever."

"Much to my own mother's dismay. And I must say, I hardly think that a gentleman of Badley's disposition or ambitions shall much care for a girl who speaks her mind, who is less than demure in society. But you," Addy rose, crossing the room to grasp Eloise's hand. "You will dazzle him. With your mysterious quietude, your quizzical expressions..."

Eloise burst out laughing, shaking her head. "Oh Addy, you and your teasing!" Her expression turned serious then, and she grasped Addy's other hand, fixing her with a pointed look. "Now, you must promise not to go mad when I tell you this, but Mother has also invited Viscount Lord Dowden and his mother, Lady Dowden."

Addy stared. "You don't mean—you can't possibly mean—"

"Yes, one and the same as James' schoolmate and friend."

Addy let out a shriek, closing her eyes tightly. "You don't mean it!"

When she opened them, Eloise was clearly fighting a grin. "I do."

"Eloise," Addy wrung her hands, "Alistair Dowden is the greatest stick in the mud of all the sticks to exist in this world."

Eloise choked on a laugh.

"All he seems to excel at is disapproving of everyone and everything he sees. I cannot bear him. I wish you had not told me, so I could have but a little longer to enjoy peace. This party will be abominable enough, with your mother and her matchmaking. But *Alistair?*"

"Oh Addy, perhaps he is changed."

"Changed? He is as fussy as an old woman, and as priggish as my mother. That cannot be changed. Tell me he is wed? Though, I pity the girl who weds him."

Eloise folded her arms, raising an eyebrow. "I think that you are merely dismayed because he wounded your pride. Especially since when he first arrived with James, you found him...handsome."

"I was a foolish child. And I knew nothing!"

Eloise smiled. "Well, in answer to your question, he is not attached to anyone. At least, I understand he is not. I believe that his mother and Lady Ashford both wish to see him wed Cordelia."

Something flared in Addy's chest, something she didn't know how to define exactly. "Well, I pity the girl. She will have to endure an utter prig for a husband." She flopped back onto her bed with a loud sigh, resting her arm across her flushed face.

She would never forget her dismay the first day Alistair had arrived to visit James. After dinner, he had retired to the library to read, and she'd trailed after him, peering down at him over the top of one of the bookshelves. He'd heard her footsteps, and called upon her to emerge from her hiding, so she had, rather sheepishly.

Of course, at that age, just as she still did now, she had burnt her skirts from sitting too close to the fire. And he had remarked on it as she approached, his handsome face marred by a haughty half-smile, half-scowl.

It had caused her temper to flare, and that was that. After that, he had seemed increasingly perturbed by her mere presence, and that in turn wounded her. Not that she would ever voice any of this aloud, except to Eloise, her confidante in all things. Perhaps she did find him handsome, at first. But that had been overshadowed by his prudish, rigidly moralistic nature.

"When do they arrive?" she inquired after a moment, sitting up.

"Early on the morrow, if my memory serves—that is when most everyone will be expected. And tomorrow evening, Lord Badley and Captain Crawford are meant to arrive."

"Well, this shall be a merry Christmas indeed," Addy murmured. What a gathering! She would have to spend the next fortnight enduring Alistair Dowden all over again? "Alistair is a viscount?"

Eloise hurried over to the door to return to her room, saying that she needed to ready herself for dinner as well. "His father died when he was but eighteen. Ever since, he has been the head of the Dowden estate."

Addy returned to her seat at the vanity, where Gemma continued to arrange her hair. "His father? I recall that Alistair practically worshipped the ground his father walked."

"So many men do," Eloise shrugged, before slipping out. Addy turned her gaze back to the reflection in the mirror and apprised herself for a long moment. Her hair was as curly as ever, though now tamed into a rather fetching arrangement atop her head. The tendrils about her face didn't need much crimping, as they tumbled about her cheeks and forehead all on their own, as was the fashion. She was hardly the same girl she had been, the one that Alistair likely remembered.

How long had it been since she'd last seen him? At least...six years or more. He had only visited Fairfield but twice. She turned around to inspect the back of her skirts, relieved to find they were not singed at least. Were any of her other dresses marred by her carelessness? She wanted to flounce her skirts.

Why was she worrying about such a thing? Simply because of Alistair? She would not care what he thought. Not a whit.

She was certainly taller than he remembered, though one could not describe her as tall and willowy. She was more on the short side, with curves her mother told her were fashionable, though Addy was certain her mother, for once, was just sparing her feelings. Her skin was tanner and more freckled than was fashionable, certainly, and she couldn't even count the number of times on her hands that her mother had mourned her complexion. *"You must wear a bonnet each time you go out riding!"*

Addy sighed and left her bedroom, stepping into the hall, where she met Eloise, now dressed in a beautiful seafoam gown that complemented her hazel eyes. Her hair had been arranged, and she and Addy shared a conspiratorial smile before heading downstairs to dinner. They met a servant on the way down sent to fetch them, and together they entered the fine dining room where the rest of the party waited.

Chapter 4

Alistair peered out the carriage window at the vast pond that stretched out like a glass mirror before Worthington Manor. It was a beautiful home, he had to admit, despite his general lack of interest in attending the holiday party thrown by his mother's friends.

Already, several other coaches were pulled in front of the manor's sweeping steps at the front of the house, and he could see clusters of guests before it. "The Ashworths are here, I believe," exclaimed Rosalind over his shoulder, clutching his arm excitedly.

Alistair managed a tight smile before leaning back in his seat, taking in a deep breath. This visit would be over soon enough, and he could return to Dowden estate, back to his routine, which he much preferred to the exhausting demands of society.

Rosalind gave his arm a gentle pat. "You will hardly be in want of company at the house. Your old friend James will be there, of course."

Don't be dour, he told himself. *Mother is beside herself over this party—has been for weeks, nay months. And you must not ruin it for her.*

He nodded, as the coach at last pulled to a stop at the base of the stone steps. A footman opened their door and helped Rosalind down first. She was at once greeted by Lady Worthington, while Alistair followed reluctantly, not before taking one last bracing breath. He placed his hat upon his head and descended from the coach, his body somewhat stiff from the long trip.

Rosalind began to greet the rest of the party, including the Ashworths of course, who lingered on the steps to see who the newcomers were.

And Alistair took this opportunity to observe the rest of the group. There were the Ashworths, their daughter Cordelia at her father's arm. Another family also stood there, watching their luggage get taken inside. He knew them to be the Scotts, old family friends of his parents. Their daughter Serena was quiet though smiling, a book clutched in her hand, as she listened to the conversations around her.

He did not see James amongst the party, but he did see his friend's mother, Lady Fairfield. Evidently, James, his father, and Lord Worthington had gone hunting for the day. Behind them stood Eloise Worthington, and at her side…Adelaide. Addy, as she'd always preferred to be called. He caught his breath involuntarily. She was no longer the girl he remembered.

Not a bit. No, she was a young woman now, swathed in red, her dark hair piled atop her head as was the fashion, and the look became her, Alistair noted, his stomach flipping.

Had finishing school tamed her at last? Though, he wondered if a finishing school would even take her for long.

Adelaide had been most disruptive, at least in his experience. She'd ruined a very fine shirt his mother bought him in London, and her comments had always come with barbs. She'd taken such delight in teasing him, but her tongue had been sharp, stinging. A flick on the raw.

His heart raced with dread as he mounted the steps to greet her parents next, and then turned to bow to Adelaide.

Her dark eyes flashed with that familiar defiance that he remembered so well, her lips, the colour of strawberries, parting as with a startled gasp. Surely, she must remember him as vividly as he remembered her. For a fleeting moment, he nearly addressed her by her given name, unadorned by proper title, but caught himself just in time, sparing himself the impropriety—as well as the mortification.

"Miss Fawcett," he managed, mouth dry.

"Lord Dowden," she replied, her tone as cold as the winter frost, and it pricked at his pride.

She extended her hand, and he took it lightly, bowing over her gloved fingers. With a taut smile, he released her hand and moved on, yet the warmth of her touch lingered. Try as he might, he could not shake off the sensation, and it continued to plague him as he entered the house.

***

Alistair and his mother were shown to their respective rooms upstairs, and once settled they retired to the drawing room downstairs where most of the other guests had gathered. Rosalind reached it first and he watched from the staircase as she entered the bright, festively decorated room, twisting one of the wreaths on the stairs between his fingers.

The thought of spending the afternoon with the throng of people caused his stomach to knot and twist, and he took in a deep breath, contemplating his next move. Perhaps he could slip out to the garden or the stables unnoticed, and try to find James and the rest of the party. The scent of cooking pheasant spread through the house, warm and rich, mouthwatering.

Despite the assurance he would be obliged to hob-knob that evening with the rest of the company, he did look forward to a full meal, for which the Worthingtons were evidently known, according to his mother. He heard the voices echo out into the hall where he stood, excited murmurings of a Christmas ball in two days, and his heart sank. So much for a peaceful country excursion.

With a sigh, he hurried down the rest of the staircase and slipped out the back doors leading to the terrace that led out into the gardens. The chill air kissed his face, and he was thankful he'd kept his traveller's coat on for his jaunt. He took to the hedge maze, an intricate system of pathways leading through bowers upon bowers until at last he reached its end, and then returned back through it, enjoying his solitude. He was reluctant to give it up, but he'd likely be missed by his mother if he stayed out too long. An idea occurred to him.

Perhaps, he could ask someone where James, Lord Fairfield, and Lord Worthington had gone to hunt. At least he could steer free of mindless small talk until this evening.

He would check the stables. He'd noticed them earlier as the coach rolled towards the front of the house. Perhaps a footman would know something.

As he emerged from the hedge maze, he strolled his way over to the stables, listening to the birdsong, the nightingales singing in the hedges, the hawks crying high above his head as they swooped this way and that.

At last, he reached the stables, but there was not a footman or stable hand in sight, to his disappointment. He made to exit, scanning about for a glimpse of someone to give him directions, but as he turned a corner, he collided with someone and sent this individual sprawling. It was a young woman in red...

Of course, it was Adelaide.

Her eyes widened as she stared up at him, her cheeks flushing.

"Good grief, forgive me!" he blurted and extended his hand to her to help her back to her feet. But she didn't take it, staring at his hand as if he'd just committed some sort of heinous offence. Instead, she stood, dusting off her skirts, though he wasn't sure as to why. The hem of her skirts was already covered in mud, as if she'd just trudged through a pig slough.

He was sure she had not been in such disarray earlier when he'd greeted her on the front steps.

Without thinking, he remarked, "Have you been wrestling one of your uncle's pigs?"

Her eyes widened even more, and he realised this was a mistake to say. "I see that you're still a stick in the mud," she said, lifting her chin in that defiant way of hers. He remembered it all too well.

His smile froze and then slipped from his face. He didn't bother attempting to recover it. "I did not mean to offend."

"And yet, you do it so perfectly," Adelaide retorted. "Do you practice at it?"

"No." He flashed a smile then, though there was no humour in it. If only he could think of something more clever to say. But that had never been his forte. It was hers. "If I recall correctly, you were always doing something or other to your skirts."

Her eyes flashed. "And if I recall correctly, you were always a prig."

A prig. Ah, of course. Her favourite name for him. "Good day, Miss Fawcett." He would take the high road.

He wouldn't humour her love of contention. But when he side-stepped to walk around her, she murmured, "Do take care and pray do not bore poor Miss Ashworth to death."

Alistair stopped short, his face going hot, and turned to glare at her. "And I implore you not to exasperate whichever poor fellow your parents hope to marry you off to."

She let out a disdainful laugh. "Exasperate?"

"Yes, exasperate," he wheeled about to face her, digging his nails into his palm.

"I do not exasperate anyone."

"Forgive me, but I recall you endeavouring at every turn to drive me mad when I came to Fairfield to visit your brother."

"So, you still haven't let that go?"

"Hardly! How could I? All you did was call me prig whenever you got the chance."

"Well, you are a prig," Adelaide snapped.

"Alistair?" Both of them turned to see James approach, a riding switch in his hand, a hound on his heels. "Is that really you?"

He and James embraced before the latter stepped back, shaking his head. "Heavens, I scarcely recognised you!" James glanced at Adelaide, his smile growing. "I see the two of you have reunited."

Adelaide huffed, rolling her eyes, and made as though to hurry away, but James detained her. "Tell Aunt Agatha that we've caught some more pheasant for her table this evening. She was hoping we would be able to."

Her back stiffening, Adelaide hastened on out of sight, though Alistair's heart continued to pound as he took a deep breath, relaxing his clenched hands. James turned to him, grinning, and clamped him on the shoulder firmly. "Come now," he said eagerly. "We must catch up! It has been far too long, has it not?"

Alistair managed a smile of his own at last, though in the back of his mind, Adelaide's cutting words continued to replay. *You were always a prig...*

He fought to hide a grimace, wondering if everyone saw him in that same light. It was disconcerting nonetheless, and only made him wish to avoid the rest of the week if at all possible. Of course, he did not want to be labelled an unsociable...prig. But if it meant avoiding another encounter with Adelaide...

James' voice cut into his thoughts. "What do you say we join my father and uncle in the billiard room for some brandy?"

"I—I don't take brandy." Adelaide's voice sang through his head. *Prig.* "But I should like to learn how you've been."

James didn't bat an eye at learning of Alistair's abstinence, though his smile widened. "No matter. Come." Together, they made their way slowly toward the house, still chatting, and entered through the back entrance. They wandered down the hall toward the billiard room.

As James retired to his room to change out of his riding clothes, Alistair lingered alone in the billiard room, which he found was attached to the library. It was an impressive library, certainly. One of the finest that he had seen.

The library shelves rose high above his head, and he began to peruse them thoughtfully, before rounding a corner and stopping short at an unwelcome sight and recoiling until he was sure he was out of sight.

It was Adelaide, in a big armchair, looking quite cosy with a book in her lap. From what he could tell she was reading a novel. She looked remarkably peaceful there, flipping to the next page, her cheek resting on her hand.

He peered at her through the stacks, feeling rather odd to be doing so in such a secretive manner, yet he found himself utterly fascinated.

How could such a contentious young woman appear so idyllic, so peaceable, when less than half an hour earlier, she'd been flinging barbs right and left at him? He stepped back, swallowing hard, his mouth strangely dry. With a sigh, he turned on his heel and hurried away as quickly as he could, back to the billiard room next door.

There he did his best to entertain himself until James, Lord Fairfield, and Lord Worthington arrived together in their evening dress. The butler brought a bottle of brandy and some glasses, and the other three men poured themselves generous glasses of the drink as they began a game of billiards.

They thankfully did not tease Alistair for abstaining from the drink, as so many had in London last year, when he'd gone with his mother. Instead, they plied him with questions about his journey and his doings for the past few years. Lord Ashford and Lord Scotfell joined them presently, and it wasn't long before the room filled with pipe-smoke and raucous laughter.

Alistair sat at a nearby table with James once they finished their first game, and together, they caught up on everything they'd missed of each other's lives for the past several years.

Since they'd parted ways, Alistair learned that James had taken to helping his father run their country estate, as well as their London townhouse, though the Fawcetts only infrequently visited the city. Alistair relayed to him the circumstances surrounding his father's death, the untimely heart attack, and how he'd been managing the estate ever since. "It can be quite tedious, can't it?"

Alistair wouldn't call it tedious—but the desire to live up to his father's name wore on him, more than a little. He said as much to James

"I only met your father once, but I remember him to be a fine man. His tenants have been known to speak well of your family. In fact, I wonder if ours are jealous at times, though we do our best," James smiled.

"I fear that I will disappoint them one of these days, through some oversight, or something of that nature."

"Oh, hardly. You're the most capable fellow I know."

Alistair appreciated James' comment, though lately, his struggle to keep up with all the duties and responsibilities made him wonder if he was fit for the task.

"Thank you, Fawcett," he said softly.

"Of course! To be frank, I rather dread the day my father's estate comes into my hands. I fear I shall bring everything he's built to ruin."

Alistair nearly winced. "That is something I fear myself."

"Well, I can't imagine it ever happening to someone such as yourself. Why, when we were in boarding school all those years ago, you were one of the only fellows to finish lessons quickly, and the rest of us were jealous over your capability."

"Ah, yes. I was labeled a bore by most of the fellows at the school, since I'd rather read than play a game of cricket."

James chuckled. "I truly believe that teasing was born of envy."

Alistair tried to smile. As much as he tried to forget it, the mockery from all those years ago continued to haunt him, despite his best efforts. He didn't like to think of it, but it had truly affected him, and that continued to last to this day. He overthought everything, no matter what.

He took a deep breath, trying to wrench his mind away from this train of thought.

Perhaps he should hire someone to manage the estate. Yet, his father had never done it, and he refused to as well. It just stung, to realise that he floundered where his father had flourished.

Chapter 5

The day of Aunt Agatha's famed Christmas ball dawned bright and promising, with a hint of snow. Addy awoke rather late in her vast four-poster bed, stretching her arms and yawning. Her stomach twisted at the thought of that evening, the crowd that would gather, as those invited would arrive from near and far for the party. The last two days had been strange as it was, as she'd attempted to avoid Alistair, his piercing eyes, his dismayed expression whenever he saw her.

Her bedroom doors opened and Mother rushed in, hastening to the window to throw open the curtains.

"Mother!" Addy groaned.

"Time to rise, my dear. It's nearly noon, and you must begin to ready yourself for this evening. The ball begins at *four*." Mother hurried over to where Addy lay, all warm and cosy beneath the blankets, and ripped them back.

Addy groaned louder in protest, sitting up and rubbing her eyes, her hair a tangled mass of curls.

"Now, I've let you sleep in terribly late. Do you know that Lord Badley arrived late last night? I am certain he is eager to meet you!"

"Isn't Aunt Agatha eager for him to match with Eloise as well?"

"It is his choice, is it not? Not Agatha's!" Mother snapped.

Addy stood as her mother called out for Gemma, before flinging open the wardrobe. "Red becomes you best, my dear. So I think this red silk evening gown would be just the thing for tonight. After all, I ordered it from London for just such an occasion as this."

"Yes, Mother." Addy crossed the room to splash water on her face, peering into her reflection and wincing as she found that sure enough, her hair was a horror.

"That hair of yours will take at least two hours to tame," Mother sighed from behind her, approaching to scrutinise Addy critically.

Gemma joined them at the mirror, and eyed Addy's hair as if taking in the challenge she was about to tame. "Have a seat over here, Miss Adelaide," she told Addy with a reassuring smile, that was more maternal than Mother could ever hope to be.

"Tell me more about this Lord Badley," Addy sighed

The rest of the hour flew by until Addy's hair was somewhat presentable, enough to be drawn into a neat bun atop her head. Once her hair was ready to Mother's satisfaction, Addy was allowed to join Eloise and the other girls across the hall. Gemma would put the finishing touches on her hair right before the ball began.

Addy had enjoyed getting to know Serena and Cordelia over the past two days, though Serena was considerably more interesting to converse with than Cordelia. Cordelia had no interests of her own aside from finding a suitable suitor. But Serena loved novels as much as Addy did, and she also shared Eloise's more studious interests in matters like history, and the great poets.

None of them dressed yet, but sat chatting together in Eloise's room as their maids prepared their clothes for that night, laying out each of their dresses upon the bed. Eloise would wear a deep blue dress of the finest silk. It would be a wonderful complement to her porcelain skin, hazel-blue eyes, and dark hair.

Serena's was a deep emerald green, covered in black lace and beaded brilliants that sparkled in the afternoon sunlight slanting in through the window. It paired perfectly with her green eyes and auburn hair.

And Cordelia's was a gentle seafoam green that accentuated her strawberry-blonde locks. The conversation turned to the gentlemen who would be in attendance. Evidently, Captain Crawford had arrived that morning, and if Addy were honest, she was curious to meet the famed hero of Waterloo herself. The stories he must have!

"I hear he's quite dashing," Cordelia giggled, perching on the edge of Eloise's bed.

"As do I," Serena nodded, clasping her hands. "I wonder if he has any scars from his battles."

"Scars!" Eloise laughed softly. It was evident she still struggled to open up to others outside of her family, but she was trying. She'd admitted to Addy last night after dinner that she did not wish to be a wallflower this winter ball, though she had been at the past Christmas parties.

And to her credit, she'd started off well, taking pains to converse freely with the other two young women. Even if it was like getting a tooth pulled as far as Eloise was concerned.

Serena wasn't so dissimilar, as she'd confessed yesterday that she preferred a good book to a ball any day. And that had immediately raised her in Addy's estimation. She and Serena clearly thought alike.

Cordelia hastened over to the window to peek out. "Guests are arriving!" she cried excitedly, clapping her hands. "Come see! There are ever so many carriages!" Serena rushed over to join her in surveying the scene.

"It's nearly four, isn't it?" Eloise sighed, glancing at Addy. The two girls exchanged a resigned smile, before joining the others at the window.

Addy raised up on tiptoe to see over Serena's shoulder. "I believe that Aunt Agatha has outdone herself this year," she murmured.

"Oh yes, she's been planning this party for almost *six months*. She's taken great pains with the guest list, the menu, the orchestra," Eloise laughed, linking her arm with Addy's. "She is determined to make this her most impressive party yet."

"I count eight and ten coaches already!" Cordelia said, her voice rising giddily.

Addy wondered if Alistair was drawn to the girl. Of course, his mother and Cordelia's hoped to see them wed by next summer, surely. But would such a serious person as Alistair care for someone like Cordelia? It was difficult to ascertain his opinion of her, though she'd been secretly watching his interactions with Cordelia Ashworth over the past two days since their arrival.

It's none of my concern, Addy told herself. *Anyways, she seems most eager to please, and that should suit his stuffy nature.*

She shook off these thoughts about Alistair and she and the other girls took turns dressing behind the screen in the corner of the room.

Gemma appeared and began to arrange little sparkling pins in Addy's hair, while Eloise's maid fastened on a beautiful necklace of sapphire stones around her cousins' throat.

Presently they were all dressed and ready to descend, and the music from the orchestra had already begun to float up the stairs, filling the halls of the vast Worthington Manor.

Addy's pulse quickened as the atmosphere in the room shifted to one of heady excitement for the festivities. The chatter turned to dancing, as they wondered how many sets would be had throughout that evening. Addy's mother poked her head in the room, her feather hairpiece fluttering high above her head, as she urged them to make haste, the guests were already assembling downstairs.

The four girls followed her into the hall to the grand staircase, where voices of the people below rose, the sound of clinking glasses bouncing off the panelled walls.

The entire house was dazzling, festooned in wreaths and ribbons, and glittering candelabra. Yes, Aunt Agatha had certainly outdone herself. It was always mesmerising to watch how the somewhat dour Worthington manor transformed into a festive blur at Christmas.

Time to parade before the suitors, Addy thought dismally. Her stomach formed into a heavy knot as she followed the others down the stairs, and the room hushed as the music swelled. Addy kept her hand on the staircase railing, tightening her grasp on the polished mahogany as she scanned the room below.

Her eyes landed on Alistair, where he stood near the wall beside her brother and his mother, Rosalind. And then, his eyes met hers, and her face warmed. His expression was, of course, unreadable.

He stood tall, pompous as ever, his hair perfectly coiffed, his cravat pin gleaming just beneath his throat. Why did that emerald-green coat he wore look so…splendid…on him? Addy tore her eyes from his, butterflies erupting in her stomach, and continued on, hoping she didn't trip and make a fool of herself.

At the base of the stairs, she joined the others, and Addy tried her best to forget about Alistair. Her pulse thudded heavy in her ears as she surveyed the room, and listened to Cordelia whisper about how beautiful the house looked tonight. "Oh, I can't wait for the dancing to begin!" she whispered to Addy and the others.

Addy managed a smile, just before her aunt swooped in, on her heels two tall and handsome young men. One of them wore a blue navy uniform, the other dressed fashionably, in a maroon coat, black waistcoat, and black silk cravat. His jet-black hair was arranged voguishly, with strands curled artfully at his cheeks and temples. And his eyes were a brilliant blue, as blue as Addy imagined the Mediterranean to be.

"Good evening, my dears," Aunt Agatha said to Addy, Eloise, and the two other young women. "Permit me to introduce Lord Sebastian Badley and Captain William Crawford."

She then introduced each of the girls to the two young men, who each curtsied to them in turn.

Cordelia, chatterbox as she was, began to ramble about the music and the garlands above their heads.

"You have such magnificent taste, Lady Worthington!

Aunt Agatha beamed, obviously gratified by the fulsome comments, and said sweetly, "How sweet of you, my dear Miss Ashworth. I do believe that Lady Dowden was looking for you."

Cordelia's eyes widened, and she beamed. "Was she?" She excused herself with a curtsey and disappeared into the crowd. Agatha drifted off to greet more of her guests, leaving Addy, Eloise, and Serena with the two young men.

The orchestra music changed just then, signalling that the dancing was to commence. Addy turned to glance at Lord Badley, Aunt Agatha's match intended for her, and found those pale eyes on her already, the corner of his mouth twisting up into a smile. She couldn't decide if she found his eyes unnerving or arresting.

He stepped forward, bowing, and extended his hand. "I should be honoured to have this first dance with you, Miss Fawcett."

Addy met Eloise's eyes, and her cousin barely suppressed a grin, nodding that she should go ahead and accept. Addy did so, and let Lord Badley draw her towards the centre of the floor where other pairs had begun to gather.

Addy glanced over her shoulder to see Captain William invite Eloise to dance with him. She caught her breath, wondering if Eloise would accept. Or, would Aunt Agatha materialise and sweep her off to another suitor?

But no such thing happened, and Eloise nodded, letting the captain bow over her hand, and brush his lips against it. Eloise's face turned red.

"Miss Fawcett, I am told you enjoy riding." Lord Badley's silky, deep voice cut into Addy's thoughts.

She stiffened, hastening to take her place across from him, and offered a polite smile as she nodded. "That is true. It is one of my favourite repasts."

"I too delight in the sport," he told her, returning her smile. She caught her breath, feeling pinned beneath his intense gaze.

Out of the corner of her eye, she noted James accompany Serena onto the floor, and they took their places further down the line, next to none other than Alistair and Cordelia. Cordelia kept sending Alistair coy glances, her mouth twitching as she glided forward, flawlessly moving through the set.

What did Alistair think of her?

"Miss Fawcett, is something amiss?" It was Lord Badley speaking to her.

She wrenched her attention back to Lord Badley. "I hear that you have ambitions to join Parliament?"

"That is true," Badley's eyes brightened, if that were even possible. They were blinding as it were. "I confess, I am an ambitious man. Some would say too much so."

Addy smiled politely at that, though she was uncertain how she felt about the way his gaze lingered upon her during the dance. His eyes flickered to her mouth as she sailed past him, their hands joining, and her stomach flipped. He was certainly handsome, she couldn't argue that. But his stare was intense, too much so.

As per the steps of the dance, she was passed off to the next gentleman in line, and then to the next, and all the bright dresses and people in their evening best blurred past until suddenly, she found herself staring up into Alistair's eyes.

She'd at last reached him in the line, and they circled one another, and he grasped her hand in his tightly. Addy caught her breath, heart leaping into her throat. A strange tension settled over the room, sending her head spinning. Her chest went tight, causing her breath to seemingly stay trapped in her lungs.

Addy managed to give Alistair a taut smile and he returned it, though his eyes never wavered from hers. She did not understand the way those butterflies beat to life again as she found herself all too conscious of the way his warm palm pressed against hers, the way his fingers wrapped about hers in a firm grip. It was a heady kind of exhilaration, one reminiscent of that day so many years ago when she'd first seen him on the steps of her parents' home.

A shiver ran down her spine. "Lord Dowden," she blurted out, her tone stiff.

"Miss Fawcett." His words came out clipped as well.

"You're looking very..."

"Priggish?" he interrupted, a humourless smirk playing at his sensitive lips.

Addy scowled. "That isn't what I was going to say. But now that you mention it...yes. You do look rather stilted."

They parted for several moments to circle around other dancers before coming back together again in the centre of the floor.

Alistair arched an eyebrow. "I'm amazed that your dress isn't burnt. Is it new?"

Addy glared at him. "Is it so very difficult for you to be pleasant?"

"I should ask you the same thing," he flashed back. And just like that, they parted ways, onto the next partner. Before long she was back beside Lord Badley.

"Would you like some punch after this, Miss Fawcett? You seem rather flushed. This crowded room makes it rather stuffy, doesn't it?" He murmured to her as they promenaded down the centre of the room in time with the music.

"I should like that," Addy nodded. "My aunt Agatha insists upon keeping that fire lit at these parties. Though we hardly need it, with all the people in here."

Lord Badley chuckled. "You are very witty, Miss Fawcett."

"Thank you," Addy replied, casting a glare towards Alistair several couples down the row. Alistair returned the look with a glare of his own, mouth tightening. Heavens, he was a maddening man.

At last, the dance was over, and Lord Badley led her off the floor to the refreshments table, where her cousin and Serena had already gathered with Captain Crawford and James. Lord Badley handed her a glass of punch, and Addy sipped, thankful.

She glanced up, and caught a glimpse of Alistair across the room, with Cordelia at his side, speaking with her uncle Richard and Cordelia's father.

To her surprise, Alistair turned then, and his eyes locked with hers. She caught her breath, her heart beginning to pound in her chest as she found herself unable to tear her gaze from his. She could not read his expression, of course. "Addy, Lord Badley has asked you something," James' voice cut into her thoughts, and she turned hastily, hoping nobody noticed who she was looking at.

"Forgive me, Lord Badley. What did you say?"

Annoyance flashed in Lord Badley's eyes for but a moment before it cleared, and he smiled. "Ah, I pray I do not bore you, Miss Fawcett."

"Not at all." She had affronted him, she realised.

"Well, I was merely inquiring if you had spent a season yet in London."

"Only once, when I was eighteen," Addy admitted. "My family quits the city most of the year, so we do not participate in the season but rarely."

"A pity. I am certain you would be the most dazzling girl in the Ton."

She had to admit that Badley excelled at compliments. His was a silver tongue. "Thank you, sir."

"Would you do me the honour of another dance, Miss Fawcett?"

She accepted, trying to hide the reluctance from her tone. She glanced over to see her mother watching them like some sort of falcon eyeing its prey. She nearly rolled her eyes but refrained Lord Badley took her hand and led her onto the floor for the next dance and away they went as the music started for the reel.

A flicker of irritation crossed his face again when, after the dance, another young man approached her to ask for her hand in the next set. Something possessive sparked in his pale eyes, and this irritated her. He did not own her, but clearly, he already believed she was his. She accepted the dance offer and was thankful to be swept away by the gangly young man, a Lord Collins, who stumbled through half the set.

"Forgive me, my lady. Good heavens, I am a dreadful bungler, aren't I?"

Addy swallowed a laugh, only barely. To her dismay she noticed Alistair watching the whole dance, a smirk tugging at his mouth. She flashed him a defiant look, irritated by his obvious glee at her suffering. What did the prig want with her? Why did he always have to watch her like that? She lifted her chin, determined to keep her dignity throughout this humiliation ritual.

Halfway through the dance, she glimpsed her mother and aunt through the crowd, conferring with one another. They looked quite annoyed that she had abandoned Lord Badley. But Addy told herself she didn't care. She would dance with whom she pleased. As handsome as he was, Lord Badley unnerved her. She was grateful when the dance at last ended and she could escape Lord Collins. She retreated to a private alcove where Eloise found her.

Eloise handed her a glass of punch, offering a sympathetic smile. "My mother and yours are very cross, I'm afraid. They think it was very unnecessary of you to leave Lord Badley to his own devices."

"He seems rather annoyed as well," Addy grimaced, gratefully taking the punch from her cousin.

"He's very handsome though, is he not?"

"Oh yes, certainly. He does enjoy talking about his political ambitions—he did so nearly the entire dance, and scarcely asked me any questions."

"Perhaps he is just nervous."

"Perhaps." Addy peered over the heads of the crowd to glimpse Lord Badley near the refreshments table, standing with Captain Crawford and James.

Serena appeared a few moments later, her eyes bright, her cheeks flushed. "I saw you with Lord Collins," she giggled to Addy. "Did he step on your toes? I have heard he does that often."

"Yes, and my feet do not thank me for it," Addy laughed.

"Lord Badley is your arranged suitor? He is quite an arresting gentleman, isn't he? He's only just recently entered the marriage mart in search of his perfect match, so I hear. He is very genteel, isn't he? What did you think?"

"Even if I were impressed, I can hardly imagine myself the wife of a politician. I would mortify him at every party."

"Well, you are well-connected and so is he. I can see why Mamma paired the two of you."

"I ought to thank her," Addy said sarcastically.

Serena and Eloise burst out laughing. "Oh, poor Adelaide. She suffers greatly at the hands of my mother."

"What if he were to press his suit? Would you accept?" Serena's eyes were wide.

"If I want any peace, I should," Addy muttered. "Anyways, you and my brother seem to get on quite well."

"Indeed, we do! We have already danced twice, and he is most enjoyable to converse with."

"Now, you must take it to heart. My brother is not overly fond of dancing, even if he excels at it. But it is a testament to his high esteem of you since he is dancing with you so often."

"Really?" Serena's eyes went wide, sparkling with delight. "Well, I confess your brother is most handsome. And he never fails to make me laugh so with his cleverness."

Addy grinned at the other young woman. One thing she knew for certain—she would be delighted to have Serena as a sister. She turned to Eloise. "And you and the captain? He was most eager to dance with you, wasn't he?"

Eloise turned pink. "It seemed so. I do hope he doesn't find me too quiet. It's simply that I get so tongue-tied, and I forget what I mean to say. And he is quite patient about it."

Something wrenched in Addy, though she wasn't sure why. She was happy to see her cousin excited about someone like this, truly. She might struggle to grasp the lure of courtship and marriage, but she did love Eloise dearly and it was heartwarming to watch this romance unfold with Captain Crawford.

Speaking of whom, the captain approached them and bowed low over Eloise's hand. "I pray I am not imposing," he said gently, gazing at Eloise with open appreciation. "But I should be honoured to have this dance with you."

Addy and Serena grinned at each other as Eloise accepted and let the young war hero lead her away towards the centre of the hall.

Chapter 6

All fifty of the guests gathered for dinner in the great dining hall of Worthington Manor, evidently the pride of the Worthington family.

Alistair took his place at the table, not far from James, and beside his mother, to his relief. But his pulse leapt when he noticed Adelaide take a seat across from him, though she was distracted and did not notice him at first. Cordelia seated herself on his other side, to his dismay, though he greeted her cordially with a tight smile. "Miss Ashworth."

She flushed, batting her eyes at him, and returned his greeting, reaching up to push a lock of blond hair from her ivory forehead. Seating herself beside him, she let out a breathless giggle and asked him how he had found Worthington Hall thus far. Nothing too stimulating, though he disliked himself for thinking in that vein. She was truly a sweet girl. Very sweet. She sought to please in everything she did, and here he was, wishing she would just leave him be.

But throughout dinner, he could not keep his attention from wandering to Adelaide, seated between her cousin, Miss Wortham, and Lord Badley, who, he noticed, had already asked her to dance twice that evening. For some reason, the realisation that she was being courted by the "devil of London" turned Alistair's stomach. He couldn't quite understand it, however.

He tried to focus on his mother's conversation with Lady Ashford who sat diagonal to them, though his gaze wandered rather frequently to Adelaide, listening to Lord Badley tell her of London, the latest season, all the latest gossip in town...she listened with great interest, her eyes bright, her smile contagious.

"You will never believe it. This Lord Brambury is the most eligible suitor in the Ton, and he has fallen for one of his father's servants!" Lord Badley told her. Adelaide's eyes widened with shock.

"He didn't!"

"Indeed, he did. And now the two are to be wed, if you can imagine. His parents of course are in quite high dudgeon about the whole matter."

Does the man know nothing but gossip? Alistair wondered coolly.

"You miss out a great deal on the London scene, Miss Fawcett. It is a pity. You ought to quit the country and return to the city. You shan't be in want of entertainment whatsoever if you do. I can't imagine the boredom you must suffer in these country estates year-round."

Adelaide stiffened visibly, and Alistair nearly smirked down at his plate. "I should hardly say I'm bored, Lord Badley. In London, there is no means to enjoy nature, to take long walks through the meadows, or rides about the fields."

"Good heavens," Lord Badley's eyes widened as he realised he'd misspoken. "I did not mean to cause offence, Miss Fawcett."

Adelaide smiled tautly, and Alistair nearly chuckled.

Her vibrance sparkled in the dimly lit dining hall, and he caught himself comparing her to the sweet but somewhat insipid Cordelia Ashworth at his side. Self-reproach rose in him, and for a moment, he craved a good stiff drink of brandy, even though he'd sworn it off years ago. His father's admonition back then had struck such a deep chord within him that he still avoided it.

"Miss Ashworth," he forced himself to focus on the young woman beside him, who pushed food around on her plate as if she lacked an appetite. She perked up when he addressed her. "Tell me, what are some past times that you enjoy?"

Cordelia laughed softly, shaking her head and sending her blonde curls dancing about her cheeks. "Oh, Lord Dowden. I mentioned earlier when you asked me that I am fond of the pianoforte, and of embroidery. I embroidered a pillowcase last week before we came here."

"Ah." Alistair felt himself turn red. "Forgive me. I confess I am not at my finest at parties such as this."

"But why not? Balls are ever so wonderful."

"Of course." But Alistair had never been fond of balls. This stemmed mostly from one particular occasion—he'd been at his first ball following his graduation from the university. He had made an utter oaf of himself trying to remember the complicated steps in the dance, trying to not step on his partners' toes. But he succeeded in treading on his dance partner's feet, to his mortification.

She had been furious about it and refused to stand up with him again after that.

"And what of you, Lord Dowden? What do you take special pleasure in?" Cordelia inquired, flashing a bright smile at him.

"Ah. My leisurely pursuits are few and far between these days. I spend much of my time attending to the estate my father left in my charge.

But when I have a spare moment, I take pleasure in going on rides about the country, and reading."

"Reading!" Cordelia repeated, wrinkling her nose. "I confess I am not a great reader myself. I simply think there are ever so many more interesting things to do."

Just then, Adelaide burst into laughter at something Lord Badley said and it drew Alistair's attention. His stomach twisted tighter, for some reason, the sight of her conversing so freely, so merrily with Lord Badley sent another flare of annoyance through him. He pulled his gaze from them again, though his grasp on his glass tightened, involuntarily. Dinner couldn't be over soon enough. In fact, this entire visit couldn't be over soon enough.

***

After dinner, James found him watching the dancing from the sidelines, leaning against one of the panelled walls beneath a large garland of fir and pine.

"Where is Miss Ashworth?" James asked him, imitating Alistair's stance of leaning against the wall.

"Dancing," Alistair nodded towards the throng at the centre of the great room, to the quick-footed form that was Cordelia Ashworth. He had to say one thing for her—she excelled at dance. He did not recall a single misstep throughout his two long dances with her thus far.

They were quickly joined by Lord Badley and Captain Crawford. "Your sister is a remarkable young lady," Alistair heard Badley say to James, wonder in his voice. He clenched his jaw and took a sip of his punch.

"She's a lively one," James grinned. "I should say. I've been raised with her. There's scarce a dull moment with Adelaide around."

"Do you suppose she will accept me for another dance?"

"Oh, certainly. Perhaps you ought to ask her."

Lord Badley strode away in search of Adelaide, and Alistair could not explain the sinking sense within him. He wrenched his gaze from the man's retreating and listened to Captain Crawford admit to James, "Your cousin Miss Wortham is a delight. I must confess I am most intrigued by her."

James chuckled. "To be frank, I am astonished that she has danced with you, and more than once at that."

"I take it that she does not do so often?"

"She is somewhat of a retiring young lady. But her eagerness to join you in the dance is a testament, I think, to her enjoyment of your company."

Captain Crawford's eyes lit, clearly relieved by James' words. "And here I was fearing that I'd lost my touch. I've been on the seas so often as of late, and now that I'm land-bound, I fear I will come across as something of an oaf in society."

James waved his hand. "Hardly. And even if you do blunder, I am certain your standing as a hero of Waterloo will predispose any young lady to overlook it."

Captain Crawford laughed. "I shall take that to heart." He raised his glass of wine and took a swig of it, before setting off across the room in search of Eloise. This left James and Alistair to themselves.

"Pray tell, what do you think of Miss Ashworth?" James asked Alistair softly, mouth twitching.

Alistair could barely suppress a sigh. "She is a sweet girl, surely. And a wonderful dancer. She is everything a young lady ought to be."

James frowned. "And yet?"

Alistair lifted one shoulder, taking another draught from his crystal glass of punch. "I don't know," he murmured. "There is something missing. I can't put my finger on it. She is indeed my mother's choice for me."

"And my aunt's," James nodded.

"I do not believe I am ready to pursue her further," Alistair admitted after a long beat, not before checking to ensure no one was listening to them talk. He would hate for Cordelia to be told by another person of his uncertainty regarding her.

"I understand. Though, I never knew you were something of a romantic." James let out another laugh.

Alistair couldn't suppress a smile of his own, feeling his face warm. "Well, what of you and Miss Scott?"

James flushed, his eyes at once wandering to the pretty auburn-haired girl enjoying a minute with another guest. "I am averse to admitting my aunt matched me well, but she did indeed match me well with Miss Scott. She is arresting, truly, and I enjoy my conversation with her considerably. I should be eager to court her if she is willing."

"You've scarcely taken your eyes from her all night," Alistair smirked.

James' flush deepened. "Ah, yes, you were always an observant one, weren't you?"

"You can't stop staring at the girl."

The two men shared a laugh as Alistair wondered if he should divulge his concerns about Lord Badley. The man had a reputation for ruthless ambition, and for being something of a devil on the London social scene. And of course, he came from an old, prestigious family with much wealth to their name.

But would he truly be a good match for Adelaide? He wondered if she yearned to be a politician's bride— to host parties and cut a swath alongside her husband in society.

The ball lasted until the wee hours of the morning, and the last of the guests departed just as the sky flushed with dawn's pale glow.

Alistair was thankful for the chance to retreat to his room and find some peace in the solitude of his room. He'd scarcely seen his mother all evening, though he was certain she'd enjoyed herself. It had certainly been an impressive ball given by the Worthington family, yet it was hardly the end of their stay. They had another week at least of merrymaking as Christmas drew close. It was but three days before Christmas eve, after all. The day passed quietly, as everyone recovered from the party the night before.

Alistair woke later than he usually did and crossed the room to his window, which overlooked the stable yard. The sky hinted at more snow, though a thin layer already covered the ground. It must have fallen sometime in the early hours of the morning.

As he peered out, he noticed a young woman hurrying down the path towards the stables. The sight of her loose dark curls told him that he was watching none other than Adelaide Fawcett. She wore a wine-red cloak over a white dress, and she kept glancing back over her shoulder, as if determined to keep her venture furtive.

She must be sneaking out for an early evening ride. He found himself watching her with interest as she vanished inside the stable. But a few minutes later, she emerged again, this time on the back of an impressive steed that would give Alistair pause. Her command of the beast was impressive, and he caught his breath as she rode out of the yard on the horse's back, her dark hair flying out behind her.

What was it about her that so fascinated and frustrated him? Perhaps he envied her ability to be herself so unabashedly, regardless of society's expectations. And this could be on account of her carelessness, but something in him sensed that she merely sought to remain true to herself.

Her words from the night before drifted into his mind. *You look rather stilted.*

With a small sigh, he admitted to himself that she wasn't wrong. He did tend to be uptight, and perhaps that accounted for his inability to connect with Miss Ashworth. She was a kindly girl, but conversation with her was difficult, almost strained.

And yet, he was somehow able to banter with ease with Adelaide, despite the barbs behind every word.

He watched her ride until she was out of sight. Despite her quarrelsome tendencies, she was an exceptional horsewoman.

Something tugged in his chest, a strangely intense longing that he did not understand. Ever since he'd first seen her three days earlier, it had kept happening, bewildering in the extreme. Alistair stepped away from the window and called his valet to get dressed.

***

Adelaide was not at breakfast that morning, nor were a great many of the other guests staying at Worthington Manor. Even the lord and lady of the manor were absent, likely recovering from the festivities of the night before. The only ones present were James, his and Adelaide's parents, and Alistair's own mother. Lord Badley did make an appearance towards the end of the meal, and he offered Alistair a tight smile as he took a seat across from him.

Alistair and James spent the rest of the morning in the billiards room, and then they, Lord Badley, and Captain Crawford set out for a lively hunt. James took several of his uncle's hounds along and they each chose a horse in the stable to ride on their outing. Alistair wondered if they would happen across Adelaide on her morning ride. He was somewhat surprised she'd managed to sneak out, but now he could see how—half the house was busy resting.

The hunt lasted the better part of the day until it began to snow again heavily, and then they retreated to Worthington Manor. They only caught two quails—James and Captain Crawford each shot one.

By this point, Alistair was eager for a bite of dinner, though he was rather disappointed to have not seen Adelaide on the hunt. For what reason, he could not say.

He and the other men retired to their bedrooms where they changed into their evening wear, before returning downstairs to join the rest of the party in the drawing room.

"How was your hunt?" his mother asked him as he entered the spacious room. A fire blazed in the grand hearth, and more garlands decorated the mantle.

Cordelia Ashworth played an aria on the pianoforte, her clear, sweet voice carrying through the home.

"It was a good repast for the day," Alistair told Rosalind with a smile, as he joined the other young men at the sideboard. He took a moment to survey the room. Lady Scotfell, Lady Ashford, Adelaide and James' mother all sat together at a whist table by one of the great windows.

The younger women sat on the settees before the fire, and the fathers, Alistair assumed, were in the billiards room sipping port and chatting about their respective estates. Sure enough, they crowded in just a few minutes after he arrived, chortling over this or that.

Alistair again refrained from accepting a glass of port from a footman, and stepped closer to the fireplace, turning his head and meeting Adelaide's brown eyes. Tonight, she wore a plain but attractive muslin that complemented her figure, highlighting its subtle curves in a tantalising fashion.

He pulled his gaze from hers, mouth dry, and stared down into the fire that blazed blithely, sparks leaping out from the grate.

"How was the hunt, brother?" she called to James from her seat beside Eloise Worthington.

"Cold, but fruitful," James replied, his eyes twinkling. "As you have probably seen it began to snow, and we were forced to retreat."

"Retreat," Captain Crawford echoed, his eyebrows lifting. He joined Alistair beside the fireplace. He laughed, and winked at Eloise, causing her to blush. "Hardly. We merely decided we did not which to endure the bitter cold a moment longer. But we will never admit defeat. Perhaps tomorrow we will attempt again."

"Unless there is a dreadful storm that determines to strike then," amended James.

"And how did you ladies entertain yourselves this fine winter's day?" Lord Badley asked the throng of young women.

"I confess, I slept a good portion of the day," Miss Scott admitted, her gaze flickering towards James. Alistiar didn't miss it. He hoped that the two would come to an understanding. It was pleasing to see how well the two suited one another.

"Ah, then at the very least you were able to stay warm. I would not be astonished if it were to turn into a dreadful storm this night."

The tinkling music from the pianoforte paused then. "Lord Dowden," cried Cordelia, "I am in need of a page-turner. Would you be so kind as to aid me in this?"

"But of course," Alistair nodded, managing to maintain a courteous air. Out of the corner of his eye, he noted Lord Badley assume his own station at the fireplace, but a small distance from Adelaide, and Adelaide's laughter carried throughout the room.

He could see clearly just how much Lord Badley seemed eager to station himself close to Adelaide, and again, irritation prickled in Alistair's heart. He wrenched his attention from them to focus on Cordelia in front of him at the pianoforte.

Chapter 7

Addy slept little that night, tossing and turning as she kept reflecting on the strange tension drawn taut as a bow string between herself and Alistair Dowden. It confused her, for she did truly enjoy conversing with Lord Badley. He was clever, silver-tongued, handsome. And yet...

With a soft groan of frustration, she flung back the covers and rose in the pale light of dawn. Hurrying over to the window, she checked the weather outside. Another thick layer of snow had fallen at some point during the night, but that hardly meant she would abstain from a good ride. She needed it. Or else she would cry out of pent-up energy that needed release. She just needed to clear her mind.

Alistair has quite poisoned my mind, truly. Ever since I've met him again, he won't stop creeping into my thoughts. The prig.

She dressed quickly, in an older, faded gown, one singed by her poor habit of sitting too close to the grate. No matter. The cloak she settled around her shoulders would conceal it. She hurried down the back staircase to one of the back doors, and as soon as she pushed the door open, the cold air bit at her skin, taking her breath away.

Even if she did not ride, it would still be wonderful to escape the confines of the house, spend some time with her uncle's newest horse, a beautiful Arabian stallion with long slender legs, a beautiful grey colour-- Adonis. Addy stroked Adonis' silky muzzle, pressing her forehead to his. *Why am I so restless?* She couldn't answer her own question, and settled for asking one of the hands for a brush so she could tend to the horse.

"What I wouldn't give to be a Joan of Arc, to do something worth remembering." It didn't matter if Adonis couldn't understand. Sometimes she believed that horses knew more than they let on. "But I am a mere woman, who cannot do a thing worth remembering evidently." *Why do I keep thinking of Alistair?*

He was as irritating as ever. Clearly age had done nothing to soften his sharp disapproval in everything around him. And perhaps it was unfair to owe it entirely to his nature, but he had been like that even before his father had passed. And yet...

She sighed and began to run the brush through Adonis' mane. The scent of hay and leather hung over the stable, a heavy but comforting combination of scents. She preferred it far more to the thick perfumes that permeated her own bedroom. Aunt Agatha was very fond of Parisian perfumes.

Sebastian Badley...what was it about him that put her off so? It was hardly the same as it was with Alistair. Alistair was a prig, certainly, but Badley...she could not wholly be at ease around him, and not because she feared his disapproval, but because of the calculating sharpness in his eyes.

Not many could intimidate her, but Sebastian could. Last night, he had walked her to the bottom of the staircase and kissed her hand for a long moment. Told her in a whisper that she should call him by his given name, which surprised her. Eloise and Serena sailed past just then, flashing them curious glances. Addy's heart had beat faster, but not in a pleasant way, exactly. She couldn't explain it even now.

With a soft exhalation, she turned to call a hand to bring her a saddle. Once Adonis had been prepared to ride, she led him from the stall out onto the path. The world around her sparkled and glistened after the latest flurry covered everything in white crystalline blankets of snow.

Suddenly, Adelaide could not bring herself to care if Mother upbraided her for sneaking out so early. Mother had not even noticed her excursion the other morning.

Addy whispered soft endearments to Adonis, who neighed softly in response. He was a splendid horse, truly. She pulled herself up into the saddle and let out a deep breath. How good it was to be back atop a horse. She ached to fly across the heather-covered fields.

But as she rounded the corner of the stable, she stopped short at the sight of none other than Alistair.

Alistair, in a long heavy coat, a woolen scarf around his neck, gloves on his hands. A plume of frosted breath appeared in the air before his lips, and he stared at her, a mixture of surprise and amusement written across his features.

But to her surprise, she couldn't read an ounce of deprecation in his expression.

"Lord Dowden." She dipped into a slight curtsey; certain her smile had frozen on her face.

"Is this a habit of yours?" he nodded at the steed whose reins she gripped so tight that if it weren't for her mittens, her knuckles would show white.

"Going for a morning ride?" she replied somewhat stiffly.

"Yes. I—" he paused then, as if hesitating. "I did not know you took such pleasure in riding?"

Addy's smile dropped. "Is there something amiss with that?"

He blinked, his forehead creasing. "It is rather singular."

"Singular! And how might that be?"

"I hardly meant to offend. I merely meant—"

"You think that someone of my breeding ought not be at liberty to take morning rides?"

"No, no—" Alistair's eyes flashed as Addy lifted her chin, hoping he could read the challenge in her stare. Would he meet it? "I simply meant it was singular."

"And pray tell, what do you mean by that word?"

Alistair's face hardened. "I think that you derive offense from what I say, though none is meant."

"And I think that you cannot restrain yourself from presenting your judgements, even when they are supercilious encroachments upon others."

"I ought to take leave," Alistair said, his voice low and taut.

"Must you?" Addy flung out, unable to help herself.

Alistair stopped short then. "Miss Fawcett, may we at least attempt civility with one another?"

"I should like that very much, but it may prove too much of a challenge for one such as yourself."

"Are you calling me contentious?"

"I am saying that you breach civility by presenting your judgements where they are not sought or desired. I go riding. Is that so great an abomination in your eyes?"

"It suggests a want of propriety, perhaps, to venture out without a chaperone."

"And you sir, are not my father, nor my brother. Nor my mother, though you and she are dangerously similar to one another."

"Ah!" Alistair reddened at that. "Similar?"

Just then, Adonis tossed his head, eyes rolling. They must have startled him with their raised voices. Before Addy could comprehend it, the horse reared up on its back legs, letting out a frightened whinny.

Gasping, she held on to the saddle desperately, her body beginning to topple sideways, but just then, large strong hands came up to grasp her leg and foot in the stirrup, as Alistair attempted to steady her. She caught her breath, a shiver going down her spine again. Just as it had been the night of the dance, her hand in his, their eyes locked as they flung out barbed words at one another.

Except now...she was frozen in place, as Adonis calmed, stamping his feet and snorting loudly in the bitter-cold air. And Alistair's hands lingered on her skirts, his throat moving up and down as if he'd swallowed hard.

Addy jerked herself from the spell of his touch, tightening her grip on the reins, and pulled her leg from his touch. But confusion spread through her, molten heat coursing through her veins. Her face burnt as she glanced away from him, taking in a shuddering breath, and Alistair stepped back, letting his hand fall back to his side.

"Thank you," Addy heard herself whisper, before nudging Adonis in the side and sending him into a trot. She couldn't resist the urge to turn, glance back at Alistair over her shoulder.

He stood there on the path, very still, his cheeks flushed brightly in stark contrast to the snowy ground. Addy urged Adonis into a canter, her lungs tight enough to burst. Her head swam as she tried to make sense of what had just happened. Why did someone like *Alistair Dowden* have such a terrible effect on her? One moment he had her fuming, the next...

She rode on and on for perhaps an hour or more, until at last she knew her mount needed to rest. The world around her sparkled with ice and snow. One thing Addy could say about her aunt and uncle—they had a beautiful estate. Even more so than her mother and father, she sometimes thought.

With a small sigh, she turned Adonis toward their manor, and took off flying, her hair whipping about her face as she soared over the ground. Adonis' hooves crunched on the icy ground.

She at last made it back to the stable and took care to remove Adonis' saddle and bridle and give him an apple or two as thanks for the ride. She scratched him under the chin, but nearly jumped when Eloise spoke from behind her.

"I thought you'd snuck away for a ride," her cousin smiled, wrapped in a plaid shawl. "Mamma sent me to find you. It's time for breakfast."

Addy couldn't help but smile back. Seeing her cousin always put her in a better mood. She accepted Eloise's arm and together they exited the stall. Reluctantly, Addy left behind the comforting scent of leather and hay as she and Eloise left the stable and hurried down the path.

"I noticed that you and Captain Crawford seemed to take to one another considerably well," Addy teased as they strolled along through the frost-covered garden to the terrace.

Eloise blushed. "He is a kind man. He might be a dashing hero, but he has this way of getting me to talk, without me even realising. He listens to me as if he truly enjoys listening to me. As if he doesn't tire of it."

"How could he not? You are an utterly fascinating creature. I am certain he only accepted your mother's invitation so that he might see you again. You must have smitten him in Bath."

Eloise laughed. "Well, what do you think of Lord Badley? He seems most taken with you."

Addy sighed, earning a concerned glance from her cousin. "Lord Badley is a genteel sort of man. It is clear that he has ambitions beyond upholding his family name. And I admire him for that."

"He is handsome, certainly." And then in a whisper, Eloise added, "Not nearly as handsome as Captain Crawford, I must say."

"Would your mother object if the captain wished to court you?"

"Now, don't you attempt to distract me from my inquiries regarding Lord Badley. But in answer to your question, I am not certain. She has not broached the subject with me yet. I believe she is resigned to it. And I am certain my father would not object to having the hero of Waterloo in the family. He also comes from a good noble family, and that also recommends him."

"Oh yes, Uncle Richard would be delighted by the prospect of having a hero for a son."

The two of them giggled before they paused at the base of the terrace steps. Eloise glanced around and turned to face Addy, grasping her hands.

"What is it about Lord Badley that gives you pause?"

"I—I don't know."

"Is it Lord Dowden?"

"Lord Dowden? Alistair?" Addy hissed, her heart lurching. "Certainly not. He drives me mad."

"*O brawling love! O loving hate!*" Eloise's eyes crinkled into a mischievous smile.

Addy glared, turning away and continuing up the steps. "I beg you not to use Shakespeare against me so, cousin."

"I could not help but note the two of you during the dance. How you seemed quite enthralled with one another."

"I should say it was less enthrallment and far more of a contest of wit and slights. We have always quarrelled. This you know all too well, Eloise."

"Come," Eloise hastened up the steps to join Addy on the terrace. "Don't be cross. I was only teasing."

"Well, I am resigned to the fact that he and I shall always be at odds, no matter what. We can never seem to see eye to eye."

"And yet, your eye is drawn to him often."

Addy hoped her face wasn't too flushed now. But once they entered the house and she hastened upstairs to change into a morning gown, she checked herself in the mirror. Sure enough, her cheeks were ruddy from both the cold and mortification at her cousin's comments on her and Alistair.

What does Eloise know? But Addy's mind flew back to that spark that passed between her and Alistair this morning as he steadied her mount, the strange look in his eyes. His expression had matched how she felt. Stricken.

"Good heavens, don't tell me you've gone riding again. And without a chaperone?" Mother's voice caused her to jump and turn, wide-eyed. Mother stood in the doorway, her face dark with irritation.

"I did not wish to trouble Gemma. It is quite cold out and—"

Mother huffed and hurried forward, snatching her by the wrist. "Never mind. We shall discuss this later. Come, or you will be dreadfully late for breakfast. Your aunt is eager to divulge the plans of the day."

Sighing, Addy let herself be pulled along, knowing there was no use in protesting. "Lord Badley has been inquiring after you. He fears that you are unwell," Mother told her as they dashed down the hallway to the grand staircase. "He is most enchanted by you, my dear. Quite so. And he could have any girl in England that he pleases. Yet, he finds *you* the most charming. I don't know how you've done it, but you may very well secure a proposal in the near future."

Addy grimaced but didn't hide it soon enough before her mother caught sight of it and fixed her with a severe look. "Now, you could do much worse than Lord Badley. He is dashing, well-appointed, of a good family. And he has such ambitions. Just think. The finest home in London. The most fashionable clothes..."

Addy stared at her mother. *Does she know me so little? Or does she simply not care what I truly desire?*

Before she could speak, however, Aunt Agatha met them, her eyebrows raised. "Ah, sister! There you are! Come, breakfast is nearly ready, and we are all in the drawing room."

Addy let her mother propel her into the drawing room where at once all eyes rested on her. She had not paid heed to the time today, and now she would suffer for it.

"Good morning," she told the gathered company in her cheeriest voice, lifting her chin. Lord Badley approached her, a cup of tea in his hand.

He bowed, and she didn't miss the way his vivid eyes flew over her, taking her in. Her stomach knotted, but in a way that was unsettling. "May I say that you look quite well this morning," he told her, in just above a whisper.

"As do you," she forced a grin but made the mistake of letting her gaze wander over for a moment to Alistair. He stood in the window with her brother, a cup of tea in his own hand. His expression was strange, taut. It sent her heart fluttering.

Lord Badley took a seat next to her on the settee, and leaned close to her, too close for Adelaide's comfort though she remained carefully composed.

His gaze followed Adelaide's to Alistair across the room. "Does Lord Dowden always exhibit such a severe countenance, Miss Fawcett?"

Addy stiffened but managed to keep her tone light. "In my acquaintance with him, I have noticed that he indeed does."

"It is rather daunting, is it not?"

"You mustn't let Lord Dowden daunt you. I have known him since childhood, and it is simply his nature."

"Since childhood you say?"

"He and my brother attended the same school growing up."

"Ah! So he has always presented himself so sternly?"

"Indeed," Addy wondered if Alistair could hear that they were talking about him. If he did, he did not reveal it in his expression or glance.

Chapter 8

Alistair stiffly took his seat at the breakfast table, quite purposely arranged so that he sat next to Cordelia Ashworth. She plied him with questions about his morning, about whether he favoured bohea or hyson tea. And then she launched into a monologue about the merits of hyson, which he scarcely heard, to his mortification.

His attention was drawn primarily to the young woman further down the table, seated beside Badley. Her hair was done up rather messily, but it hardly detracted from her bright eyes, her expression inscrutable. What was she thinking? He wished he knew, which was strange to realise. *Has she bewitched me somehow?*

He picked at his food, listening to Cordelia give up on conversing with him about tea and begin to chat with Miss Scott across the table. Alistair tried to distract himself by watching James and Miss Scott exchange polite conversation across the table, their manner noticeably warmer than with others. He'd known James for years, and this was his first time to see his old friend truly smitten with a girl. The man enjoyed flirting with girls, certainly, but Serena Scott arrested him.

Smothering a wry smile, he took a long sip of his tea and strove to focus on his plate of food. Breakfast at the Worthington Manor was an extravagant affair, complete with all sorts of pastries and rich meats. He usually took a simple piece of bread and butter, but Lady Worthington had taken great pains to ensure her guests were well-fed.

His appetite, however, was feeble, and when he glanced up, he found his mother watching him with a soft frown. He offered her a reassuring smile and took a bite of figgy pudding. Towards the end of the meal, Lord Worthington stood at the head of the table where he'd been sitting, poring over a newspaper, and announced to the guests that a game of charades would be played that evening.

"What better way to pass a winter evening than to play a good game of charades? Huzzah!" He lifted his cup of coffee with a broad smile, and excited whisperings began around the table. "In the meantime, I beg you all to enjoy yourselves. The library is at your disposal, of course, as is the billiards. For my part, I mean to challenge my good brother here," he gestured to Lord Fairfield, "a game of billiards."

Once he'd settled back into his seat again, Cordelia turned to Alistair. "Don't you love a game of charades?" she exclaimed in that fluttery voice of hers.

Alistair nodded politely, though he didn't. "But of course, Miss Ashworth," he murmured. His heart sank. He was a dreadful actor. He'd participated in a play years ago at Fairfield Manor, his second visit to see James. And he'd been abominable. Of course, Adelaide had teased him for it wretchedly.

He excused himself and retreated to the library, citing a need for some air. The rest of the guests dispersed as well to entertain themselves for the day.

Alistair found himself a cosy seat in the library by one of the large windows there and began to flip through a book of natural history. It was quite a good book, but presently he heard the familiar voice of Badley drifting from somewhere else in the library, as well as someone else, and he perked up, shutting his book. Standing, Alistair drew closer to the voices, listening intently.

At the mention of Adelaide's name, he froze, and strained to hear more from his position behind one of the shelves. They must be just inside the library door. "Miss Fawcett is not only lovely, but her political connections make her quite the advantageous match."

Alistair caught his breath. Anger surged within him as the meaning behind Badley's words sank in. *The man is a social climber. To him, Adelaide is nothing more than a pawn.*

He ought to warn her. She clearly took pleasure in his company, and Badley had been fawning over her for the past several days, shamelessly. The man was a master at charm, but it was all for show. He did not truly care for Adelaide.

Something protective and dark coiled heavily in Alistair's stomach. He turned on his heel and slipped out of the library, his head swimming. Should he tell her? She deserved to know before she forever vowed herself to the man in matrimony. And it was clear that everyone around them designed for Adelaide and Badley to marry.

But it wasn't his business to meddle. And something in him ached at the thought of divulging the truth of Badley's intentions.

He needed to take a good long walk. He stepped out into the bitter air, the sky heavy with storm clouds, the wind beginning to pick up. It scraped against the skin of his face but he barely noticed. Alistair strode onward until at last he came to a pause beneath a large, barren oak. For the first time in at least a week, he withdrew his pipe and took a draw, thinking things over. Perhaps it would be overstepping to inform Adelaide of her suitor's words.

Besides, would she even believe him? Or would she scoff and laugh at him as she seemed so inclined to do?

After this morning, he wondered if she would question his own motives. Or, had she been as affected by that moment as he had? It was rather impossible to tell. She was truly a study of contradictions, a perfect, bewildering storm that bemused him at every turn.

He never knew what she might do next. And right now, that brought him up short as he contemplated broaching her about Lord Badley's words. He did not wish to quarrel with her again. But everything he did, at least in her eyes, was offensive. And he did not know how to amend that.

After an hour of hiking through the thin layer of snow that covered the ground, he returned to the house, gave his coat to one of the staff and headed back to his room to change. But as he emerged from the bedroom and hurried down the hall, he turned a corner and found himself face-to-face with Eloise Worthington.

"Good afternoon, Lord Dowden," she curtsied, smiling. "How are you faring this day? Are you eager for the charades game tonight?"

"Ah—charades. Yes," he managed stiffly. This only made her chuckle.

"You are under no duress to play," she told him, her voice gentle.

"No, no, I shall," Alistair hurried to say. He did not wish to be a spoilsport.

Eloise kept walking as if to continue down the hall, but then she stopped and turned. "I may be presumptuous to say this, but for two people who disdain one another so greatly, you and my cousin certainly do pay one another a great deal of attention."

Alistair's chest tightened, his face heating. But before he could think of something to say, Eloise hastened on down the hall and around the corner out of sight. He stood stock-still, her words sinking in.

Confusion roiled through him as he sought to compose himself and continue to his bedroom. Once inside the room, with the door closed, he closed his eyes, before crossing the room to look out the window. So far today, he felt he had already lost his footing in more ways than one, and he struggled to reconcile the conflicting emotions inside him.

***

The rest of the day passed quietly until that evening, when, after dinner, everyone gathered in the Worthingtons' large drawing room for a game of charades. Alistair stationed himself near the window to watch the proceedings, bracing himself for the inevitable moment when he would be expected to participate.

He did not exactly anticipate the game, though he would not say as much. He did enjoy seeing his mother's spirits lifted thus far on their visit. She'd needed this excursion, he knew, and it pleased him to know that at the very least, he could do his duty by her, as Father requested, and see after her happiness. Her eyes gleamed with delight as she sat on the sofa beside Lady Ashford and Cordelia.

Lady Worthington divided the guests into teams, and Alistair found himself on a team with Adelaide, Cordelia and her parents, Captain Crawford, Eloise, and Lord Fairfield, while the rest of the party was relegated to the other team. Alistair's stomach knitted itself into knots over the prospect of performing in front of others—he'd never been partial to the game.

Once everyone parted to their respective sides of the room, Lady Worthington, who declared herself to be the arbiter of the game, handed out the slips of paper to the first contestants. Adelaide was selected first, and she stationed herself before the hearth, her cheeks flushed, eyes bright. The colour red truly became her, and Alistair could not help but note it matched her fiery temperament.

She was striking to watch, commanding the room with a natural predisposition towards the dramatics, and Alistair could not tear his gaze from her. She read the first verse, and Cordelia cried out, clapping her hands, "An opera singer!"

Adelaide gestured as if to indicate that Cordelia was going in the right vein of thought.

"A soprano!" called Lord Fairfield, chortling.

Adelaide nodded, grinning, and took a small bow. The rest of their team erupted into laughter and applause, while the other team groaned in good-natured dismay.

Alistair tore his eyes from the young woman, with curls dancing around her face, her dark eyes like golden embers. Next to perform was

Miss Scott, and she read the next riddle to the room. Alistair noticed James admiring her, pressing a fist to his mouth as if to smother the smile spreading across his face as she endeavoured to coax the answer from her team.

But at last, it came time for Alistair's turn, and his stomach churning, he strode to the front of the room to take his slip of paper from Lady Worthington. He read his riddle aloud, "My first is a wandering act. My second is a minister's home in fact. My whole is a true love tract." He stumbled several times through the reading and was sure his face was a burning bright red.

But he'd scarcely finished when Miss Wortham cried out, "A romance!"

He nodded, unable to keep from smiling. "That is the answer." He at last permitted himself to glance in Adelaide's direction, finding her watching him intently, her mouth curved into a smile he couldn't decide was sardonic or perhaps, something softer. He presumed the former—to guess the latter would be rather audacious.

Alistair returned to his place by the window, exhaling a sigh of relief, though his heart continued to flutter. After that morning in the stable, he had no idea what to make of things between himself and Adelaide Fawcett. Was she repulsed by him? Or was it something else?

She truly had to be the most confusing girl he'd ever met in his life.

But in no time whatsoever, it was his turn again, and on shaky legs he returned to the appointed spot in front of the fireplace, reading the next riddle. And once again, he floundered, halting, an oaf. Lord Badley chuckled behind his hand from the back of the room, where he leaned, arms crossed, and Alistair was certain he'd gone beet red.

To his surprise, he noticed Adelaide cast Badley an irritated glance before turning her attention back to his performance.

At last, it was over, but that observation lingered in the back of Alistair's mind, even after he'd retired to his bedroom for the night. He tossed and turned, unable to sleep. His head raced as he contemplated the weight of his duty. It was clear his mother favoured Cordelia—she practically fawned over the girl since arriving. But he had yet to see her conversing easily with Adelaide.

Adelaide alarmed her, if he wasn't mistaken. And Cordelia was everything one ought to seek in a woman. She was the girl any man worth his salt would desire—she was accomplished, comely, sweet. But she was pale and insipid next to Adelaide.

It had only been five days since arriving at Worthington Manor, and already, he felt spent, his mind hazy from the onslaught of conflicting emotions and feelings. Why couldn't he remove Adelaide Fawcett from his mind? Why couldn't he put her far from his thoughts? Before he'd come, he'd dreaded the idea of seeing her. And now?

So much had changed.

Chapter 9

Addy slept in that day in fact, she woke early, and lay abed until late morning when breakfast was meant to be served. She yearned to venture down to the stables for a ride, but the possibility of seeing Alistair there knitted her stomach into a dozen knots, none of which would come undone, no matter what she told herself.

He is exactly the same as he was all those years ago. Stiff. Stern. Uptight.

Yet, she could not ignore the flutter of excitement his presence stirred within her, how his gaze seemed to light a warmth in her cheeks and send a faint tremor through her frame.

Today, instead of venturing down to the stables, she lay in her bed, staring up at the ceiling and wondering what the day would hold. Last night, Aunt Agatha announced after the charades game that, if the weather permitted, they would go ice skating on the nearby frozen pond that Uncle Richard loved to fish in during spring and summer.

Addy stole to her bedroom's vanity and perched on the stool in front of it, staring at herself in the mirror. Then, she hurried to the large cable hanging to ring for Gemma. Presently her maid appeared, and asked with her usual pleasant air, "What can I do for you, Miss Adelaide?"

"I'd like to ready myself for breakfast," she told Gemma, to her maid's surprise. Gemma was more than accustomed to Addy's habits of sneaking out and getting in late, often at the expense of her hair and dress.

"Of course, Miss Adelaide."

Gemma set about arranging Addy's hair, artfully styling her natural curls around her face in a way that became her features and selected a gown to wear for the day. It was a deep emerald colour that would be warm enough for the weather outside, for skating. One thing Addy loved only slightly less than riding was skating.

She shoved aside her turmoil of feelings concerning Alistair, how everything had shifted between them in the past week since arriving. Her mind drifted back to the night before, how he'd looked nervous and vulnerable, presenting his riddle to the gathered company. Something like sympathy twinged in her, alongside the realisation that perhaps, his tendency towards stiffness was born out of shyness.

Guilt twisted in her. She'd done nothing but taunt him about his severity since their first meeting all those years ago. And yes, Alistair could be a prig. But last night had been more of a revelation than anything. *Is he truly so uptight because he's nervous in society?*

Another thought flitted through her head. *But he is so cruel to me about my supposed lack of decorum.*

"Is something amiss?" Gemma's voice cut into her thoughts as she tightened the fastenings of Addy's stays.

Addy forced a cheery smile. "No, no. Nothing is amiss. It's simply...I fear I have misapprehended someone's nature. Of course, I could be right about this person, but still..." she sighed, twisting a loose strand of hair around her finger. "If I was wrong, I have been dreadfully cruel. But am I less cruel if this individual was cruel in turn to me?"

Gemma's forehead knitted as she finished tying Addy's stays. "Methinks an apology goes a long way, Miss Adelaide."

An apology? Addy's throat tightened. She wasn't sure if she was ready to resort to *that* yet. But she would continue to observe Alistair closely. It didn't help matters that he was dreadfully handsome.

***

When Addy entered the breakfast room, she was ushered to her seat, today between Serena and James, which proved amusing, as the two of them engaged in light, playful conversation throughout the meal, as though she were invisible. She had half a mind to bump her foot against James' under the table for good measure but refrained today.

As usual, Aunt Agatha outdid herself with breakfast, serving an array of pastries, meats and eggs in an attempt to impress the Scotts and the Ashworths. Lord Badley was seated across from her, coincidentally beside Alistair, whom she tried desperately to ignore throughout the meal. On Alistair's other side, of course, Cordelia sat. She'd been clinging to him like ivy since the ball.

But as she sat down, heat spread over her skin as her eyes flickered into his. And she scarcely noticed Badley throughout the rest of breakfast, which Mother and Aunt Agatha would find displeasing.

Lord Badley inquired if she slept well, and she nodded with a smile. "Very." Though, that was a lie. She'd slept horribly. The last few nights she'd tossed and turned to no end.

Aunt Agatha, seated at one end of the table, rose and clinked a spoon against her glass. "After breakfast, we shall traverse to the pond north of our house. It is frozen solid, and will make for a wonderful rink for the young people to skate upon."

Everyone began to murmur excitedly, and Addy of course didn't miss the coy smile Serena flashed James. The two of them were becoming insufferably smitten with one another, which must please Aunt Agatha greatly. But of course, James always was perfect in her eyes. The same couldn't be said for Addy. In fact, Aunt Agatha might even prefer James over Eloise, since by virtue, he was the son she'd always wanted.

She turned her attention to Eloise and Captain Crawford further down the table. Captain Crawford was seated across from Eloise, and it was clear that the two were drawn deeply to one another. He was saying something to Eloise, and she'd cast her eyes down shyly to her plate, her cheeks flushed prettily, a soft smile curving her lips. Captain Crawford said something else, which caused her to laugh. A pang went through Addy.

She might despise the idea of marriage, but in moments like this, she wished desperately she could connect with the man selected for her as smoothly as Serena and Eloise did. But instead, she was drawn to the man directly across from her, intended for Cordelia Ashworth.

Addy propped her chin on her hand and began to stir her tea with more aggression than was necessary, earning her a sharp look from Mother.

With a sigh, she laid down her spoon and waited restlessly for breakfast to be over so she could go skate. When she glanced up, she found Alistair watching her, his expression, like always, inscrutable. *I don't understand you, Alistair Dowden. Not one bit.*

At last, breakfast ended, and everyone departed on foot for the pond, all but for the older women and men, including Addy's parents, who came by sledge. Laughter rose up from the party as they slogged through the thick snow to the pond, and a footman accompanied them with the skates in tow. Another pair of footmen brought several benches for the skaters' use.

The young women pulled on their skates first, all of them bedecked in heavy coats and woollen scarves and mittens. Mother scurried over to where Addy sat, tying her laces. "Lord Badley is captivated by you. See how he stares at you now?"

She nodded to the tall, black-haired man across the pond, already gliding across it on his sparkling blades. He flashed a smile that should have

Addy's knees buckling. But instead, she felt nothing. Just a cool disinterest. "I overheard him telling Captain Crawford that you are a ravishing creature," Mother whispered in Addy's ear.

Addy rose, smoothing her skirts, and took a deep breath, stepping onto the ice. Nearby, James sped over to where Serena sat, lacing up her own skates, and offered her his hand once she'd finished. Addy could scarcely smother a smile at the sight.

"I'm afraid I'm a dreadful skater," Cordelia's shrill voice rang across the ice. Addy turned to see her sitting on one of the benches, as Alistair stood poised in front of her and his mother.

Rosalind Dowden beamed between Cordelia and Alistair, satisfaction flashing in her eyes. Over the past several days, she'd done little to conceal just how much she'd like to see a match form between Alistair and Cordelia.

"Take care," she was saying to the two of them as they set off together, across the pond. Lady Dowden touched her mouth, her eyes twinkling as she watched the pair depart. And truly, they made for a handsome pair. Alistair was tall, with his dark curling hair and deep blue eyes. Cordelia's blond hair, porcelain skin, and angelic features complemented his features.

Addy's heart sank when she turned to see Lady Dowden now gazing at *her*, her expression turned cold. Addy swept onward, a pit yawning in her stomach. Did Lady Dowden suspect something afoot between her and Alistair? She needn't worry. A surge of defensiveness rose in Addy.

The woman needn't worry. Not one bit.

With a small sigh, she turned her attention to skating, perhaps going a little faster than she should, but her body ached with pent-up energy, and she loved the exhilaration of soaring across the ice. It was almost as heady as flying on horseback across an open field.

She paused for a breath on the edge of the ice, lowering herself onto a bench on the banks, when Lord Badley skated over to her, his mouth curving as he peered down at her. He extended his hand towards her. "You are an exceptional skater, Miss Fawcett," he told her, his voice silky and deep. It should send Addy's heart fluttering. But as she turned her head, her eyes met Alistair's across the ice. His expression, of course, was unreadable.

And just like that, the butterflies burst to life inside her.

She tore her gaze from his, focusing on the man beside her. "Thank you, Lord Badley," she murmured in her most demure voice, her mouth dry.

"You possess a grace on the ice that rivals any I have seen," he continued, as they moved across the pond, following close behind Eloise and Captain Crawford. Eloise nearly slipped just then, but Captain Crawford caught her, and the two burst into laughter. A pang went through Addy, and for a terrible moment, she longed for Alistair to be beside her instead of Lord Badley.

She clenched her teeth, willing this thought away. But it didn't scatter. Instead, it lingered in the back of her head. Addy stole another glance towards Alistair, and the weight of his gaze nearly knocked her off balance. A shiver went down her spine. *I wish I could have the chance to understand you better.*

But all we do when we're together is despise one another. Surely it would be fruitless to pursue anything with him. Not to mention the fact that his mother's cold look earlier indicated it would be an unwelcome match.

At last, everyone retired from the pond, cold but merry, and began the long walk back to the house. The sky had darkened over the past two hours, hinting at a snowstorm. Aunt Agatha and the rest of the older people sped past in their sledge, and Aunt Agatha called to the young people that hot chocolate would be served back at the manor.

Addy's mouth watered. She loved hot chocolate. And it would be welcome after the skating.

Lord Badley fell into step alongside her. "What can you not do?" he asked her, his eyes glinting. Again, she glimpsed that spark of possessiveness in his expression, and it dismayed her.

"I'm afraid I am hardly accomplished as a young lady of my station ought to be," she told him, wondering if Mother would materialise out of the mist and scold her right then and there for saying such a thing.

Lord Badley's expression, however, did not waver. "Ah, you mustn't speak of yourself in such a fashion."

His voice deepened then, and he paused, and she did as well, although somewhat reluctantly. "Miss Fawcett, you are truly exceptional. You are nothing like the girls back in London, nothing whatsoever." He shook his head, his gaze skating over her. "You are everything a lady ought to be. You would shine like a star in the London social scene. Especially its political sphere. As my…" and here he cut himself off, lowering his gaze to the ground. The rest of the party fell away from them, leaving them behind in the cold air.

"Addy!" Eloise and Captain Crawford paused a little further ahead, and past them, Addy noticed Alistair stop in his tracks as well, staring back to where she and Lord Badley stood together.

Her pulse leapt and she managed to cast Lord Badley another polite smile and hurried on, but he matched her pace. "I hope I did not overstep, Miss Fawcett."

"No, no." But Addy suddenly wished she could be alone again, in her room. Her thoughts blurred together, a cacophony of chaos. But then again, chaos had always trailed her, no matter where she went or what she did.

"I understand you are partial to your independence," Lord Badley continued, crunching through the snow beside her.

"And that did not trouble you?" Disappointment flickered through Addy. For a moment, the words, *I do not wish to marry, but if I did, it wouldn't be to you,* balanced on the tip of her tongue. She swallowed them hastily.

"Hardly," Lord Badley smirked.

Her mother's voice swam through her head. *You could not do better than Badley.*

At the very least, he was not put off by her flagrant behaviour. In fact, he seemed charmed by it.

As far as she knew, Alistair viewed it in quite an opposing light.

So, why am I so drawn to him?

"Pray, explain your lack of alarm. I should like to know," she said, using her most charming smile.

"Well, as a politician, I shall be frequently occupied with my endeavours in parliament, as you can imagine. And I should desire a wife who will not fault me for being frequently absorbed in my career, in social expectations, and so on."

"Ah." Now Addy could see why her aunt had paired her with Lord Badley. On paper, they made a perfect pair. His expectations aligned with hers, and if she were to ever marry, she could not hope for a better husband. He would leave her to her own devices, and he clearly wished to be left alone to his own. But she couldn't shake the unsettled sense that lurked in the back of her mind.

***

Back at Worthington Manor, Addy changed into an evening gown and joined Serena, Cordelia, and Eloise in the hall. They were all whispering together excitedly over the events of that day, the romantic excursion upon the ice with their respective suitors.

"My cousin is besotted," Eloise was grinning, and Serena blushed, shaking her auburn ringlets. "I've never seen him so besotted before"

Addy nodded in agreement. "Truly."

Cordelia sighed loudly. "I confess, I wish it were easier to make out Lord Dowden's feelings about me. He is so aloof, it at times is beyond me, to discern his intent."

"He was most attentive to you on the ice," Serena offered, eager to reassure her.

Addy dug her nails into her palm and excused herself to fetch her wrap that she'd left there, as an excuse to flee this conversation. She didn't have anything to offer Cordelia in terms of encouragement. Even if she did, the words would stick in her throat.

But when she returned, she froze at the sound of voices floating down the hall, from the top of the staircase where Alistair and his mother had paused to speak in private. They did not notice her pressed against the wall nearby, listening.

"Miss Ashworth is a remarkable skater, is she not? And she is drawn to you, my dear. Charmed!"

"Charmed," Alistair let out a soft, humourless laugh.

"And did you not hear her play the pianoforte the other night? Her voice is like that of an angel's!"

"Indeed." It was difficult to detect any sort of emotion in Alistair's voice. *What does he truly think of Cordelia?*

"She is gentle, sweet, polished in every way. Her parents have reared her admirably. I cannot say the same for..." Addy's stomach churned as Lady Dowden whispered her name. Alistair did not speak, but his mother drove on. "Alistair, you could not hope for a better match than Miss Ashworth"

"We ought to join the others downstairs," Alistair at last replied.

A lump formed in Addy's throat, and she remained rooted to the spot, her eyes stinging as Lady Dowden's slight sank in. Yes, she'd not been mistaken earlier, when she'd found the woman glaring at her across the pond.

Chapter 10

Alistair's mother continued down the stairs, leaving him alone on the steps. He inhaled deeply, tamping down a rush of annoyance at his mother's comments, her praise for Cordelia and her disparaging remark about Adelaide. There was something pointed about her words, as if she'd noticed something between himself and the Fawcett girl.

He at last stirred and continued down the stairs, but at the bottom, he turned to see Adelaide descend, gliding her hand along the bannister as she moved with surprising grace, just as she had earlier on the ice. Admiration rose in him, and his throat tightened as he stared, unable to tear his gaze from her. Longing pricked behind his ribcage.

She at last reached the bottom of the steps as well, pausing just a few steps above him, and he couldn't move, mouth as dry as an African desert.

"Lord Dowden," she murmured, and this time, she spoke his name without the usual acerbity.

"Miss Fawcett." His thoughts ran together in a tangled mess. "You—" he paused, considering his next words. "You are a wonderful skater."

Her eyes widened, her lips parting. "My! A compliment from Alistair Dowden?" But for some reason, her sarcasm did not send a flare of irritation through him this time. Perhaps it was the lack of derision in her brown eyes that dulled the edge of her words. Instead, his heart began to thud wildly in his chest. "What have I done to merit such a marvel?"

A laugh bubbled in his throat, and her cheeks bloomed with a bright flush. "I am not endeavouring to tease you," he hastened to tell her.

Her brow furrowed as she studied him for a long moment, as if trying to ascertain if he was being truthful.

"Adelaide—" A dozen words sat on the tip of his tongue, but his mouth was too dry to speak, and he cut himself off.

The moment ended too soon; his opportunity was lost. At the top of the staircase, Cordelia and her parents appeared. "Lord Dowden!" Cordelia cried. "I am relieved to find you did not catch a cold today."

Adelaide skirted past, her expression shuttering closed, barring him from reading her. His heart sank, and he resisted the urge to watch her cross the grand foyer to the drawing room. "Miss Ashworth," he bowed as Cordelia reached the ground, and offered him a gloved hand to kiss.

He knew he was meant to escort her to the drawing room, and reluctantly offered an arm to her. Behind them, he glimpsed Lord and Lady Ashford exchanging pleased smiles.

In the drawing room, Lady Worthington announced a game of whist would commence, which explained the tables set up around the room with four chairs at each. Alistair led Cordelia to the nearest one once Lady Worthington finished with her announcement.

Cordelia giggled. "I fear I am a poor hand at whist," she admitted to Alistair.

"Surely not," he replied, maintaining an air of polite attentiveness. To his surprise, Lord Badley and Adelaide joined them, though it wasn't by choice. They'd been relegated to this table by Lady Worthington.

"Oh, but I am!" she cried, resting a hand on her heart. Her eyes twinkled. "

A strange tension hung in the air as the game commenced.

Alistair struggled to keep his gaze from Adelaide as the cards were dealt, but jealousy plucked inside him as he noticed Lord Badley's open admiration of her. The man was a charlatan. He didn't truly care for Adelaide, not in the way he should. This was merely a political move, in his eyes.

He clenched his jaw and centred his attention on the game. But to his surprise, Adelaide laid down a clever play at the end of the first match, her eyes sparkling with excitement.

"Good heavens, Miss Fawcett. You have a mind for this game!" exclaimed Lord Badley, offering her an arch grin.

"That is very kind of you, Lord Badley."

"But of course."

The rest of the afternoon passed quickly, with Adelaide winning most of the matches at their table. Alistair couldn't help but be impressed by her quick mind and her witty quips as she laid down her cards, each play putting the rest of them to shame. Badley held his own, however, winning almost as often as Adelaide, and he was clearly amused by this, frequently casting her worshipful glances.

Alistair pretended to ignore this.

He and Cordelia talked the most, Cordelia about London whist parties and the opera, while Lord Badley took it upon himself to enlighten them on the ins and outs of parliamentary elections and his hopes for the next election when he intended to run. Alistair asked polite questions about the political scene, though each word stuck in his throat.

As dinner drew close, the tables switched, and Alistair was grateful for the chance to separate himself from Cordelia, ending up at James' table. Adelaide and Lord Badley remained at the same table, however, joined by Eloise and Captain Crawford. Alistair laid down a successful play, wishing for a moment he could've done so at Adelaide's table.

James leaned over, stealing a look towards his sister and Badley at the neighbouring table. "Adelaide may have met her match at whist."

"I did not realise she was so masterful at the game," Alistair admitted under his breath.

"Ah, yes. Adelaide is full of surprises, isn't she?" James chuckled; his smile pointed. Alistair flushed, realising that his friend was reading him like an open book. Was he really so obvious?

"Indeed, she is," he murmured.

Serena and her mother joined them at their table just then, cutting off their conversation.

Laughter rang out just then and he glanced over to see Adelaide and Badley chuckling over something. An intimate joke told by Lord Badley for Adelaide alone. It sounded like some sort of limerick for Adelaide's ears alone.

For a long moment, he wondered if he ought to share his suspicions about the man with James. Surely James would agree with him, deem Lord Badley less than honourable to pursue his sister purely for political gain.

Perhaps Crawford had said something already. And perhaps, James did not deem it significant enough, though Alistair doubted it. James had always loved his sister dearly, so if he suspected anything amiss with Badley, surely he would baulk at the arrangement.

At last, the party dispersed to ready themselves for dinner. Alistair lingered in the drawing room, taking a moment to enjoy the warmth of the fire in the hearth, blazing away merrily. Out of the corner of his eye, he noted Adelaide also hang back, pausing to sniff a bouquet of Christmas roses that adorned one of the marble-topped tables in the room.

His heart leapt, and he turned, bracing himself, approaching her quietly as she straightened, her eyes widening slightly as she realised he had hung back.

"Lord Dowden," she said in a tone he couldn't decipher.

"Permit me to say that you are a wondrous card player," he managed, throat nearly closed.

Her eyebrows rose, and she let out a soft, somewhat shaky laugh. "What have I done to deserve not one but *two* commendations from Alistair Dowden?"

"Truly," he said, breathless. "I—" he stopped short, noticing that Adelaide's maid had slipped into the room to monitor them. "I pray you forgive me for my uncouth words the other day at the stable."

He half-expected her to say something mocking; to laugh and inform him she didn't regret her own part. But instead, she nodded, a flush rising up her throat. "And I must ask you to pardon me, for my own unkindness." She gave her head a small shake. "I confess, I was clinging to our childish quarrels, and that was hardly fair of me."

Alistair blinked, startled. "Ah, yes. Our quarrels. You know, I am still astounded that you possess such incredible aim. How far did you send that cherry? It was halfway across your parents' lawn."

Adelaide's flush deepened, her sooty lashes sweeping her cheeks. "Good heavens. I don't know what possessed me. I suppose I felt left out. You and James wanted nothing to do with me, and it made me quite cross." She drew her fingertips against the petals of one of the roses, before at last lifting her eyes to his. Alistair's breath caught in his lungs.

After a long moment, she spoke again. "I am most sorry about the loss of your father. I know that I have never expressed my condolences since we met again. And that is unforgivable."

Alistair strained to keep his eyes from drifting to her lips. He opened his mouth to speak when Adelaide's maid cleared her throat, and he stepped back, remembering himself. Somehow, without realising it, he'd drifted close to her. Too close for propriety.

"I—I ought to retire to my room to ready for dinner," Adelaide whispered, and his heart lurched when her eyes drifted down to his own mouth. It all happened so fast he could scarcely comprehend it, and then she'd turned and hastened away, out of the drawing room, leaving him alone.

His knees shaking, he followed her after a few moments, struggling to compose himself. Once back in his room, he closed the door and paced the floor, heart racing again. What had just transpired? He did not know how to even begin making sense of it.

At last, he sank into the armchair in the corner of the room, resting his head in his hands. His father's words haunted him, resounding through his head on repeat. *Do not forget, my boy. You must put duty above all else. The Dowden estate is in your hands.*

For the first time, he baulked at those words. Cordelia might be a perfect match for him, but that did not change his burgeoning feelings for Adelaide. She might not be the prim and proper lady that Cordelia was, but that did not change her family's standing, their repute. The Ashworths were, of course, prominent in London society, and it would be advantageous to marry her. But did that not make him as disingenuous as Lord Badley?

And furthermore, did duty necessitate a lifetime of misery married to the one he did not love?

Even Father had married Mother for love. And yet…

Alistair groaned into his hands, and stood, crossing the room to splash water on his hot face in the porcelain basin of the commode. Of course, Father did not have a grieving mother who depended upon him. And Mother had her heart set upon Cordelia. She could not make it clearer that she found Adelaide wanting.

She did not forget, either, how Adelaide had launched a cherry at Alistair's shirt all those years ago, her headstrong nature, her tendency to run about Fairfield Manor barefoot, hair unkempt, skirts caked in mud.

She'd hardly been impressed by Adelaide Fawcett, that much was certain.

With a sigh, he called his valet to help him ready for dinner, watching in the mirror as Jenkins arranged his silk cravat about his throat, smoothing the jacket upon his shoulders until he was presentable for the evening meal.

Dinner was another challenge in itself. At the table, Alistair was seated beside Adelaide, which hardly helped his predicament. Across the table, Badley sat, heralding Adelaide with a story of his recent trip to Venice, how underground carnival parties were held since they'd been outlawed a while ago. She listened raptly, her eyes bright in the glow of the candelabra. Alistair pushed around the food on his plate as he listened to her ply the politician with question after question.

Footmen brought out a platter of roasted pig, causing a gasp to rise from the group at the table.

"What of you, Lord Dowden? Do you travel much?" Badley asked Alistair as a footman began to carve the pig.

"Not much," Alistair admitted. "Though, I should like to. As heir of the Dowden estate, however, I can scarcely account for frequent absences."

"Ah. Well, should you ever venture south, do take an opportunity to visit Assissi. An idyllic town in the Perugian mountains, if ever there was one."

Alistair managed a tight smile in thanks for this recommendation. "I shall consider it."

Adelaide sighed, her dark eyes flickering into his. "I should like to venture to the continent one of these days. I dream of seeing the Far East as well. Perhaps our colonies in the Far East! Or Athens! Perhaps even the West Indies."

"The West Indies!" Captain Crawford turned then from his conversation with Miss Wortham. "I'm afraid the West Indies are all plantations and pirates, Miss Fawcett."

"Pirates," she echoed, her eyes shining. Alistair smothered a grin. Ah yes, he well-remembered her adoration of adventure. It lived on, strong as ever. Hardly stamped out by polite society. But then again, Adelaide Fawcett would never be moulded by societal expectations. Not the Adelaide he knew.

"Adelaide!" Lady Fairfield exclaimed, further down the table. She began to laugh, a forced sound. "Good heavens, she says the most outrageous things?"

Adelaide's cheeks flushed, but she lifted her chin defiantly, still not cowed by her mother's statement.

Admiration flared in Alistair's chest. He envied her unapologetic brazenness and wished he was more capable of that sort of attitude. But he'd always been flustered so easily, eager to fall in line and do as was expected.

"I should like to see Paris, but only if it is at peace," Miss Wortham spoke up then, sharing a smile with Adelaide.

"Paris!" Lady Ashford shuddered. "What a gruesome place."

"Notre Dame is, of course, magnificent, but yes, it is a place filled with rats and waste," added Lady Scotfell.

"I should like to visit Moscow one of these days," James announced. "Before it was ransacked by jolly old Buonaparte."

"Hear, hear!" Lords Scott and Ashford agreed.

Cordelia set down her glass of wine. "For my part, I am quite content in Bath. Surely no place comes close to the refreshing waters of

Bath." The room stilled for a second before others around the table nodded their agreement. *Bath? Of all the places in the world—Bath?* Alistair glanced over at Adelaide, and her expression matched how he felt.

"I for one am delighted I ventured to Bath this summer. Otherwise, I might have never made acquaintance with Lord Worthington and his daughter," Captain Crawford spoke up, in an effort to break the awkward silence, but genuineness rang in his words. Miss Wortham flushed, dropping her eyes to her plate bashfully.

Not long after, dinner concluded, and Lady Worthington announced to the group that they should retire to the drawing room for music after the men enjoyed a game or two of billiards. "Eloise is a beautiful singer, and my niece plays exceptionally well."

Adelaide's eyes widened slightly, and she bit her lip, her brows knitting as if she did not appreciate the compliment. Intrigued, Alistair anticipated the rest of the evening. He'd never seen Adelaide play the pianoforte as of yet, not once in their entire acquaintance. He had no idea she even played it to begin with.

Chapter 11

Addy confronted her aunt once all the gentle sex had retired to the drawing room. "Aunt Agatha, you know I despise playing," she sighed, falling into step alongside the older woman.

"Oh, Adelaide. Must you be so difficult about everything?"

"Mamma, if she doesn't wish to play—" Eloise began, as she waited for them at the double doors of the dining room.

Aunt Agatha waved her hand. "Posh! She has done very little to recommend herself to Lord Badley, and I fear that he will abandon any attempts at pressing suit if he thinks her utterly lacking in accomplishments. The only thing she has shown herself to excel at is riding and skating."

She spoke as if Addy wasn't right there, and fury flared in her chest. She clenched her hands and took a deep, steadying breath. "Very well, Aunt Agatha."

Eloise grasped her by the hand and drew her towards a dark and quiet corner of the drawing room before everyone else reached it.

"I must tell you something," Eloise whispered, as they came to a pause behind a potted plant, softly enough that no one would overhear. "Captain Crawford kissed me!" Between the whist game and dinner earlier...and it all happened so suddenly, I did not expect it, or know what to do. But it was—it was heavenly, Addy. Heavenly!"

Addy grinned. "Does your mamma know?"

"Heavens, no! She would have a conniption."

"That is very true."

"Then, does he mean to wed you?"

"He said he would like to," Eloise covered her mouth, shaking her head so hard her curls flounced about her rosy cheeks. "I did not know a man such as him even existed, Addy. He is...he is so good, and noble, and kind. And he doesn't mind that I'm quiet, a wallflower. He somehow draws me out, with such ease, and it astonishes me, how effortless it is to converse with him."

Addy's heart squeezed. For the first time, a surge of envy went through her, that her cousin should find such camaraderie in the arms of a suitor. "Do you think your mother would object?"

"Oh, no. I don't believe she would. Which is so strange, because ordinarily she would. But she spoils me, Addy. And I think she'd given up on me ever marrying anyhow. I am so quiet."

"But he understands you, does he not? He sees beyond that." Wistfulness rose to choke Addy. Her mind flew to Alistair, to the moment they'd shared in the drawing room earlier, fraught with a heat and longing she didn't even think possible.

"Alistair and I spoke for a moment, earlier. In the drawing room, before dinner. He asked for my forgiveness for our childish quarrels, and I asked for his. I never imagined such a thing would happen."

"Addy!" Eloise whispered, unable to stifle a giggle. "I think Alistair is mad about you."

"He isn't! He can't be." Addy didn't dare believe it. It was futile, regardless. His mother wanted him to marry Cordelia Ashworth. For a moment, she considered telling Eloise what she had overheard on the stairs earlier, but bit back the words. She didn't wish to cause any sort of spectacle or turmoil. She tended to be disruptive enough as it was.

"Girls!" Aunt Agatha's voice rang shrilly from across the room. "What are the two of you whispering about over there?" She and the other ladies had just entered, and they all took their seats about the room.

"What song do you mean to play, Adelaide?" Serena asked as she situated herself beside her mother.

"I—I think O Come, O Come, Emmanuel should suffice," Addy told her, taking a seat at the pianoforte.

"Such a beautiful song," declared Lady Scotfell.

Addy began to flip through a book of compositions on the pianoforte to find the right one. At last, she discovered it and set up the book on the stand. As she did so, she glanced up to find Lady Dowden eyeing her closely, one eyebrow lifted. Her features were taut as if with vexation, and Addy offered a careful smile, which was not returned. Wonderful. The woman despised her.

She counts me a threat to her plans for Alistair and Cordelia.

With a small sigh, she began to play. She might detest playing, but she'd always excelled at it. It certainly wasn't her first choice of pastimes. She'd much prefer to be riding or running across a field. Behind her, Eloise began to sing, her beautiful voice ringing out through the room.

The gathered women gasped and murmured praise for their playing, and Addy glanced over to see Mother, beaming in pride for once. She'd hardly wear that expression if she knew that Addy was developing feelings for someone other than Lord Badley.

When they finished the song, applause filled the air. "Wondrous players!" exclaimed Lady Ashford. "Nearly as wondrous as my dear Cordelia."

Cordelia preened beneath her mother's statement and Addy just barely refrained from rolling her eyes.

It wasn't exactly fair, since Cordelia Ashworth was a sweet young woman. But something about her grated on Addy's nerves. And the girl's parents certainly didn't help either, with all their fawning

Lady Scotfell glanced over at Aunt Agatha. "Eloise ought to have been an opera singer."

Aunt Agatha laughed. "Isn't she marvellous?"

"Play another, Adelaide. I think another carol would do," Mother said from her own place on one of the settees.

"Ah, the gentlemen are coming," said Aunt Agatha, tilting her head as if to listen closely.

Addy and Eloise decided next on "Silent Night", and as the gentlemen entered the drawing room, Addy began to play, letting instinct take the helm. Her fingers flew over the ivory keys as she began the song, and Eloise sang the first verse.

Addy made the mistake of lifting her gaze again from the piano, and this time, her eyes locked with Alistair's. He had taken his customary station at the window nearby, and his intense gaze caused her stomach to squirm strangely.

It was a good thing she was seated. For she doubted her legs would hold her up. She withdrew her gaze from his, heart thundering wildly, and glanced towards Captain Crawford to check his expression. He was rapt. Positively enthralled. Eloise captivated him desperately, and it was heartwarming to watch.

What is happening to me? Before this trip, she'd been so set upon despising romance and everything it represented. She might enjoy a romance novel or two, but it was an entirely different matter to experience it on the page rather than in real life. It wasn't nearly as terrifying and dizzying.

She continued to play, their audience remained hushed, spellbound. Eloise's voice lifted in a crescendo as she reached the bridge of the song, and she heard gasps from the rest of the guests. Pride surged in her, and for a moment, Addy wondered if she herself ought to pursue the stage. Of course, that would horrify her mother.

At last, they finished the song and Eloise excused herself to take a seat on the settee beside Serena, her cheeks as red as holly berries. The room erupted in a loud volley of applause.

Addy rose as well, simultaneously relieved and disappointed that the performance was over. For the first time, she'd actually enjoyed playing. Instead of joining her mother on the settee, she retreated to the back of the room where her father stood. Father grinned, patting her arm. He whispered in her ear, "Wondrous playing, my dear."

"Magnificent," Lord Badley stepped closer, beaming at her. He shook his head, his silky voice almost a purr. Perhaps another girl would swoon, but Adelaide did no such thing. She managed a bright smile and latched her arm with her father's, now not daring to glance towards Alistair until a few moments had passed, and quiet conversation rose in the room.

Addy retired early, along with Eloise and Serena. The three of them climbed the staircase, giggling amongst themselves. Addy had never understood those giddy girls who chattered nonsensically after a party, but tonight, she did. She looped arms with her cousin. "Well done, my fellow performer," she told Eloise.

"Captain Crawford couldn't take his eyes off you," Serena told Eloise with a grin.

"And my cousin can't take his eyes from you."

Serena laughed, sighing. "You are too kind to me."

"Truly. I meant it when I informed you my brother is captivated," Addy interjected.

"Mamma is delighted to have made a match!" Eloise paused at her door, and Addy crossed over to hers. Serena floated on down the hall, a giddy smile upon her face, and Addy at last slipped into her bedroom, relieved.

She needed to contemplate everything that had happened that night, to make sense of her conversation with Alistair, that bewildering moment when they'd nearly kissed in the drawing room. Suppose they had? What would have been the aftermath of it?

"Silly conventions," she sighed to herself, ringing for Gemma. "If only it weren't so frowned upon to broach this matter with him, straight out. I despise this beating about the bush business."

Gemma appeared presently and helped her dress for bed, and Addy climbed beneath the covers. Sleep of course eluded her tonight. She kept flip-flopping back and forth until she sat up with a groan and snatched her robe. A glance at the clock told her it was nearly midnight. The rest of the house seemed quiet and peaceful. She could slip down to the library and peruse the shelves.

Find some solace in a book there, though she doubted that her aunt owned any novels. Aunt Agatha considered them wicked. It was a wonder Eloise had managed to sneak any past the woman.

Addy instead settled into the armchair before the window, not before lighting a taper. Then she began to read the novel she had packed in her own trunk. It was a new novel, one of several that James had snuck her a month earlier, somehow managing to smuggle it past Mother. Addy wondered if her mother had overlooked it since she always overlooked what he did, regardless of how mischievous

The romance in this particular novel was a forbidden one, set in a monastery in the Alps. A friar and a young nun burned with love for one another, despite their callings to their religious orders. Addy read it until dawn's first light, the wind howling through the trees outside her window. A blizzard rapidly approached. Which meant everyone would be trapped indoors for the day.

Addy nearly dropped her book when the door creaked open and Eloise stuck her head in through the crack. "You're awake, Addy?"

"I never slept," Addy admitted with a sheepish laugh.

Eloise hurried over to the bed and fell upon the downy mattress, reaching out her hand. "What are you reading?"

"A novel. Courtesy of James."

"Ah! Is it romantic?"

Addy stood and crossed the room to flop onto the bed beside her cousin. "Very. It is a tale of forbidden love."

"Something you know a great deal of," Eloise murmured.

"Certainly." Addy sighed. "Alistair's mother dislikes me, I think. I believe she suspects something is afoot between us."

"Which it is."

"Indeed. But she needn't worry. Alistair is committed to duty. This is nothing more than a silly tryst to him. I am sure. What else could it be?"

"Perhaps, he doesn't care for Cordelia. Perhaps he just wants to court you?"

"We might have forgiven one another, and put our quarrels in the past, but he surely doesn't deem me a suitable match. And—and it frightens me. The idea of love. It means surrendering to—" Addy closed her eyes tightly. "He is all duty, and I have my ideals."

"Your ideals, I think, are simply that you yearn for respect. But take your mother and father. Your mother would never be one to be ignored by your father. She is, I think, even more opinionated than you. And your father adores her."

Addy paused, frowning. "But that is so rare. And—and I do not think they loved one another when they wed all those years ago. *If* I were to ever wed, it would only be for love."

"What if you are falling for Alistair?"

Addy burst out laughing. "Falling for Alistair! I couldn't be! No. Eloise, that is ridiculous."

"Is it?" Eloise narrowed her eyes.

"Yes! Indeed, it is! Very." Addy lowered her face to press it into the blankets beneath her. "I cannot...we are much too different. He is stilted and inflexible. And I am—"

"Stubborn. Very stubborn. And you bring him to life. I think he would lead a very dull life if he were to wed Cordelia."

"They are *meant* for each other!"

"But are they?" Eloise sat up, shaking her head. "If they were, would these desires even exist? Especially on his part. I don't think he cares for her. His mother might desire it, but he does not. It is clear to me, and I am certain Lady Dowden noticed it as well. Why else would she glare at you so?"

"So, if I were to wed him, I would be forever bound to a contentious mother by marriage?"

Eloise scrunched her nose. "Well, you did torment him so as a child."

"It is hopeless, Eloise. Hopeless."

"Perhaps. Or perhaps it isn't."

"Come, let us speak of you and Captain Crawford. I cannot believe he kissed you! How did he kiss you?"

"As I mentioned, it was most sudden. And quick. But it was," Eloise touched her lips. "It was magnificent."

The two of them burst into laughter.

"I cannot believe it. Though, I always suspected you would be the first of us to be kissed. In fact, I imagined you would be the only one of us to be kissed."

Addy battled down another surge of envy. If only it could be so simple for her as it was for Eloise. Though, Eloise deserved it. She was the kindest, sweetest person Addy knew, and she ought to have a true love like the dashing Captain Crawford.

A pang went through Addy. *Alistair and Cordelia will wed, and I will die a spinster.*

Chapter 12

After breakfast, during which Addy resolved not to look once in Alistair's direction—and succeeded—everyone retired to the drawing room, where several long tables had been erected, laden with ribbons, evergreen boughs, and pinecones.

Aunt Agatha announced to guests that they would be making garlands for the tree they'd cut down later that day, as it appeared the blizzard had quelled, at least for the time being. Everyone assembled at the tables, excited chatter rising, and Addy hurried to find a place beside Eloise. Of course, Captain Crawford joined them, as well as Serena, Lord and Lady Scotfell, and James.

Addy tried to centre her attention on the task at hand, through her wreaths were woefully dismal creations, her bows all uneven. She made the mistake of glancing over at Alistair across the room, where he was crafting garlands with Cordelia. She held one wreath up to him, giggling boisterously, and his chuckle reached Addy across the room.

"Is it tolerable, Lord Dowden?" she asked, tilting her head almost coyly.

"Quiet," he agreed, though his smile didn't quite reach his eyes.

"I have decorated my parents' home countless times. They say I've become quite proficient at it, wouldn't you say."

"Indeed, you have," Alistair replied.

She wrenched her gaze from them and tried to enjoy the chatter between Serena and Eloise—it was comforting to have their camaraderie this week, more than she'd expected.

The three of them burst into laughter as Addy held up her pitiful garland, with its droopy bows and withered leaves. "I'm afraid that wreath-decorating is *not* my forte," she admitted with a shrug. James and Captain Crawford joined in their laughter, and to Addy's dismay, Lord Badley left the other table to see what the mirth was about.

"Ah, but you could never do ill with anything," he exclaimed, dampening the merriment. Addy struggled to smile again then, wondering why it was so difficult to receive anything he said. Something about his words always fell flat—they lacked a kind of sincerity, though it was difficult to put her finger on it.

She smiled tautly and started to tie another ribbon. Her fingers were sore from being pricked by pine needles, yet she scarcely noticed as she wished that Badley would just leave her be.

She stole a glance towards Alistair, and a shiver trickled down her spine when she found him already peering at her. He held her gaze for a moment before turning to help Cordelia with fastening a trinket to their wreath. Envy rose to choke her and she tried to focus on Eloise and Serena who were discussing the most delightful Christmas sweetmeats.

"Cherry trifle," Serena declared.

James chimed in to second her opinion, much to Addy's amusement. Truthfully, she had never seen James so captivated by a young lady before. It was, she had to admit, quite endearing.

Eloise pondered for a moment. "Gingerbread is truly delectable."

"Gingerbread!" Captain Crawford, standing beside her, smiled down at Eloise, with such fondness that Addy's chest ached.

I'm supposed to despise marriage and all its entanglements, she thought bitterly. *And yet, here I am, envying my cousin her romance.*

Lord Badley brought his lips close to her ear, but not too close, for propriety's sake. "And what tickles your fancy, Miss Fawcett?"

She tried to laugh, though it fell unconvincingly in her own ears. "A great many things, I must confess. I've always had something of a penchant for sweet things. And reading."

"I can testify to that," James chuckled. "At Christmastide, when Addy was but a girl, she was wont to creep down to the kitchens and ask Cook for scraps of gingerbread."

Addy's face heated but she couldn't help but laugh at her older brother's good-natured teases. The others also laughed uproariously at this story, before Aunt Agatha interrupted, clinging a spoon against her glass in her customary bid for attention.

"Since it seems the blizzard has passed by without circumstance, I believe it would be a perfect day for the young men to venture out for a Christmas tree. The Worthington estate boasts a fine forest for just such an undertaking."

James raised a toast to this, earning him an exasperated but amused glance from Aunt Agatha. Addy stole another look at Alistair, beside Cordelia. She was sending him these coy looks beneath her lashes, her lips forming a pout. Something in Addy snapped.

"I shall go along as well. It's a beautiful winter day for a jaunt," she cried out.

Aunt Agatha's mouth went slack, but to Addy's delight, Eloise spoke up, "I shall as well!"

"Heavens!" Aunt Agatha began to protest, but then Serena added, "And so shall I!"

Addy hoped that Cordelia would not decide to go, and to her relief, the young woman did not volunteer.

It was clear the idea of going out into this cold weather dismayed her. So much the better, Addy nearly smirked. "I fear I ought not to go along—it is much too cold. And I fear I shall catch my death I do."

When Addy turned her head, her eyes locked with Alistair's once again. His cheeks flushed, and the corner of his mouth twitched. Was he pleased? Or did he find her uncouth?

She would have to find out on the hike if she got the opportunity. As she moved to follow her cousin and Serena upstairs to dress for the excursion, she met Cordelia's eyes and was taken aback by the usually sunny-natured Cordelia's hot glare.

I think she despises me now.

It didn't take long to find warm garments to cover herself for the hike out into the woods. When she returned downstairs to the drawing room, it was mostly empty, save for Lord Scotfell, dozing on the settee, and Alistair, standing at the window, evidently his preferred place in any given room. He gazed out, his forehead knitted, but he turned when Addy entered.

For a moment she paused, catching her breath as their eyes met. "Lord Dowden," she curtsied, and drifted further into the room, pausing at the table to fidget with one of the ribbons there. Footsteps sounded behind her, and suddenly Alistair was just beside her, picking up a pine cone and twisting it this way and that between his fingers.

"Miss Fawcett, did you happen to steal any gingerbread from the cook downstairs?"

Heat rose into Addy's face. "You overheard James' story?" she huffed, a laugh spilling off her tongue.

"I confess, I did," Alistair grinned. *Is this truly the same man I despised a little more than a week ago?*

"Has it forever established me as a shameless gingerbread indulgent?"

She and Alistair shared another laugh before she dropped her gaze again, afraid that if she kept looking into his eyes she'd fall into his arms. And someone could walk in any moment. And he might not want her to…yet…what could explain the way he looked at her across the room these past few days?

Eloise slipped into the room just then, and with a grin, said, "I'm rather cold. I must warm myself by the fire." She stayed across the room in front of the hearth, holding her hands close to the leaping flames. A surge of gratitude rose in Addy for her cousin, and she glanced back up at Alistair.

"If you will believe it, I once ate so many shortbread biscuits that I made myself ill," Alistair murmured.

Addy shook her head, scarcely able to believe that this was one and the same man as the boy she remembered, with his disapproving curl of the lip and shrewd eyes.

"Mother!" Eloise's voice sent them staggering back apart, just as Aunt Agatha rounded the corner and stood in the doorway, peering at each of them closely, her eyes narrowed.

"Well, Adelaide. I beg you to take care. I am not certain what possessed you to propose that you and the other girls accompany the men on this errand. It is not quite suited to a lady's capabilities, you understand?"

"I thought the walk would be welcome, after spending most of the morning within," Addy raised her chin defiantly. Out of the corner of her eye, she was startled to see Alistair smother a grin, which he attempted to hide by ducking his head.

Aunt Agatha's mouth tightened. "Very well. But take care. A Christmas tree hunt can be most perilous."

Addy almost rolled her eyes. "Yes, Aunt Agatha."

"We will be in good hands, Mamma," Eloise spoke up, by the fireplace.

Aunt Agatha sighed but nodded, and bustled over to peck a kiss to her daughter's cheek. "Off you go."

***

Addy, Serena, and Eloise clustered together on the snow-covered terrace. Excitement hung in the crisp air, and Addy was still in shock that Aunt Agatha had permitted them to accompany the gentlemen on this trip.

"I've never been to find a Christmas tree," Serena admitted beside her.

"Never fear!" James cried, grinning. "I shall see to it that you are well-looked after."

Serena laughed, biting her lip as she peered up at Addy's brother. She might find it revolting, their shameless trifling, but she liked Serena too much. Addy would not mind at all having her for a sister.

The door opened behind them as the last member of their party emerged—Lord Badley. Addy barely swallowed a sigh in time as he stepped up beside her.

"Lord Badley," she managed in an overly bright tone. Eloise gave her a knowing grin and Addy nearly made a face.

As the party climbed down the steps, her irritation faded as she met Alistair's eyes, and he fell into step alongside her. Suddenly, the day didn't seem so dismal at all.

Chapter 13

The bitter air stung Alistair's face as he trudged through the snow, trying his best not to watch how Lord Badley hung about Adelaide like a fly in the heat of summer. It turned his stomach, though triumph squeezed his chest as he noticed that Adelaide kept close to her cousin and Miss Scott, as if reluctant to remain alone for too long in Lord Badley's company.

This did not please Alistair. Not one bit.

The world around them sparkled, the ice and snow crunching loudly beneath their feet as they delved into the wooded portion of the Worthington estate. The sun peeked through the heavy clouds overhead, sending rays slanting through the trees.

His cut twisted when he noted how Lord Badley hastened to offer Adelaide his hand to help her over a fallen tree trunk, following the example of Captain Crawford and James, who each aided their respective maidens past the obstruction.

Addy's eyes shone, her cheeks flushed with exhilaration, even if she barely paid Badley a second glance. She walked arm-in-arm with her cousin and Miss Scott, and the three of them sang carols softly, laughing among themselves. Alistair tried to pay attention as James and Captain Crawford debated the merits of spruce and evergreen trees.

"Spruce are superior, I think," James opined, holding up a gloved hand to his eyes to see past the sun's glare off the snow.

"There! I see one over there looming above the rest," Captain Crawford pointed northward, and sure enough, a spruce stood tall and stately. Not tall enough however to stand too tall for the Worthington entry hall. It would be a perfect addition.

"That is precisely the sort of tree Mamma would deem worthy," Eloise said to Captain Crawford, accepting his hand as he helped her down an embankment.

Alistair paused at the base of the slope as Adelaide ignored Lord Badley's offered hand and carefully manoeuvred her way down all on her own. Alistair didn't miss the exhilarated smile spreading across her face, causing him to stifle another grin.

"I am hardly astonished that you decided to accompany us this afternoon in pursuit of this tree," he told her, the corner of his mouth quirking up.

"Then you are well-acquainted with my penchant for horrifying my aunt and mother."

Before this week, Alistair might have agreed unironically. But today, he shook his head. "A good walk in the snow has never harmed anyone."

"I should say," Adelaide laughed, and it was a pleasant sound to hear. Alistair reminded himself that this may be due to the fact that she wasn't laughing at *him*—but beneath that lurked something more confusing, dizzying. They fell into step beside each other towards the tree.

Somewhere behind the group, a footman scurried with an axe in hand. But at this moment, all that Alistair could care about was that he shared this moment with Adelaide. Badley walked ahead of them but kept casting them glances over his shoulder, his forehead creasing. Alistair ignored him, watching Adelaide out of the corner of his eye, a puff of frost swirling from her lips.

She had no right to be so lovely.

Her arm brushed his as they pressed on, and up ahead, James and Serena fell into step beside each other. Adelaide exchanged a look with Alistair. They shared a smile.

"I don't suppose you recall your second visit—it was just after Twelfth Night," Adelaide watched her step as they strolled through the snow-covered forest. "And I—I don't remember why, but I was so cross. So indignant. Over something you said about my riding bareback. I made a snowball and tossed it at you. And it hit your—"

"My back. I recall. You had me thinking that James had thrown it."

Adelaide brought a hand to her mouth, sooty lashes brushing her cheeks. "Forgive me."

"It is scarcely a justification for my disagreeable manner, but I confess that I was—I am—envious of your...spirit. You were always so bold, so determined to do what you liked, and not think twice about it. And I, on the other hand, am quite dissimilar to this in more ways than one. I envy your boldness. How you can do something without thinking twice about it."

"It has caused my family great grief on more than one occasion," Adelaide murmured.

"And that is another feat of yours I can only hope to employ. To continue on, regardless of who you may disappoint and—"

"Well, it isn't something I care to do, if that is what you denote." Adelaide's eyes flashed as she stared down at the ground.

Alistair realised his misstep. "No, no. I merely meant...I did not mean it in that fashion. Heavens, I am poor with words,"

"Perhaps a little. But it is rather endearing. Don't let anyone dissuade you from that." Alistair blushed as they joined the rest of the group in the clearing ahead, within it stood the spruce they'd seen from afar earlier.

"Surely we can find something grander, more impressive," Lord Badley frowned, setting his hands on his hips.

"If we find something too much bigger, it won't fit inside the manor," Alistair blurted, earning an irritated glance from Badley.

"How would we reach the top of it, anyway?" Eloise spoke up then, beside Captain Crawford, who nodded his agreement.

"This spruce is beautiful," Adelaide breathed, shaking her head as she gazed up at it, mouth open in awe.

Alistair smothered another pleased grin. Lord Badley scowled and shoved his hands into his coat pockets. "It's scarcely impressive. I've seen trees in London double its height. And your aunt's home could surely accommodate a tree such as that."

"Sometimes prestige is not everyone's primary interest," Alistair replied in clipped tones.

Badley's face flushed, his mouth compressing, but he did not reply.

"Shall we?" Captain Crawford asked.

The footman brought forth the axe and James swung first. But after several strokes, the spruce swayed precariously.

"I've never seen a tree be felled before," Adelaide admitted, and her breath caught as the tree groaned, and then began to topple. Without thinking, Alistair lunged forward, pulling Adelaide back against him, to ensure that she would not be in the falling tree's bath.

She gasped but did not struggle to get away. A cloud of snow rose into the air, stirred by the tree's impact.

Adelaide turned about, her breath hitching in the still air, and Alistair looked up to find the rest of the party staring at them, rather stunned by the sight of him holding Adelaide tightly in his arms. He released her, his face too hot, his breath stuck in his chest.

Good God, Alistair. What are you doing?

He glanced towards Badley, who was already giving him a withering glare. Adelaide stepped away from him, her cheeks stained a vivid pink, and to Alistair's relief, the moment passed. He hurried to help the other men lift the tree and carry it back towards the manor, a long, gruelling walk that he barely noticed, unable to stop thinking of the way Adelaide had felt in his arms. Her dark curls smelled of honey, and she'd been soft and warm in his arms.

Adelaide walked just ahead with the other girls, but several times, she glanced over her shoulder at him, the corner of her mouth curving upward in a soft smile.

His chest squeezed.

At last, they reached Worthington Manor, and the footmen greeted them taking the tree from them and carrying it the rest of the way indoors. The girls disappeared indoors, and Alistair followed with the other men. Just inside, James stopped him. "Thank you," he whispered, "for endeavouring to look after my dear little sister."

He winked and continued down the hall, leaving Alistair standing, stunned, before the great double doors that opened upon the terrace. As he continued down the hall towards his room, his mother intercepted him.

Rosalind grasped his arm and drew him into a private alcove. They would be in no danger of being overheard or disturbed here, and he could see that something weighed on her.

"Alistair, I am ill at ease over the manner in which you conduct yourself—around Miss Fawcett. Is Cordelia not everything you should desire in a bride?"

"Mother, I—"

"No, listen to me. Her family is of great station and import. I have told you—you could not hope to do better than her. And yet, I keep noticing how you pay rather more attention to Miss Fawcett than Miss Ashworth."

Alistair closed his eyes. "Mother. I beg you not to think of it in such a light. Miss Fawcett is the sister of my dear friend. And that is all there is to it."

"Indeed! I am not blind. I have seen the way you gaze at her across the room, when Cordelia is right there at your side."

"Forgive me, Mother," Alistair whispered.

"Cordelia Ashworth is your perfect match. She is quiet, sweet, and very accomplished. What more could you possibly need or want? What objections could you have?"

"I don't have any," Alistair whispered, clenching and unclenching his hands.

Mother was right. He was forgetting himself, his vow to Father, to uphold the family name and estate. But while Adelaide might be well-connected, as was evidenced by Lord Badley's interest in her, she was hardly the wife he or his mother had once envisioned for him.

When he returned to his room, he sank into the armchair and buried his face in his hands. Was it possible for a heart to be torn in half? Because that might have happened to his own heart.

Remember your duty.

Father had clasped his hand tightly and gazed at him with desperate hope. Alistair nodded, promised that he would put the Dowden name in good standing, and he had also sworn he would care for Rosalind for as long as she lived.

Grimacing, he scrubbed his hands down his face and swallowed hard. Never in his life had confusion whirled through his head with such violence, sending him reeling. For a moment he wished he'd brought his own horse, to ride it across the fields in an effort to clear his mind.

Instead, he contented himself with a walk before dinner, although he'd already exerted himself earlier when hauling the tree back to the manor.

The walk lasted up until dinner, and when he returned, he paused in the entry to find it already bedecked in candles from tip-top to bottom.

How was it that just such a short time ago, he'd been certain that he desired a girl precisely like Cordelia?

But now, the thought of wedding someone else, like Cordelia, turned his stomach.

He at last came to a halt under another spruce tree like the one they'd found earlier. Leaned against its trunk and drew out his pipe. After lighting it, he savoured the relaxation that flowed over him as he exhaled several mouthfuls of the sweet smoke, closing his eyes tightly.

He was grateful to be alone at last, truly alone. To have the opportunity to review the events of that day, and contemplate his predicament. So much had changed in just a matter of a few days. His entire perspective on marriage and duty shifted, and suddenly, his duty was more of a burden than anything.

But before, he had been eager to prove himself, to show that he could be a good steward of his father's estate. Now, the costs yawned before him, threatening to swallow him whole.

Perhaps he could speak to James about this, and get his advice. Yet, he did not wish to put his friend in an awkward position. James was

Adelaide's brother, after all. And he would be torn between giving friendly advice to Alistair and keeping his sister's best interests in mind.

Who else could he speak to about this?

Alistair grimaced to himself. No, he was utterly alone in this predicament. He would need to push forward, though the outlook was beginning to appear bleak. Either he would have to follow the course laid down by duty, and suffer a miserable existence, or follow his heart and endure his mother's anguish, betray his late father's legacy.

He peered out at the horizon, straining for a glimpse of a steeple, a vicarage he might pay a visit to. He would welcome the chance to kneel in a church and turn his worries over to Providence.

But there was not a sign of one from where he stood at least. With a soft sigh, he started back towards the manor.

When he returned, he found it in a flurry of excitement over the newly erected Christmas tree. Already, several of the garlands had been hung on the tree. He gazed up at the spruce, his mind replaying the moment he'd pulled Adelaide into him. She had fit perfectly into his arms. In a way that terrified him.

The rest of the house had evidently retired either to the billiards room or the drawing room, but Alistair retired to the library where he settled into an armchair and tried to focus his roiling energy on a book rather than on his current predicament.

The Worthington library featured an array of titles on everything from natural history to political treatises. He even found some religious tracts, which he browsed through until at last a footman appeared and informed him that dinner would be served shortly.

Alistair hastened through the quiet house upstairs to his room, where he ran into Badley, to his dismay. Badley regarded him coolly, pale eyes narrowed. "Lord Dowden," he acknowledged with a dip of the head.

Alistair greeted him and continued onward, but then Lord Badley spoke again. "She deserves someone who can give her the world."

Alistair froze and turned slightly, casting the other man a hard look. "I beg your pardon?"

"Miss Fawcett. She belongs in London, in the centre of the political renown. But you would hide her away at your country estate—"

"Forgive me, but I know your sole intention in marrying her is for your own advantage."

"Sir, you speak out of turn."

"Out of turn!" Alistair let out a bark of humourless laughter. "Says the man who wants for sincerity."

"You know nothing," Lord Badley hissed. Alistair didn't bother replying then. If he remained, he would be too tempted to send the gentleman sprawling. Though, to call him a gentleman was nothing short of ironic.

"I know more than you imagine. You intend to use her merely as her pawn in your little game of political advance. Surely, I am not incorrect on that count?"

"You forget yourself, Lord Dowden. And now I beg you to watch your tongue. I find Miss Fawcett desirable, and pretty, and she shall be the star of the Ton should she wed me. What can you yourself do to elevate her station in a like manner?"

Once inside his room, he began to pace again, seething. He would teach the fellow a thing or two. At least, he yearned to.

Chapter 14

The next morning at breakfast, Lady Worthington announced the plans for that day. Since the weather remained fair and free of any winter storms, they would be riding down to the village by sledge for a charitable event and Christmas shopping, if it should suit them.

Alistair found himself consumed with wondering what Adelaide was thinking. Was she dismayed by yesterday's events? Had her parents objected to her behaviour? Would they disapprove if they knew what had truly transpired? To his disappointment, Adelaide scarcely looked at him today, which caused his stomach to knot up tightly in his belly.

Sledges were brought around for the excursion into town, and Alistair watched as

Adelaide boarded one with Miss Scott and Miss Wortham, her brother, and Captain Crawford. He was designated to one with Cordelia, of course, her parents, and his mother.

They were given blankets to lay across their laps for the ride to the nearby village, and off they went. The ride was pleasant, but somewhat awkward, with Cordelia plying him with questions about his plans for the new year.

"Mother, Father and I may go to Scotland," Cordelia told him, her eyes sparkling as the sledge sped along. "You and Lady Dowden are welcome to accompany us should you so desire."

Before Alistair could speak, Mother assented. "Oh, how kind of you to invite us. We should be delighted to accompany you! When was the last time we visited Scotland, my dear?"

"Ah—I am not certain." Alistair tried to distract himself by watching the trees that flashed past, searching for a glimpse of some woodland creature amongst the trees and bramble.

"It has been far too long. Certainly, before your father passed, if I am not mistaken."

"Father bought a castle in Scotland but a year ago," Cordelia informed Alistair, batting her eyes at him.

"A castle!" Mother cried.

"Indeed," Lord Ashford replied, smiling proudly. "One of the oldest on the moors."

"Oh, I should love to see that."

Alistair couldn't speak, the words sticking in his throat. His future seemed already mapped out, but it wasn't entirely clear whether he would allow it to sweep him along or fight against the current. Was this an inevitable path, or was it a war he could still win? He could not say.

"Lord Dowden?" inquired Lady Ashford.

He jerked his attention back to the conversation. "No, no. I'm not—hardly. I am simply tired. I did not sleep well last night."

"A pity! I do hope it is not those goose-down mattresses. I've been doing my very best to talk Lord Worthington into purchasing some new ones. Ours are getting quite lumpy."

"No, no. It was not the bed. I simply could not sleep."

Thankfully, the conversation turned from a potential visit to the Ashworths' Scottish castle to the village, its shops, and the charitable event at the church they would participate in. Lady Worthington announced they would make food baskets for the impoverished to hand out. Everyone chattered eagerly about this task.

As the sledge reached a crest, the village came into view, its twinkling lights visible from their snowy perch in the grey, wintry morning. The sky had been fully hidden by heavy clouds. Alistair caught his breath, impressed by the cosy town before him. It was bigger than Dowdenshire, certainly. Even the church was larger and more ornate.

"What a sweet little town!" Cordelia said to Alistair, beaming.

"Indeed," he managed softly.

"You are rather pale, Lord Dowden. Are you sure you are not unwell? Perhaps you ought to have remained home. It is not advisable to be around such people in any sort of poor constitution."

"I should like to go on and help in what ways I can," Alistair told her in a harsher tone than he'd intended. Her lips parted in surprise but she nodded.

"Well, it is most admirable that you should be eager to help. I confess I'm rather nervous. I wore my mother-of-pearl necklace today, and I fear it shall be taken right off me amongst these people."

Alistair didn't know what to say to this. He was simply stunned that someone could be so short-sighted regarding these people in need.

The sledge wound down the road until at last they reached the main street of the village, speeding over the bridge at its entrance. Down the narrow streets they went until at last they reached the church, where the rest of the sledges had stopped to let out their passengers. Alistair helped the ladies down, though Cordelia nearly tripped, and he was thus obliged to catch her lest she fall, face-first, into the snow.

She giggled softly, her cheeks darkening, and lingered in his arms for a long moment. Alistair smiled tightly before setting her upright on the church steps. His mother cast him an approving look, her mouth curving into a fond smile. Again, that sinking sense welled within him. He fell back a few steps, watching as the rest of his party ventured into the church, taking care not to slip on the icy ground.

Once inside, his gaze instinctively sought out Adelaide across the room at a table beside Miss Scott, together distributing food to several bedraggled families shuffling through the church. The rest of the Worthington party was spread out through the drafty room, assigned in clusters to various tables where they gave soup, bread, and other victuals to the local indigent.

Alistair distracted himself with setting to work beside James and Captain Crawford, though once or twice, he met eyes with Lord Badley, hovering near Adelaide, and the politician's expression shifted into one of derision, his lip curling.

Shouting arose from the other end of the church where Adelaide worked with her cousin, Miss Scott, and Lord and Lady Worthington, as well as her parents. Alistair frowned, trying to ascertain the cause of this tumult. A young boy broke into a run, barrelling past Adelaide and knocking her to the ground where she lay very still. Several cries rang out as Miss Wortham and Adelaide's parents rushed over to attend to her.

Alistair, James, and Captain Crawford dashed over, and James managed to catch the boy before he could flee the chapel. He thrashed wildly, shouting obscenities and causing the older women in their party to gasp, bringing their gloved hands to their mouths.

"Enough!" Captain Crawford rapped out as he took the boy's other arm. The parish vicar hastened over, his face pale and tense.

"What is the meaning of this?" he exclaimed.

"There is no need for thievery, my boy," James told the child in his arms. "We are here to give you and whoever else anything they may need. But you have injured someone!"

Alistair knelt beside Adelaide, where she was already being tended to by Miss Scott, Miss Wortham, and her parents.

Adelaide was pale, her cheek bruised as she blinked hazily up at Alistair.

"Oh, Addy! Your head—how are you?" Miss Wortham grasped Adelaide's hand; her eyes wide with concern. Alistair stared, a helpless sense welling in him. The sight of Adelaide's pale face shook him to the core.

She was helped to her feet by her father, bringing a hand up to her cheek. She winced.

Her eyes met Alistair's, and she managed a weak smile that wrenched him. He wished he could take her in his arms, reassure himself of her safety and somehow give her comfort. But he could not go near her. Even in a friendly manner.

It would bring the censure of his mother upon him, and as for Adelaide—he had already overstepped the day before. Since then, she'd withdrawn from him, avoided eye contact, as if disturbed by his lack of propriety yesterday when felling the tree.

"My dear, are you well?" her mother fretted, smoothing her skirts and checking her for other scratches or bruises.

"Mother," Adelaide recoiled from her mother's fussing. "I am quite well. It was a simple fall. Nothing more."

Everyone's attention turned to the boy. The vicar reassured him that he and his family would receive the help they needed but gave the boy a stern rebuke. "There is no cause for attempting to misappropriate the items we give out today. They are free for you to take."

"I beg your pardon, ma'am," the boy said to Adelaide tearfully.

She shook off her mother's fretful grasp and strode forward, in her usual bold manner, and took him by the hand with a warm smile. Murmurs rippled through the rest of the party, but she acted as if she did not hear them. Alistair's heart squeezed.

"No need for a pardon," she told him gently. Alistair's heart fluttered as he watched the scene unfold. He'd not yet seen this side of Adelaide's nature, but it was inspiring to behold.

Adelaide guided the boy to one of the tables and handed him a basket full of food, as well as a blanket. "Should you need anything else, do not hesitate to return and ask us for it," she told him gently.

"I'm most sorry ma'am, for my impudence." The child began to weep and threw his arms around Adelaide's waist. She didn't push him off or try to extricate herself. Instead, she wrapped her arms around him as well and held him as he tried to calm himself. More gasps rose in the air, but Alistair could not take his eyes off Adelaide, her smile radiant as she tried to console the boy clinging to her.

At last, the vicar stepped forward and drew the boy away, gently telling him to stop by the church should he be in want of any further aid.

Nodding and begging thanks, the boy shuffled off, and everyone returned to their tables. Alistair joined Adelaide at her table, along with James and Captain Crawford.

He suddenly did not care a whit what the rest thought. He just wished for Adelaide to know that he admired her for her kindness, her gentleness, and her compassion for that child. Somewhere behind them, he heard Lady Ashford whisper, "I cannot believe she let that sooty child cling to her so!"

Adelaide stiffened as she packed the next basket full of food. "They are people, are they not? People in want."

"Do not pay heed to her, Addy," Miss Wortham urged her in an undertone.

"Indeed. You showed that child kindness," Captain Crawford agreed. "It is one thing to pack a basket for the destitute. It is another to show them true compassion."

Alistair nodded. "Precisely. Sometimes a simple kindness is all that is called for."

Adelaide lifted her eyes to him, her expression changing into one he had never seen. Something between gratitude and wistfulness. Alistair ached to reach over and cover her hand in his, to touch the bruise on her cheek and kiss it. To tell her how greatly he admired her.

"Thank you, Lord Dowden," she murmured after a pause. He opened his mouth to speak, but he was suddenly tongue-tied.

He clenched his teeth when Lord Badley sidled over to join their table. "What a shame, that such violence should be exhibited in the face of an act of charity," he clucked his tongue, and Addy's face flushed with anger.

Alistair recognised that flash in her dark eyes.

"The child was desperate, Lord Badley," she told the man in a cool tone. "He was afraid, and starving."

"Be that as it may, he ought to be taught a lesson for his impudence."

"Perhaps he simply needs to be extended compassion."

Lady Worthington passed by but paused, as if she'd noticed her niece's irritation with Lord Badley. "Adelaide, a word?"

Adelaide set her shoulders, her eyes flickering to Alistair. He didn't bother to hide the sympathy in his expression as she followed her aunt away towards a private corner of the church. Her aunt frowned as she seemed to scold her niece for scolding Lord Badley.

After finishing with the event, everyone dispersed to explore the village. It was late afternoon by now, and the sky had darkened even more, hinting at severe weather that night. But it was fair enough to enjoy a walk through the town, though Alistair was not at liberty to accompany Adelaide and her group through the streets. His mother called him before he could attempt to. She stood on the church steps with the Ashworths and Cordelia of course.

Alistair swallowed a sigh and extended an arm to Cordelia, offering her a courteous smile she met with a bright one of her own. They commenced on through the streets to the shops, where they would enjoy some Christmas shopping.

The lampposts and windows were festooned with garlands of evergreen and holly, interspersed with sprigs of mistletoe. In the centre of town stood a towering tree, decorated just as brightly, and that evening, the townsfolk would gather to admire the adorned branches, their bright trimmings reflecting the joy of the season.

Cordelia was eager to explore the shops, and the first one they entered, they discovered that Adelaide's party had already entered, and were browsing the various ribbons and trinkets the shop carried. As Cordelia rifled through the ribbons, Alistair turned to meet Adelaide's gaze. She ducked her head, but the corner of her mouth twisted up in a hidden smile.

His stomach flipped.

"Lord Dowden, what do you think of this bow? Do you think it becomes my complexion?"

Cordelia's voice cut between them, and he turned to inspect the ribbon Cordelia held up. When he turned back to look for Adelaide, she and the rest of her party had slipped out. His heart sank.

Cordelia purchased the ribbon and together they returned to the street where the rest of their party waited, admiring the village's decorations. Onward they walked until they passed a milliners' shop. In the window of the brightly lit shop, Adelaide tried on a bright hat with feathers spreading from it. She and her cousin and Miss Scott began to laugh together, but the sigh brought Alistair up short. He nearly lost his footing.

His mother cleared her throat, dragging his attention back to Cordelia beside him. "I see a mask shop! Oh, Mamma, we must throw a masked ball, don't you think?"

"Indeed!" Lady Ashford nodded.

"Alistair, you have not been to a masked ball, have you?" Rosalind's voice pulled Alistair's attention from the milliner's shop window.

"Ah, I have not."

"A shame, Lord Dowden!" Cordelia sighed.

They resumed their walk down the street, Cordelia slipping her arm through the crook of Alistair's once again. The rest of the party fell behind them, and once they were far enough ahead, she spoke. "My mother and your mother were saying that come spring, we ought to venture to Bath together. Does that sound agreeable to you?"

"Ah—in the spring, you say?" Alistair searched desperately for some sort of excuse but fell short.

Cordelia prattled on, tossing her head. "Bath in the spring is quite lovely. But it would need to be late spring, of course. It is quite rainy too early in the season."

At last, they returned to the church where the sledges waited and climbed into one to return to Worthington Manor. Adelaide and her party climbed into the one just ahead, laughing gaily amongst themselves, and again, wistfulness pricked in Alistair's chest. Lord Badley was at her side this time, and as he helped Adelaide into the sledge, he locked eyes with Alistair, a smirk flickering across his features.

Alistair clenched his teeth as the conversation he'd shared with the man surfaced in his memory. It was maddening to think that he should hold himself in such esteem, that he should regard himself the righteous match for Adelaide. She deserved to know. And no matter what, he would endeavour to tell her.

"Is something troubling you, Lord Dowden?" Cordelia asked softly, directly across from him.

"No, no. Nothing is amiss," he lied.

"Wonderful. I was afraid you did not enjoy sleigh rides."

"Oh, no, I do enjoy them. I'm simply somewhat tired."

Cordelia managed a smile. "Well, haven't you been waking quite early? I confess I do not rise early most days as you do."

Alistair flushed, wondering if he'd been observed running into Adelaide in the gardens as well. "Ah, do not censure yourself over it. I am something of an ascetic when it comes to my daily life. I have a routine I abhor to break."

Cordelia laughed softly at that. "You are a rather odd man, Lord Dowden."

They sped off from the village as the sun set somewhere behind the clouds. The village behind them sparkled in the snowy night, and Alistair watched it vanish from view, his future a paralysing mystery he could not ascertain. That alone frightened him deeply.

Chapter 15

Addy descended from the sledge, helped down by Lord Badley, of course. He kissed her hand and led her up the manor steps until they were inside the warm entry hall. In the warm, golden-lit hall, she began to pull her coat off, giving it to a footman. Turning, she nearly collided with Alistair, her face almost in his chest.

He flushed and apologised, stepping back. Ever since the incident in the forest the previous day, he'd been more distant than usual, almost as he had been when they were children. It stung.

But it didn't matter. She would not be tricked into surrendering her independence. No matter how much she might enjoy Alistair's company or how handsome she found him. It simply did not matter.

He was clearly unwilling to attach himself to her. She wasn't exactly a suitable choice to run the Dowden estate. She wasn't polished, and she could be too impulsive, too bold. Too outspoken. Too much of everything.

And that likely mortified him. Even if he did find her desirable. But before she could retreat to her bedroom, he spoke in a low voice meant for her alone. "Miss Fawcett—Adelaide—I must commend you for the way you dealt with matters today. I admire your composure, your care for those beneath your station."

Addy's eyes widened. "It was merely the right thing to be done." She tried to laugh.

"How is your cheek?"

"Oh, I can scarcely feel it," Adelaide's heart climbed into her throat. "Truly." She searched his face. There were dark smudges beneath his eyes, and his blue eyes were dark, piercing.

Alistair chuckled. "I expected you might say that."

"Adelaide!" Mother's voice startled her, and she stepped back, face hot. "Come! Dinner is nearly upon us." She swept down the stairs towards them. "Lord Dowden," she chirped, rather coolly. "My sister tells me there is to be dancing after dinner, Adelaide. And dinner is in but half an hour. Scarce any chance to prepare yourself, making yourself presentable."

Addy nearly sighed and joined her mother on the stairs. But she turned, unable to resist stealing another look at Alistair. Her heart ached as she let herself be led away from him, and her pulse quickened when his mouth curved in a smile meant for her alone. Once they made it upstairs and out of sight, as well as presumably out of his earshot, Mother said, "And here I imagined you were above marriage."

Addy squared her shoulders. She was more than certain that it would be futile to attempt to explain her reasoning to Mother. Mother would laugh, scoff, and wave off her grounds. She was wont to do this in every sundry matter, no matter how significant.

"What were you and Lord Dowden speaking of?" Mother demanded as they reached Addy's bedroom door.

"He was merely telling me he thought I dealt with the incident this afternoon quite well."

"Well, he's a well-bred young man. It is a shame his family is not so well-endowed as Lord Badley's."

"Lord Badley is an opportunist," Addy blurted. "Is anything he says sincere?"

Mother grasped Addy by the arm and drew her into the bedroom behind them. When the door had closed, she hissed, "Now, what are you speaking of, Adelaide? It's pure foolishness. I've had enough of your folly. It must stop."

Addy's eyes suddenly pricked as she stared at her mother. "Did you marry for love? Or if you did not, did you hope to?"

"I had a duty to my family, Adelaide. As do you. As women, it is our portion to marry whoever is chosen for us. To secure the future of our families through an advantageous marriage."

"I shall not marry, if it is not on my own terms."

"Then you are far more thoughtless than I imagined."

Mother released her arm, and swept out, shutting the door hard behind her.

Addy walked over to her bed on wobbly legs and let the tears fall. Perhaps Mother was right. She was thinking of herself. And if today had shown her anything, it was that she was far better off than some. Some, like that boy today, could scarcely eat or keep warm.

And here she was, miserable over the prospect of marrying a man she did not love—and yet, he was wealthy all the same. She would want for nothing.

Someone knocked on her door, and she considered telling them to go away, wiping away her tears. But presently, the door cracked open and Gemma, her maid, stuck her head in. "Miss Adelaide, I've come to help you dress for dinner."

"Come in," Addy choked out. She took in a deep breath. Mother was right. She was a fool, with ridiculous ideals and hopes for something impossible.

Gemma entered and helped her into an evening gown, before having Addy sit at the vanity to fix her hair.

Alistair's intense gaze kept replaying in her head on repeat. How close he'd been. His soft smile. The earnestness in his tone. And she compared it to the manner in which Lord Badley spoke to her. Handsome though he was, his words always fell flat.

Downstairs, she joined her cousin and Serena in front of the tree. "Tomorrow, we shall decorate it, I believe. But in the meantime, we must admire it for its grandeur. It's nearly as high as the ceiling. I'm astonished our footmen managed to get it in." Eloise shook her head.

"It might have fallen upon you if it weren't for Lord Dowden," Serena whispered to Addy. She flushed, and Serena laughed softly.

"Forgive me, but it was quite endearing to see how he nearly swept you into his arms."

"Serena!" But Eloise was giggling as well.

The three of them together entered the dining room, where most of the party had already gathered for the meal. Addy pointedly ignored her mother, heart hammering. Mother's words ran through her head in a continuous loop. *You are far more thoughtless than I imagined.* The contempt in her mother's eyes chilled her.

She could barely eat, picking at the food on her plate. Several times she glanced up to find Alistair watching her, a slight crease in his forehead. How was he able to read her so thoroughly? It was as if he could see right through her.

"How are you faring, Adelaide?" Aunt Agatha inquired from the head of the table.

Addy pushed a pea across her china plate. "Just weary," Addy replied, for once wanting to sink into the ground as everyone else turned to regard her curiously.

The night could not end soon enough. This entire visit could not be done soon enough.

"Well, you are scarcely eating. It makes one thing the food is dreadful."

"That wasn't my intent, Aunt Agatha."

Aunt Agatha clicked her tongue and Addy swallowed down words that would likely draw gasps from the gathered guests.

***

Dinner ended without much circumstance and as was per custom, the women retired to the drawing room while the men went their separate way to the billiards room. In the drawing room, Cordelia began to chatter on about the merits of a Bath visit and how the waters there did such wonders for the skin and constitution.

Addy said little tonight, her spirits dampened. Her head spun as she tried to make sense of the conflicting feelings that raged in her heart. There was no doubt that she was drawn to Alistair.

Despite their contentious beginnings, all those years ago, she now couldn't help but think that her connection to him was strong. Yet, both had expectations pressed upon them by their mothers, by their families. In his mother's view, she was not good enough for him. And in her mother's view, it was the inverse. How ironic.

"What are you smiling about, my dear sister?" James' voice cut into her thoughts. Addy jumped, turning from her place by the window.

"I was trying to see if it was snowing," she lied.

"Something is troubling you," he murmured. He turned to look in Alistair's direction. Alistair stood across the room beside his mother. Cordelia was on his arm of course. Then, James turned back to give Addy a pointed if not sympathetic smile.

"I think that this spring, I shall convince Father to let you go on an excursion. What do you think?"

Before this Christmas, Addy might have been beside herself. But right now, she could only summon a watery smile. "I should like that very much."

Lord Badley approached them then. "Miss Fawcett, I should like to request the honour of this evening's first dance with you."

Addy took in a deep breath, glancing up. Mother was watching her intently, her mouth pursed. At last, she curtsied and nodded. "Very well, Lord Badley. I am all yours."

When Badley left them again to converse with Captain Crawford, James leaned close to Addy. "You needn't promise him a thing if you don't wish."

Frustration sparked in Addy. It was easy for him to say when he could have his choice of wife. He could even choose not to marry, and nobody would bat an eye.

Yet, if she in turn chose to remain unmarried, she would be declared a spinster, a pariah of society. And she would never know a day of peace if she decided to flee Badley's advances.

Regardless of her choice, she would be stuck in a mire.

And Alistair...Alistair had his own duty to consider. Even now, Lady Dowden watched Addy with a circumspect purse of her mouth, and an arched brow.

"I shall play a few songs. All dancers adjoin to the centre of the room," called Aunt Agatha.

She sat down at the pianoforte, and Badley found Addy once again, offering her his hand. When she turned, Alistair was watching, jealousy smouldering in his expression. It was enough to send her pulse thundering, so fast she lost her breath.

Badley led her through the steps, so fast that the room spun around them in a blur. Addy tried to smile up at him as she followed him in the dance, and at the other end of the line, Alistair and Cordelia followed the same pattern of steps.

As the music reached its crescendo, she whirled past them in Badley's arms, but instead of paying attention to her partner, her eyes met Alistair's, and his mouth parted as if in a silent gasp. As they continued to circle the drawing room, their eyes kept meeting.

When the dance concluded, Addy excused herself for a moment and fled through the house until she at last pushed open the doors leading onto the back terrace. The cold hair was a balm on her warm face as she swallowed in large mouthfuls of air, trying to compose herself. *Why am I so drawn to him?*

She began to shiver, wrapping her arms around herself as tears snaked down her cheeks.

"Addy?" It was Eloise.

She turned to see her cousin approach, a shawl around her shoulders, and another one in her hands. She handed it over to Addy and Addy took it, grateful.

"I just needed some fresh air," she whispered, voice trembling.

"Oh Addy," Eloise pulled her into a tight hug. "It's dreadful to see you in pain."

"I shall be—I shall be quite well. He will wed Cordelia and I—I shall marry no one. I care not what my mother and father say. I shall die alone, and it shall be exactly as it must. I never wished to marry, anyhow."

Eloise drew back. "I ought to have brought a handkerchief."

Addy laughed through her sobs. "I am fine, truly. Truly. I always wanted to be independent."

"Come, let us get inside. You're trembling dreadfully."

Eloise led Addy back inside and they started towards the back staircase of the house. The one Addy usually took to steal out to the stables. Captain Crawford met them before they reached the stairs. He bowed, offering Addy a sympathetic smile. "Miss Fawcett, Eloise."

Eloise beamed up at him softly. "Addy is tired. I was going to retire with her for the night."

"I have something to tell you, if I may. Well, Miss Fawcett, to be precise. I know that your family intends for you to come to an understanding with Lord Badley, but earlier this week, he said something to me that gave me cause for concern. He voiced his desire to wed you stems from an eagerness to further his own political career. You are, of course, of a notable family. Forgive me for putting it so indelicately, but I thought you should know, given he is courting you."

Addy stiffened. "He is not courting me. Especially not now." Something in her shattered. Of course, she'd suspected Lord Badley of these motives, but to hear it confirmed. It was a blow to the gut.

"Thank you, William," Eloise whispered.

"I wondered if you already knew," Captain Crawford murmured, frowning. "I was certain that Lord Dowden would have said something."

"Lord Dowden? What cause would he have to say something?"

"He overheard the entire conversation. I imagined he would have mentioned it."

Addy shook her head, unable to believe this. Why had Alistair not said anything? Fury surged in her. "I've been such a fool," she choked. And she took off in a run towards the back stairs, running until she at last reached her bedroom and flung the door open, slamming it shut. Leaning back against it, she squeezed her eyes shut as sobs wracked her body.

She was confounded that Alistair had not even mentioned it. Not once. If he had known something, why did he fail to bring up Lord Badley's words?

Chapter 16

At breakfast the next morning, Alistair asked Captain Crawford if anything was amiss with Adelaide.

"I'm sure she will be well in due time. She just needed some rest," Crawford replied with a reassuring smile.

I hope she has not fallen ill. Alistair reviewed the events of the night before. Just after the dance in the drawing room, Adelaide had fled, followed shortly by her cousin, and then Captain Crawford.

Beside him, Cordelia began to rhapsodise on the merits of Italian opera as opposed to French opera, and he noted that Adelaide's parents seemed hardly concerned about their daughter's absence. He'd observed her mother's contempt for the girl, and her father's doting fondness for her, despite his unwillingness to intervene when Lady Fairfield was scolding Adelaide for whatever reason.

And James was occupied with Miss Scott, discussing with her the best parks to visit in London in the spring. They'd been lost to the world for the past few days, swiftly falling for one another as the week progressed. He would not be surprised if James proposed by New Year's.

Just then, Adelaide herself sailed through the dining room French doors, her head held aloft. She sat further down the table and did not look towards him once. Neither did she acknowledge Badley, to her mother's obvious dismay.

"Lord Dowden, have you ever been to the Paris opera?" Cordelia's voice interrupted his thoughts.

"I am afraid that I have never yet been to Paris."

"Never been to Paris! Why, that must be amended."

Dowden was stunned when Addy called down the table, "I beg you to spare yourself the trouble, Miss Ashworth. Lord Dowden is scarcely the sort to travel. Why, I would not be astonished if he has not gone further south than London."

Cordelia gasped. "Why, you are rather severe upon Lord Dowden, Miss Fawcett."

"Am I? I imagined I was merely stating a matter of fact." Adelaide flashed Alistair a derisive look, and he blinked, stunned. What had brought on this sudden turn? Just last night, she'd been transfixed as much as he even as they danced with other partners. It had been strange, haunting.

Terrifying. And at the same time, he felt himself coming to life after what must have been a very long slumber.

And now…she smirked at him, lifting her chin with that defiance he knew so well, before taking a sip of her tea.

He frowned, but she turned then without bothering to respond or answer his silent question. Alistair's appetite dwindled and he pushed his food about his plate, restless.

"Are you unwell, Lord Dowden?" Cordelia inquired under her breath, her forehead knitting with concern.

"Oh, no, no. Hardly." But he had no desire to eat any longer. He wanted to speak to Adelaide and ask her if something was amiss. Was she to accept Lord Badley's hand? Had her parents given her a talking-to? An ultimatum?

His thoughts swirled in confusion as he endeavoured to unravel the answers to this perplexing puzzle, a pang of hurt striking him. Were he to be entirely honest with himself, he would confess that he was deeply wounded—wounded by her coldness.

At last, breakfast ended and Lady Worthington told them all that games would be held in the drawing room again later that morning. "I believe that a snowstorm is meant to start this evening. At least, the weather suggests it. So if you should like a walk about the grounds, do so now. I fear we may be relegated to amusing ourselves within the manor for the next day or so."

Alistair took her up on this suggestion, venturing out into the gardens, the sky above dark again as if threatening snow.

Adelaide's words echoed through his head. Where had this sudden return of malice come from? He ought to ask her directly, but right now, he simply needed to wade through a mire of hurt and steady himself.

As fortune would have it, when he returned inside, he stole to the library, thankful for a little more time to spend in solitude. He rounded one of the towering shelves and found himself staring at Adelaide herself, in one of the big armchairs there, a book in her hands. When she saw him, her forehead creased, expression flattening.

Gone was the warmth and eagerness of the past few days. Instead, she rose and made to move past him. He stepped into her path, heart hammering. "Miss Fawcett. Adelaide." He took a deep breath. "Is something amiss?"

"No," she replied, but her expression hardened. Her jaw tightened, and furious tears sparkled in her dark eyes.

"Adelaide," he whispered, nearly reaching for her. But he pulled his hand back.

"What? What could you possibly have to say to me?" Her voice came out in a hiss.

"I thought—I thought we were past this. Was I mistaken?"

"And I thought—" Adelaide shook her head. "I thought that I could—I could trust you. But I was simply naïve. A fool."

"What do you mean?"

She didn't reply. Instead, she swept out of the room without another word, leaving him rooted to the spot, a chill working through his bones.

He forced himself to return to the drawing room after discarding his coat and scarf, where the rest of the party had gathered for an afternoon of chess and whist. Outside, the trees started to toss and the wind began to howl, hinting at the coming storm.

Adelaide was at a table playing cards with Miss Wortham, Captain Crawford, and her brother James, and Alistair took a place at the window to watch the storm roll in. The sky was already dark, and snow had begun to fall, swirling across the windowpane.

Cordelia called to him, imploring him to join her table for a game of whist, which he conceded to after a pause. He glanced towards Adelaide, but she'd already looked away, her expression inscrutable. Later yet, she excused herself from her game and stationed herself at the chess board, moving pieces about the board, her brow creased in a pensive frown.

When Lord Badley approached her to converse, she replied in clipped sentences, Alistair noticed. At last, the man gave up and joined a whist game nearby with Lady Scotfell, Lady Ashford, and Lord Worthington.

Cordelia began to play on the piano, plunking out the tune of "God Rest Ye Merry Gentlemen". Alistair rose from his seat on the sofa and unable to help himself, crossed the room to sit at the chess board. Adelaide stiffened, her lips tightening.

"Ah, Lord Dowden. Are you prepared to be thoroughly flounced at chess?"

Alistair tried to smile at this, but her eyes were sharp, piercing into him. "Show me your worst, Miss Fawcett."

He ignored his mother's frown from across the room, and Cordelia's dismayed expression from her seat at the piano.

He and Adelaide began to arrange their chess pieces to start the game, and thus it began. Since she had taken the white pieces, it was her first move. She started by moving a pawn forward first in the middle of the board.

Alistair moved forward one of his own middle pawns. He had always excelled at chess. It was one of his favourite games, even as a boy he had enjoyed playing it. Especially with his father. Father had adored the game, and shown Alistair it was a wonderful way to learn strategy, to think ahead always.

He strove to anticipate Adelaide's moves, but at every turn, she surprised him. Just when he thought she would move her rook, she would move her knight. And when he expected her to drag her bishop, she swept her queen forward, felling his rook. It sent his head spinning and bespoke of her chaotic nature. Tempestuous. Arresting.

More than once he had to remind himself to focus on the game, to not let himself be distracted by the way she dug her teeth into her lower lip, the furrow of her brow as she concentrated on her next move. Her knack for strategy astounded him.

There was so much about her that he wanted to know, yet his heart sank with every withering glance she cast his way after each play. *What has happened? What has changed? Why is she so incensed with me?*

When she put his king in check, her smirk sent him into a tailspin. "Why do you look so astonished? Did you think I was a poor chess player?"

Alistair shook his head, moving his king to safety. "I made a grave error in my estimation, I suppose."

"Is that a habit of yours?" Adelaide demanded softly. Thankfully they were alone on this side of the room. He lowered his voice even more. "Have I done something to offend?"

Adelaide tossed her head and swept her queen forward, again putting his king in check. "I would focus on the game if I were you, Lord Dowden. You are about to lose your king."

He took the necessary action to preserve his king. "Very well. What do you say best out of three matches?"

"If you wish to be flounced dreadfully, then of course."

Alistair's face heated, irritation twinging in him. Was she really so fickle? *What has changed?* He wondered again.

"Very well," he took a deep breath. "I cannot make you out. Whatsoever."

Adelaide glanced over towards the pianoforte. "Take care, Lord Dowden. Miss Ashworth appears disconcerted that you are engaging me in this game."

Alistair clenched his jaw, moving his bishop into place to take her queen. His queen was long gone now.

"You confound me, quite."

"I could say the same about you," she retorted. He stared in surprise as she swept her queen forward and knocked his bishop off the board.

She bested him that round, of course, and the next. When he looked up again, the room was nearly empty save for them, Eloise, and Captain Crawford, who sat together on the settee, very close, speaking in low voices to one another.

"Where has everyone gone?" Adelaide stammered.

"To ready themselves for dinner," Eloise replied, on the tail end of a laugh she'd shared with Captain Crawford.

Alistair stood, hoping he could have a moment to speak with Adelaide in private now. But she swept out of the room before he could open his mouth, and he was left standing alone, stunned.

He excused himself and hastened into the hall, but Adelaide was nowhere to be seen. As he reached the top of the staircase, his mother rose from a nearby alcove that overlooked the gardens, her mouth a grim slash across her face. "Alistair, come," she beckoned him into the alcove, and he joined her, heart sinking. "Yes, Mamma?"

"Cordelia was most hurt by your actions this afternoon. You were utterly engrossed in your silly little game with Miss Fawcett. Did you hear nothing I said the other day?"

Alistair opened his mouth to speak but could think of no reply. "I—forgive me." Though, frustration welled in him. As dearly as he loved his mother, he was confounded by her lack of understanding. For a moment, he considered telling her of his confusion about Adelaide's behaviour. But she would say something along the lines of, "What did you expect from such a fickle, strange girl as she?"

He took in a deep breath and swallowed. Turning, he murmured, "I am going to try to rest before dinner."

"Consider what you will say to Cordelia this evening. She was almost in tears. She is certain you're going to pass her over for Miss Fawcett. I reassured her that you would not, but it would be more reassuring to hear it from you yourself."

Alistair closed his eyes, nodded, and began to walk back towards his room, but his mother said his name again, and he stopped in his tracks. "You are a good young man. Upstanding. You hold honour in high regard. Your father and I raised you to do what is right in all things."

"Yes, Mother," he whispered. But in the back of his mind, he wondered how it was possible for one to love someone, whilst ignoring their pain. A silly thought he pushed away, but it kept resurfacing as he stared out at the stormy landscape, the trees tossing to and fro as more snow began to swirl down.

***

Dinner was awkward, to put it briefly. Cordelia scarcely spoke to Alistair, and even worse, Adelaide wouldn't look at him. His mother's pointed stare urged him to engage Cordelia in conversation, though he could think of little to say to her. More and more, he wondered if he was taking his duty too much to heart—it came at the expense of so much. His heart weighed in his chest like a stone, and his head swam as he tried to weigh through social niceties. But the conversation swirled on around him, and misery gnawed at him.

After dinner, everyone retired to the drawing room, as was customary, with most of the men discussing the storm raging outside, speculating on how many inches of snow it might bring. "It appears to be a proper blizzard," Lord Worthington declared, his brow furrowing.

"I pray it doesn't last through Christmas in but a few days," exclaimed Lady Ashford, her husband grunting his agreement as he sipped a glass of port.

"Adelaide, will you play us a carol or two as I try to think of what we can do to entertain ourselves?" Lady Worthington demanded of her niece. Her voice brooked no room for argument. Adelaide's eyes flashed but she nodded and rose, crossing the room to sit at the pianoforte. She began to play "Greensleeves", the melody swelling through the room. Lord Badley joined her, hovering over her and turning the pages for her. Alistair noticed how Adelaide's mouth twisted with annoyance at his nearness.

Lady Worthington and her sister murmured together in low voices in a corner of the drawing room while Lord Worthington brought out another bottle of port. "This occasion calls for another round of drinks," he cried, his face flushed red. It was clear he was a little tipsy.

"Hear hear!" cried Lord Ashford.

"Ah! I've got it!" Lady Worthington and Lady Fairfield turned to face the rest of the room. "We've decided upon a game of snapdragon!"

"Snapdragon!" echoed Lady Scotfell, placing a hand over her heart. "What a singular idea. I love it."

"I'll grab a set of matches," Eloise said and hurried from the room to fetch them. Captain Crawford watched her go; his eyes dark with longing. It was endearing to witness.

"And I," Adelaide stood abruptly from the piano bench, "I will go first."

Alistair's throat tightened, a mixture of awe and worry swelling within him. He wasn't in the least bit surprised by her announcement, but he feared that, one of these days, her boldness might lead her to real injury.

"Adelaide," her mother exclaimed in a warning tone.

"I will," Adelaide lifted her chin.

Huzzahs broke out from James and Lord Worthington, much to Lady Worthington and Lady Fairfield's bemusement.

Chapter 17

James set the whiskey alight in a large glass, causing golden and amber flames to spark forth. And Aunt Agatha dropped some chestnuts into the glass before turning to regard Addy closely. "You are certain?"

Addy was surprised by the concern in her aunt's expression. "Yes," she managed, forcing a broad grin. "I'm quite ready."

"Very well." Aunt Agatha gestured at the marble-topped table where the burning glass sat.

Excited whispers and murmurs broke out through the room as she braced herself for the first round of Snapdragon. She had only played once before, as a child, with James and some of his schoolmates. Truly, she was astonished her aunt had even proposed it, though she imagined it was intended to be more of a lark for the men present.

Glancing up, she found Mother staring at her, a furrow between her brows. She could almost hear her, knowing exactly what she'd say. "What possessed you to do such a thing?" That would be an inevitable question she'd have to answer later.

Taking a deep breath, she paused before the glass, not before lifting her eyes to Alistair over by the window, his customary position. His eyes were wide with open worry, and her chest squeezed. Yet, she pushed the feeling aside, burying it deep, and turned her attention back to the leaping flames on the surface of the whiskey. She'd dip her hand in to pull out as many chestnuts as she possibly could.

James was smirking, hiding his mouth behind his hand, and Father's face read surprise and amusement.

Eloise, on the other hand, shook her head silently, a smile twitching at her lips. Of course, she was not surprised by Addy's decision. And neither should anyone else be. Addy was never the sort to back down from a challenge. Serena flashed her an encouraging, admiring grin, and Captain Crawford wore a similar smile.

Closing her eyes, she dipped her hand into the glass, through the sputtering flames, and her fingers at once brushed the shell of a chestnut. Closing her fist, she jerked her hand out, the tongues of flame licking ever so briefly against her skin.

Lady Dowden gasped from the settee, covering her mouth, and Lady Ashford fanned herself, horror etched across her pinched features.

Addy uncurled her fingers to reveal the three chestnuts in her palm. Applause erupted through the room.

"Good heavens, you've done it!" Father pulled her close and pecked a kiss on her forehead. "I'm all astonishment."

"Of course I did," Addy declared, setting the chestnuts on the table before stepping back. "Who is next?"

"I will go," Alistair said suddenly, and everyone turned to regard him, surprised.

Addy's heart hammered against her ribcage as he stepped up to the table and extended his hand, meeting her eyes.

"You will burn yourself!" Cordelia cried, shaking her head so hard that her blonde curls bounced. "You mustn't!"

"I will survive just as Miss Fawcett did," Alistair replied, surprising Addy. She half expected him to listen to the girl. But instead, his face hardened with resolve.

He followed her suit, not before rolling up his sleeves. It would be dreadful if his cuffs caught fire. However furious she might be with him, Addy wouldn't wish that upon him.

"You'll do splendidly, Alistair!" James called from across the room, and Captain Crawford seconded this blithely.

He took a deep breath, and then plunged his own hand down into the glass, past the flames. He scrambled for a moment, as if searching for more chestnuts before he yanked his hand out and opened his fist. A single chestnut rested on his palm and more applause broke out.

"Marvelous! Capital, capital!" Uncle Richard crowed. Alistair's mother covered her mouth, closing her eyes as if in silent relief. And Cordelia, of course, flounced over, heralding Alistair with rambling praises.

"You were wonderful, Lord Dowden!" she told him in that sweet, grating voice.

"I will go next," Lord Badley spoke up then, a smug grin pasted on his face. "I confess, I excel at snapdragon."

Addy nearly rolled her eyes.

Badley stepped up to the table and drew up his sleeve, inspecting the glass with a nervous chuckle. He doused his hand too slowly, and jerked his hand back with a cry. "Good heavens!"

Addy swallowed a laugh, though when she met Eloise's eyes, she could not help herself. She giggled. Badley cast her a wounded look as he shrank back from the table, pulling his sleeve back down. "Well, I suppose today isn't my day."

Captain Crawford went next, and to no one's surprise, he succeeded in fishing out the majority of the chestnuts in the glass. Everyone cheered again, delighted, and Addy smothered a smile as he returned to Eloise's side, giving a small bow for her and her alone. Envy sparked in her chest. She snuck a look towards Alistair, where Cordelia fawned over him, praising him and fussing over him. "You singed your sleeve, Lord Dowden," she was exclaiming,

James finally took his turn and managed to get one chestnut like Alistair. He presented it to Serena with his usual twinkle in the eye, earning a laugh from her.

Addy retreated to the window nearby to stare out at the blizzard raging on. It was impossible to see very far, and even the trees were shrouded from view by the driving snow. She jumped when a low voice said her name.

Turning, she glared up at Alistair standing just behind her now. "Somehow, I'm scarcely astonished that you tried your hand at snapdragon."

"There's nothing like a little thrill now and then," she replied airily.

"Certainly not."

"I would not have expected you to care much for the game. I half-expected you to bow out."

"As much as you may despise me, I assure you that I do not back down from a challenge."

"Oh, really?" Addy raised an eyebrow.

He lowered his voice then, casting a wary glance over his shoulder. "What is the matter? What have I done?"

"It is more about what you haven't done," she hissed.

He winced. "If you mean—" he took a deep breath, "If you mean addressing what is going on…I…forgive me for that. I am unsure of how to proceed. And you continue to alter your demeanour towards me in the blink of an eye; I scarcely know what to think."

"Are you calling me fickle?" Addy gritted her teeth.

"I am merely confused," he whispered.

"Let me put you at ease, then. Leave me be." And with that, she sailed past him and out into the hall. Once she was out of everyone's view, she took off running up the stairs to her room, shutting the door behind her. In her dark room, she took several deep breaths, fury and sadness mingling in her. *If only he'd never come this Christmas. I would only have Badley to deal with. But now, I must somehow navigate all of this.*

Her heart pounded.

Someone knocked on the door, and she opened it to find Eloise standing there, as well as Serena. "Your mother sent me after you," Eloise exclaimed. "She worries you've fallen ill."

"Hardly. I'm merely sick of her meddling," Addy gasped.

Eloise and Serena slipped inside the room and Addy shut the door again, joining them on the big four-poster bed.

"I cannot make sense of Alistair one bit, nor of myself," she confessed, her heart thudding so fiercely it unsettled her stomach. "I thought I was resolute in my wish never to marry, yet I cannot banish him from my thoughts. How foolish I have been."

"Pray do not be cross, but Eloise told me about what Badley said to Captain Crawford, that Alistair overheard it as well. Mayhap he did not want to overstep. Or did not know how to say it. Mayhap he did not wish to hurt you."

"Hurt me? All he cares about is his duty. That is all that matters to him. And Cordelia is his duty."

"Do you wish to know what I think?" Eloise grasped Addy's hand. "I think he cares for you deeply, but of course, the whole matter is made complicated by his mother and your own family. Perhaps he wished to spare you the mortification of learning of Badley's true intentions."

"You are too generous, Eloise." Addy lay down sideways on the fluffy bed, a tear rolling down the bridge of her nose.

"Mayhap," Serena spoke up then, "Mayhap you are afraid."

"Afraid? I'm not afraid," Addy cried.

"You are afraid of your feelings for Alistair, of losing your autonomy, and you seek any reason at all to push him away."

"That's not true!" Addy whispered. But deep down, Serena's words struck a chord. Her chest tightened, and more tears spilled down her cheeks. "And—and even if it were, he will marry Cordelia, they will go off to London and Bath together, just as his mother wishes. He will not defy his mother. Not for me. No matter what. And furthermore, he is a coward. I will not be bound to a coward. You, Eloise, you are courted by a hero. The furthest thing from a coward. And James is not afraid to show you how he feels, Serena."

The other two girls exchanged sorrowful glances, but let Addy continue, her voice trembling, "Perhaps I am afraid. But it does not change things. It does not change Alistair, and his devotion to duty. I should like to be left alone now."

Eloise nodded, sighing. "Very well, we shall leave you be. But we are here to talk if you would like. We will be across the hall having tea if you would like to join."

But Addy didn't join them. She stayed on her bed, knees drawn up to her chin, and watched the snow flurries outside, the panes rattling with the strong winds. It was going to be a dreadful storm.

She slowly lay down on her bed, drifting off to sleep, tears drying on her face. She just wanted to go home. She would have to tell Mother and Father sooner or later of her resolve to never marry. The sooner the better, she supposed. Because after this, after learning about Lord Badley's true intentions, she could not in good conscience marry him. She detested herself for even considering it.

Mother knocked on her door early the next morning, and entered without waiting for the still-slumbering Addy to respond.

Blinking and yawning she watched her mother perch on the edge of the bed, her expression troubled. "Lord Badley fears that you dislike his company, Adelaide."

Well, it was as good a time as any. Addy stared at the patterns swirling across her blankets in an ornate, brocade design. Drawing her fingers across the sleek, soft fabric, she tried to think of a good way to explain her decision. But none came as Mother fixed her with a searching stare.

"Perhaps I do," she whispered at last, lowering her eyes to the ground.

"You simply do not care about anyone other than yourself, do you?" Mother's words were like a slap in the face.

Addy jerked her head up. "Mother, I cannot marry someone I do not love. Someone who does not love me either. I am nothing more than a pawn to him. A tool for his use to advance himself, his career, his political influence."

Mother stood abruptly. "That is utterly ridiculous. You are simply fishing for excuses."

"No, I am not!" Addy choked out. "I am not!"

Mother's eyes snapped with fire. "I will not argue with you. But rest assured, you will marry him. He means to propose, and I had to plead with him not to think ill of you. Especially after the way you mocked him yesterday after that game of snapdragon. Which, by the way, was most indecorous of you to play."

"It was Aunt Agatha's idea, was it not?" Adelaide stood as well, trembling with anger.

"It is no matter whose idea it was. It is meant to be a game for gentlemen. Not the gentle sex."

"So many rules!" Addy burst out. "Far too many of them. I am sick of them."

"And I am weary of you. I cannot endure another decade of incessantly battling you over every trivial matter. Your brother is not half as maddening as you are."

"Thank you, Mother," Addy's throat tightened and she hurried to the window so as to hide the tears that streaked down her face.

"I am merely being frank with you. No more of this nonsense. Do you understand? Your father and I have had enough."

"If it weren't for you, I would not be compelled to marry. I'm sure he wouldn't expect such a dreadful thing of me."

"It was *his* idea," Mother snapped. "Now get dressed and ready for breakfast. Your aunt has a full day planned. And think upon what I've said. Your father is distressed enough by you as it is. Do you truly wish to plague him even more?"

And with that, she swept out, closing the door rather loudly behind her. Addy covered her face with trembling hands and let the tears come again. This had to be the worst Christmas in the history of Christmases.

Gemma was called to help her prepare for the morning meal, arranging Addy's hair in festive ribbons that matched the burgundy of her dress. A little stain on her lips enhanced her features. With a deep sigh, Addy braced herself for the events of that day. Mother would not let her escape Lord Badley's clutches without a fight.

As for Alistair, she could not let herself think of him, or she wouldn't be able to remain composed. For a moment, she wished she could talk to James about all of this. But again, he could bring it up to Mother on accident. Or Mother would draw it out of him.

So, she kept her mouth clamped shut. Perhaps she was learning a thing or two about restraint.

Chapter 18

Alistair was stunned by the heavy blanket of snow driven by swirling gusts outside. There would certainly be no escaping the house today, though he craved the chance to walk, to clear his mind.

Downstairs at breakfast, the table buzzed with excitement for the day ahead, though Alistair wondered if they felt as restless as he did.

Lady Worthington and Lord Worthington announced they would be retiring again to the drawing room for another day of games and carolling.

"At least we are not bound to spend this Christmas in our homes all alone," Lady Worthington told them with a laugh.

"Hear, hear!" Lord Ashford agreed.

"And thank heavens I am not on my ship this Christmas. This would be a dreadful endeavour, to sail through this," Captain Crawford added.

Alistair sought Addy out throughout the meal but of course, she continued to ignore him, engaging in conversation with Eloise. *Why is she so angry with me again? How can I mend it?*

Badley sat beside her of course, but he seemed wary of broaching a conversation with her throughout the meal, his tone more timid and less confident than usual. Perhaps he was learning that with Adelaide, his penchant for gloating about political prowess didn't go so far.

Cordelia,too, was cowed today, quieter than usual, and he imagined she wasn't too happy with him for speaking with Addy yesterday evening after the Snapdragon game. In due time, she may very well decide to marry someone else, and guilt pricked in him as he hoped that she would. Though, it would hurt his mother deeply.

Breakfast drew out for a long while, as everyone was at their leisure. There was nowhere else to go, after all, and the Worthingtons' ideas of what to do here at the manor were dwindling rapidly.

James challenged Alistair, Captain Crawford and Lord Badley to a game of billiards following the meal, which Alistair welcomed. It would take his mind off his dilemma, the warring desire for Adelaide, his burgeoning feelings for her, and his wish to carry out his duty to his father's estate. Furthermore, it hurt to know he would disappoint his mother should he follow his heart.

"Now tell me, Captain. Do you mean to turn my cousin into a shipman's wife?" James chuckled as he sent the balls scattering across the table.

"If your aunt and uncle should be agreeable to it, then yes," replied Captain Crawford with a smile. "And what of you and Miss Scott?"

"I mean to propose on Christmas," James replied, not before checking to ensure that Lord Scotfell was not nearby. "I mean to have a word with her father tomorrow evening."

"Huzzah, then! Her parents adore you, certainly, as does Miss Scott. I confess I worry that your aunt and uncle will not deem me suitable for your cousin."

James laughed, shaking his head. "Well, your bravery at Waterloo recommends you and my uncle should be honoured to have you as a son-in-law. Don't let my aunt dismay you."

"I will endeavour to keep that in mind. I was hoping to broach the matter on Christmas Eve."

"Then there are wedding bells in both of our futures, are there not?"

They both laughed, clinking their glasses together at that, while Alistair took aim for his shot. He managed to get two balls in the pocket, to his relief.

"What of you and Miss Ashworth, Lord Dowden?" Captain Crawford asked, stooping to take his turn.

"I—" Alistair stammered. "I am not certain."

Captain Crawford lifted his eyebrows. "Oh?"

"Has Addy besotted you that much?"

For a moment, Alistair nearly poured out everything about his conflicting desires—one for duty, one for Adelaide Fawcett. "She is truly a magnificent young woman," he murmured after a beat. "But—"

"Your mother has her heart set upon Miss Ashworth, I presume?"

Alistair gulped. "She does."

"But what is it that you want, Alistair?" James leaned on his billiards stick. "Do tell."

Adelaide. If only this were simpler.

But before he could speak, the older gentlemen entered to watch the game at hand.

The game lasted most of the morning until, at last, they finished, with James as the winner. In the drawing room, they found a game of spilikins going on. The tower of small, rectangular blocks teetered precariously as Addy withdrew one, then another, from the base of the column. Alistair watched, impressed, but when he turned his head, he was startled to find Cordelia regarding him with almost an accusatory expression. His mother too watched him with exasperation. She'd caught him admiring Adelaide, and she lifted her eyebrow in a silent question before nodding towards Cordelia, seated on the settee watching the spilikins match.

"Miss Ashworth, do you not enjoy spilikins?"

"No, not truly," she told him. "And I have no wish to mortify myself by sending the column to the ground. My hands are rather unsteady."

"Ah," was all he could think to say. Another glance at his mother told him that she was smiling to herself, pleased that he was at last attempting to engage with Cordelia.

"Lord Dowden," Miss Wortham called from her seat at the spilikins table. "Will you take my place? I must excuse myself for a moment."

He turned, realising that if he agreed, he would be seated beside Adelaide, pitted in the game against her. Without thinking, he nodded. Cordelia wilted beside him on the sofa, and he stood, heart hammering as he crossed the room and sat down beside Adelaide.

"Are you quite ready to be roundly quashed?" she demanded, her dark eyes flashing into his.

A smirk tugged at the corner of Alistair's mouth. "I could ask the same of you," he responded tautly, and this earned a careful look from her.

"Be warned, Alistair. Addy is a spilikins master," James called across the room.

"What do you *not* excel at, Miss Fawcett," Alistair murmured, loud enough for only Adelaide to hear.

She did not reply, but her eyes said a world of things he yearned to decipher. It was his turn next, and he attempted to remove a stick from the bottom of the stack. A bold move. And Adelaide's expression said as much.

The tower teetered precariously.

Next, she removed another stick, setting it on the table loudly.

Alistair took his turn then, holding his breath as the pile swayed again, and those watching let out giddy cries.

"That was rather close," he murmured.

It was Adelaide's turn to smirk. "Indeed."

She removed a stick from closer to the top of the stack, and then Alistair took his turn. The pile crashed down. "It would seem you've bested me," he admitted, smiling.

For a moment, Adelaide's expression wavered, and something like sadness settled across her pretty features. She opened her mouth to say something, but before she could, Lord Badley sat down at the table as well. "Would you like to go against me, Miss Fawcett?"

"Alistair, will you come and turn the pages for Cordelia at the pianoforte?" his mother called. Alistair clenched his hands and nodded, crossing the room to take a seat beside Cordelia on the bench there. But as he sat, waiting to turn the page for her as she ran her fingers deftly across the keys, Adelaide lifted her gaze to him, that sadness washing once again across her features.

The sight wrenched him.

With a small sigh, he lowered his gaze, wishing he could have just a moment to speak to her in complete privacy, to make sense of what was happening between them. He had so many questions about the past week, ones he certainly could not ask easily with his mother, Cordelia, or anyone else around. Moreover, Addy's mother cast him a withering look, as if she counted him an obstacle between Adelaide and Lord Badley. Did she know of Badley's ambitions? Did she know Badley truly didn't care about her daughter?

Surely, if she did, she would object as well.

Alistair straightened his shoulders. If nothing else, he would need to find some time to speak to Adelaide alone. He would need to be careful of course, and not raise any suspicions. Perhaps he could catch her at some point before breakfast tomorrow, since she seemed to favour rising early.

If only this blizzard weren't going on, and they could steal outside. It would be easier to find privacy in the garden. But in this weather, it would be foolish to step outside. They would catch their deaths, surely.

As everyone retired to their rooms to prepare for dinner, his mother once again drew him aside, guiding him down the hall to the library. There, she turned to him, her expression grave and tense. "My dear boy, I spoke to Cordelia's parents, and they were wondering when you meant to make an offer of marriage."

"An offer of—" Alistair stopped short, heart climbing into his throat. *There will be no offer of marriage,* he nearly said. But he gulped those words down.

"I was thinking that Christmas Eve would do. After speaking with Lord and Lady Fairfield, I understand that their son means to propose to Miss Scott that night as well. What better time to do it then?" Rosalind Dowden clasped her hands together, a dreamy look in her eye.

Alistair opened his mouth and then closed it.

"What is the matter, my boy?"

"I—" *I wish to marry Adelaide, if she will have me.* But the words did not come. Instead, he shook his head and whispered, "Nothing." He watched as she hurried out, a pleased smile spread across her face. A hopeless pit yawned inside him.

When she'd gone, he covered his face in his hands. Never in his life had he ever felt so...trapped. And a pang of empathy went through him. Adelaide must be undergoing the same distress.

It was clear she did not give a whit for Lord Badley. But if her parents insisted...she would have no choice. Of course, she had far more spirit than he did. She would baulk as much as she could, he didn't doubt.

With a groan he closed his eyes and wished that he could summon the courage to be honest with his mother, to inform her that he would not be marrying Cordelia Ashworth. Polished a girl that she was, he could not imagine himself wed to her, much less betrothed.

And it would be unfair to everyone if he kept silent.

As he exited the library, he paused at the sight of Lady Fairfield hurrying down the hall. She paused when she noticed him in the library doorway.

"Lord Dowden," she nodded stiffly.

He bowed and expected her to continue along. But to this surprise, she didn't. Instead, she paused and regarded him with cold eyes. "You and Miss Ashworth make such a delightful pair," she told him, something calculating beneath her tone. He couldn't put his finger on it, but his stomach churned, his tongue tying.

"Your mother is most pleased about it, I can see," she continued, as if prompting him to speak, to mention his own eagerness. *She fears I will come between Adelaide and Badley.* He exhaled slowly.

"Indeed she is," he replied.

"Well, may I offer you my congratulations?"

When Alistair did not speak, she swept onward, her mouth a thin, humourless slash.

He remained standing there, turning the conversation over and over in his head. He and Adelaide both were caught in a strange crossfire. Their lives, it would seem, were not their own to decide.

He slept fitfully that night, Adelaide everywhere in his dreams. In one, he was wandering through a great forest, towering spruces all around, And he could hear her voice calling him, pleading with him to find her. He searched for her desperately, praying he would find her before something befell her. But she was nowhere to be found. Her voice haunted him as the dream progressed until suddenly, she went silent.

Panic filled him, and he awoke then, his body covered in a cold sweat. It took him several moments to realise it had just been a dream. He rose and padded across the cold floor until he reached the window, staring out into the swirling snow. When would the storm end, he wondered. He prayed it would be soon; he would go stir-crazy if it didn't.

A glance at the clock told him it was nearly six in the morning. So he dressed and slipped out into the hall. There, he nearly collided with Adelaide herself. Her face flushed as she stared up at him, stepping backwards. "Alistair," she whispered.

His name on her lips sent his heart fluttering madly. "Adelaide, can we speak in private?" he whispered.

"Why?" she demanded in an undertone.

"Please. It is of a delicate nature." He didn't know what he was thinking, truthfully, but if he didn't at least attempt to tell her about Badley, he couldn't forgive himself. At the very least he could attempt to protect her from the man.

At length, she nodded and together they slipped down the back staircase into the library, where they took refuge behind a large shelf. "Miss Fawcett—Adelaide. What is amiss? Why are you so angry with me? I thought—"

"What did you think?" Adelaide's eyes narrowed.

"I don't—"

"Can't you just say it?" she bared her teeth, glaring up at him. "Or does your duty prevent you?"

"And what of *your* duty?" Alistair could barely get the words out of his dry mouth. "Answer me that. We both have our duties."

"I thought at least you could warn me, Alistair. About Badley."

"Badley?"

"That he is a conniving exploiter. That he didn't truly care for me, not in the way a man ought to care for his wife."

"I—how did you learn that?"

"Captain Crawford. He said that he noticed you listening, that you knew of what Lord Badley said as well about me. About viewing me as merely an advantageous match."

"I meant to tell you. Truly I did."

Adelaide's eyes flooded with tears, and she shook her head. "It hardly matters. My parents are merely concerned with me making a good match. Regardless of his intentions. At least, my mother does."

"I am sorry," Alistair whispered. He ached to reach out and gather her in his arms. But if someone were to walk in right now, they would be ruined.

He kept his hands rigidly at his sides and measured his next words carefully. But he couldn't think of anything to say. He was utterly at a loss and wished that for once, he could be suave with words. That he could have the same ease as James did when it came to conversing. But his wish did not come true.

Adelaide stepped away, a tear running down her cheek. "I ought to go."

"Are you going to marry him?" Alistair blurted.

She froze, turning large, wet eyes to him. Her expression wrenched him. "Not if I can help it."

And with that, she was gone. He lingered for a long moment, his feet rooted to the spot, trying to make sense of what she'd just said. What he wouldn't give for her spirit, her audacity.

Chapter 19

Addy had no appetite for breakfast. Instead, she lingered in bed, staring up at the ceiling, until Mother came up to fetch her and scold her for neglecting the rest of the company. "Your aunt is in need of someone to perform upon the pianoforte," she informed Addy, arching a thin eyebrow.

Addy sighed loudly and sat up. If she didn't go now, she'd never hear the end of it. So she dressed, Gemma came to arrange her hair, and she followed her mother downstairs to the drawing room, where Eloise, Cordelia, and Serena sang "Hark! The Herald Angels Sing", and Aunt Agatha arranged an assortment of desserts on the room's marble-topped table.

Lowering herself onto the pianoforte bench, Addy began to play in tune with their singing, though she could not summon any energy to make it a lively performance. Presently the gentlemen entered, smelling of brandy and pipe smoke, and she watched as James and Serena took a seat on the rug before the big hearth. Eloise and Captain Crawford found a place on the settee, supping on a serving of pudding, and when Alistair entered, Cordelia danced up.

So many things had been left unsaid last night, that much was certain. Her mind kept replaying those moments over and over again in her head, the way he'd swayed close to her, a longing spark in his blue eyes. For a moment, she'd wondered if he would gather her to him, hold her in a warm embrace. And yet, he had not. Instead, he had ended the meeting quickly, after she told him about why she'd been so peeved with him.

Despite his apologies, she was annoyed that he had delayed so long in telling her. The sincerity in his eyes haunted her, however.

From her seat, she could see him and Cordelia admiring the tree in the hall. Cordelia's arm in his, they conversed with one another about the decorations wrapped around the massive tree, as Lady Ashford and his mother looked on, exchanging pleased smiles and murmuring to each other about the pair.

"Miss Fawcett?"

Addy's stomach churned at the sound of Lord Badley's voice just behind her. "Lord Badley," she replied somewhat stiffly. Across the room, Mother watched. So she pasted a wide smile on her face, frantically racking her mind for some excuse or other to escape the drawing room. "I was speaking to your parents, and they informed me that someday, you would like to visit Venice. Is that correct?"

Addy straightened, barely refraining from shooting Mother a glare. "Indeed. I have wanted to go there for some time."

"Ah, wonderful. We shall have to arrange it, shall we not?"

We?

The afternoon dragged on, the blizzard continuing to rage outside. But at last, it was dinner time, and she excused herself to go change, along with Eloise, Serena, and Cordelia. As she set foot on the bottom step, however, her mother approached, grasping her by the arm. "Adelaide, your father and I would like to speak to you in a few minutes."

Addy's stomach began to churn. *So, has the time come?* She could try once more to tell them of Lord Badley's intentions. She prayed that they might listen.

With a small nod, she followed Mother down the hall to a quiet study, where Father waited. He smiled at Addy when she entered and pecked a kiss on her cheek. "My dear!"

"Is something the matter?" She glanced around, hoping that Lord Badley didn't emerge from the study's shadows.

"No, no, no," Father chortled. "Nothing is wrong. Nothing at all. In fact, we have spoken with Lord Badley this morning, and he is eager to press his suit."

"He is—" Addy shook her head. "What do you mean?"

"He wishes to *marry* you!" Mother exclaimed, grasping her hand tightly. So tight that Addy winced. "Is that not good news?"

"Now, now Olivia. It is her decision, after all. Though to be sure, we are certain you and Badley would make an excellent match. He is eager to take you all over with him on his travels, and you will want for nothing.

"But—what if I am not cut out to be a politician's wife?" Addy whispered.

"I think it should suit you very well," Mother waved her hand, dismissing this objection. "You must not be so hard on yourself, my dear. The man has four and ten thousand pounds a year, and you could not do better. You will travel all about the world, and your home will be one of the finest in England. He could even purchase you a castle in the north, should you so choose."

Addy caught her breath. It sounded wonderful, but that did not mean she would love him, and he didn't love her. Lump in her throat, she stared at the ground. "I don't wish to rush into anything," she at last said, vision blurring.

"But—" Mother began. Father cut her off with a wave of his hand. "Ah. Well, you may ponder on it. But you could not do better than Lord Badley."

"Yes, Father," Addy said numbly.

Her head spun as her parents left, her mother casting her one last, sharp look before vanishing out of sight. Addy's chest hurt. Her heart hurt.

She sank into an armchair in the corner of the room and stared out at the storm swirling beyond the window panes.

To be a child again, without a care in the world...

***

She didn't know how long she sat there, watching the blizzard in all its tempestuous glory. It was truly a beautiful sight to behold, but the moment ended all too soon when someone rapped on the study door and she turned to see Father standing there, his eyes creased in a thoughtful smile. "My dear, you are in low spirits, aren't you?" he stepped into the room and joined her at the window, peering down at her with a curious expression.

"Somewhat, Father," she admitted, a lump forming in her throat. She bounded up then and threw her arms around him in a tight embrace, and he brought up his arms to hug her as well. "I'm just—I know you and Mother want to see me settled. But I—" she drew back, forcing her to meet Father's eyes. "I cherish my independence. I hold it most dearly. And I cannot fathom myself marrying someone if there be no love."

"Your mother and I were not in love when we married, but it grew. It does grow."

"Father," Addy tried to swallow. "I know it can. But for me, I cannot marry if it is not there to begin with."

"Ah. I see," her father murmured. He sighed, leaning back slightly and tipping her head back with the crook of his finger. "You are a good girl, my dear. But I worry for you, for when your mother and I are gone. Your brother will inherit the estate, and I would like to see you settled in an advantageous marriage. I know you wish to be independent, but it is not practical. Don't you understand?"

"I know it's not practical," Addy sniffed. "But I don't care."

"Is this about that Dowden boy?"

"No," Addy shook her head, though it was a lie in part. "It's not."

"He is a good man, certainly. And I can see you are drawn to him. As he is to you. But he has his duty. And you have yours. The sooner you both accept that, the easier it shall be."

"Why must I accept it though?" Addy wrenched away, wringing her hands.

"Lord Badley is handsome, wealthy, and of course, he might be driven by political ambition. But he would be occupied much of the time by his career, and you would be afforded all the time you'd like to be independent, to do as you please."

"That's not the same," Addy shook her head.

"But it is what you've wanted all along, isn't it?"

"Yes. But—"

"Then what is the matter?" Father frowned.

"James—James is in love with Serena, and she with him."

"They are quite fortunate in that regard. It is rare for an arrangement to work out thus."

Addy felt a fierce urge to stamp her foot, but instead, she balled her hands into fists. "I long for that. I long for what they have—what Eloise and Captain Crawford share."

"Your cousin is only permitted to court the captain because of his recent advancement in the Ton, due to his commendation by the Prince Regent. If it weren't for that, I am certain it would not be so happy a circumstance."

Addy's heart sank. She had hoped her father would side with her, that he would let his sympathy take over and tell her she did not have to marry Badley. But she had been foolish.

"Just imagine it. You and your cousin will be married, and you can enjoy London society together in splendid townhomes. You shall want for nothing. Your mother shall be happy, as shall I. But if you continue to neglect Lord Badley, he shall move on to seek some other lady's hand, and you, my dear...you will be a spinster. And your future will remain uncertain."

Addy whirled on her heel, rushing to the door. "I do not care," she whispered, before fleeing.

***

Addy sat at her vanity that evening, watching as Gemma piled her curls atop her head. She lifted her hand to brush her fingers against the delicate band of velvet around her throat, hoping nobody noticed her red eyes at dinner. With her fortune, someone might.

Her door opened and Eloise entered, scurrying over to the bed to watch. "I saw James and Serena kissing," she whispered feverishly. When Addy managed only a faint smile, Eloise's expression fell. "What is the matter?"

She rose and hurried over, grasping Addy's hand tightly.

"Nothing. It's just—I—" Addy closed her eyes, exhaustion seeping beneath her skin, into her bones. "I'm simply tired. It has been a long week."

"Oh Addy," Eloise pulled her into a hug. "I'm sorry."

Addy's eyes prickled and she blinked her tears away rapidly. She tried to give a brave smile. "It is no matter. I am sorry to be such a spoilsport."

"No, no. Don't apologise. I am here to listen, if you need anything."

"Thank you," Addy whispered. Where to even begin though? Instead, she attempted to use a cheerful tone. "You saw my brother kissing Serena? Where?"

"In the library! They didn't know I saw, so don't speak of it. But they are very much smitten with one another."

At that, Addy couldn't help it. She began to weep. Eloise's eyes went wide and she gathered her into her arms. "What's the matter, Addy?" she pled.

Addy wiped her eyes, willing herself to stop crying. But it was fruitless. "My parents tell me that Badley means to propose. Very soon. And they wish for me to say yes. But—I don't know if I can."

"Oh, Addy," Eloise's eyes filled with tears also. "Surely they will not enforce it?"

"I pray not. But if they do, I swear I shall run away. I swear it."

"What of Alistair? Have you spoken to him at all?"

"Yes, but he is duty-bound. And he will carry out his duty, no matter what. I am not like that, Eloise. I can't do it. I just can't. And my mother and father won't listen. They just want to marry me off well. And if I were to ever marry, it would have to be for love."

"Addy," Eloise sighed. "I am deeply sorry to hear that. When is he to propose?"

"Very soon, I fear. Too soon. I must figure something out, lest I be entrapped in a marriage with him. I cannot wed him, Eloise. I cannot. But how am I to—"

Eloise gently hushed her. "Someone may hear. We must stay quiet. But I will do everything in my power to see that you are not coerced into anything."

Addy nodded, hiccupping through her sobs. Closing her eyes, she wished she could be far, far away, in another world. Another country. Anywhere but here. Of course, she would miss James, and Eloise desperately. But at least she would be free.

"It is nearly dinner time. Why don't you wash your face? I shall tell Mamma you will be down soon."

"Thank you." Addy crossed the room and splashed water onto her face over the porcelain bowl on the commode. Her eyes were still a little puffy when she finished, but not enough that it would be obvious she'd been crying.

"Let me think of something. Some way you can escape, should he propose. Yes?"

Addy nodded and followed her cousin on dragging feet down to the dining room. Taking her place, she turned and found Alistair watching her, his forehead furrowed with worry.

Taking a deep breath, she managed a tight smile, her face going warm. The thought of eating right now turned her stomach. Even worse, Lord Badley made a beeline for the seat right next to her, grinning at her. "Miss Fawcett. I pray you are feeling better."

"I—I am," she murmured, pushing some stewed carrots across her plate. Mother must have excused her abrupt exit earlier; said she was under the weather. Which she was. Never had her future seemed so bleak. Even her father, who usually favoured her, did not agree with her reluctance to marry without love.

Down the table, Alistair kept his eye on her, his blue eyes full of a gentle concern that sent a flurry of emotions raging through her. Everything from anger to wistfulness to deep, yawning sadness swirled in her chest, and she would give anything to go for a long ride, just to clear her head.

Hopefully, the blizzard will clear tomorrow morning. She could only wish for that. Perhaps, when she went for her ride, she could keep riding and never stop. She could flee to the Americas. Somewhere else. Anywhere else but here. The thought of seeing Alistair and Cordelia's marriage announcement in the papers sent a shudder through her.

That night, she sat up until her taper had nearly spent itself, fascinated by the whirling snow just on the other side of the windowpane. The glass was freezing to the touch, and she enjoyed the beautiful chaos that tore through the night. Footsteps echoed out in the hall, and she sat up, listening closely.

Slipping out of her room, she paused again, holding up her sputtering candle. Someone was up and moving through the house.

She crept down the back stairs to the library, wondering if whoever it was up had gone there.

Pushing open the library door, she paused at the sight of Alistair in a big armchair near the fireplace. It had been lit already, likely by the candle on the table next to him. When she took another step forward, he jerked around, his eyes locking with hers.

"Adelaide," he whispered.

Her heart lurched. "Alistair," she replied after a long moment. Heart thundering, she crossed the room and sank into the chair opposite him.

"You seemed distressed earlier," he whispered, shadows and light flickering across his face.

Addy kept her smile fixed. "I was quite well. No need for concern."

"Addy." He had not called her that in a long time. "I am so sorry for not mentioning Lord Badley's words sooner. I should have. But I did not wish to overstep and—"

She sighed, shaking her head. "I fully understand, and I forgive you, rest assured."

His mouth curved. "I hope I did not wake you."

"No, I was already awake. I couldn't sleep."

"Neither could I." Again, they locked eyes for a long moment, the air heavy and thick with a strange tension. At last, Addy dropped her gaze to the tips of her slippers peeking out beneath her nightgown.

"What were you going to read?"

"An atlas. The discussion earlier this week about travelling gave me cause to wonder where I would go, should I be able to travel in the near future."

"For a honeymoon?"

Alistair stilled, his jaw clenching. "Adelaide…"

"Please, just call me Addy," she leaned forward. "And never mind my question. Please. Can we at least be friends?"

His eyes widened slightly, but he nodded. "I should like that." His cheeks flushed, as he dropped his gaze to the book in his lap.

Chapter 20

Addy snuck out of the library just as the first rays of dawn streaked through the windows. Her mind reeled as she tried to understand the strangeness of her...friendship...with Alistair. They had chatted half the night about travelling. Alistair longed to visit Bavaria, and Addy yearned to see Delphi, where once upon a time, an oracle would deliver prophecies to the ancients.

"I did not know you enjoyed travel," she had teased Alistair, and he had coloured in the firelight.

"I pray you did not imagine me dull," he had sighed, earning a laugh from her.

"Not at all!" she exclaimed. "In truth, I find you most fascinating."

"Fascinating? I should say the very same of you," Alistair smirked.

She could not stop smiling all the way back to her room. At breakfast, she kept making eye contact with him, and each time her heart fluttered. Her grief from the day before melted away slightly, though it still clung to her, something in her aching whenever she watched him converse with Cordelia. Something akin to jealousy.

Aunt Agatha announced to them that they would be finishing up decorating the Christmas tree that day, since the snowstorm had not let up yet.

"I pray this dreadful storm may cease by the morrow," she sighed. "Particularly, as tomorrow is the day before Christmas Eve. In the meantime, however, we might occupy ourselves with adorning the tree. Crates of ornaments, along with strings of popped corn and cranberries, await in the entry hall. After breakfast, let us adjourn there and partake in some cheerful decorating."

A light applause broke out around the table. As Addy made to leave the dining room with everyone else, Lord Badley fell into step beside her. "I confess, I thought we needed a grander tree at first. But the one we brought has sufficed remarkably," he told her, not noticing her eye-roll.

She slipped away from him to stand near Eloise and Captain Crawford, James, and Serena. Together, they searched through the crates, picking out ornaments to hang on the tree boughs.

Addy pulled out a crystalline one, resembling a snowflake, while Captain Crawford chuckled over a little tin soldier he had discovered in the box. "How apt," he laughed. Addy made the mistake of glancing up to see Cordelia and Alistair on the staircase, leaning out to hang several bows on the tree. Cordelia's arm was flush with Alistair's, her cheeks rosy, her eyes sparkling as they laughed over having to strain to reach the tree.

Another pang of jealousy surged through Addy and she turned, trying to distract herself.

As she hung another ornament, a glistening orb the colour of emerald, Lord Badley approached her from behind, leaning over her shoulder to help her fasten the ball on one of the boughs. "Allow me," he murmured in her ear. She glanced up then to find Alistair staring at her, and his expression made her stomach flip.

"Thank you, Lord Badley," she muttered.

Somewhere nearby, James cleared his throat. Turning, she found him lifting an eyebrow at Badley, his eyes flashing protectively. She gave him a smile that she hoped was reassuring. She could handle the politician quite well on her own. If she were to swear herself to living independent of any man or marriage, she needed to deal with Lord Badley on her own.

Perhaps I can drive him away somehow.

She didn't have time to ponder on this idea. The rest of the afternoon flew by in a blur, until at last the tree stood festive and beautiful in her aunt and uncle's hall. Truly breathtaking.

At dinner, Aunt Agatha proposed another evening of dancing. Serena agreed to play the piano for the first dance, and as everyone clustered in the drawing room, Badley bowed and asked Addy to accompany him. She nearly sighed but accepted, and took their places. Beside her, Cordelia and Alistair came to stand, Cordelia batting her eyes at him. He smiled, but it didn't reach his eyes. Addy did not mistake that whatsoever.

Addy played for the second dance, allowing Serena and James to dance together. From her seat at the pianoforte, she watched the others circle through the steps of the reel, her stomach twisting at the sight of Cordelia gazing up at Alistair adoringly. But as the dance concluded, his eyes flickered to her, and his cheeks flushed brightly. Addy caught her breath, heart turning over.

She couldn't suppress a smile, lowering her eyes to the ivory keys beneath her fingers.

She didn't care all of a sudden if her mother or his mother was looking on. Confound duty! She wouldn't live by someone else's rules. She refused. And perhaps…perhaps Alistair agreed.

Though deep down, she feared he didn't.

Everyone dispersed for the night, and after getting into her nightgown, Addy crept across the hall to Eloise's room. Her cousin opened the door for her and she hurried in, and confided in Eloise the events of the night before.

"You were in the library together? Alone? Heavens, your mother would have a fit!" Eloise laughed, shaking her head. "But I did notice the two of you looking at each other this evening. Something's changed. You've forgiven him for the whole ordeal with Lord Badley?"

"I can't help it. I—I don't know, Eloise. It's so strange, but before this trip, I detested him. And now...I can't stop thinking of him. How could I marry Badley when I have feelings for another?"

"There is no doubt of where your affections lie. But many a lord and lady have wed with desire for another."

"Impossible," Addy whispered. "I shall not be amongst them."

"But Alistair may," Eloise gently said, reaching over to grasp Addy's hand.

Addy's heart dropped, and she lowered her gaze to the bedspread. "I pray not," she whispered through clenched teeth. A tear rolled down her cheek, and Eloise leaned forward, hugging her tightly. "Oh, Addy. It breaks my heart to see you like this. I want you to secure your happiness. So dreadfully."

Addy nodded, a lump in her throat. "Thank you. I'm just confused, I suppose. I imagined that I wouldn't ever fall in love. That I never wanted to. And yet, suddenly..."

"It does take one unaware, doesn't it?" Eloise smiled. "I understand completely. I did not expect to fall in love with Captain Crawford. Of course, when I met him this summer, I found him dashing and handsome. But I did not imagine..." she sighed, a dreamy sparkle in her eye. "He told me that he yearned to know me, the first time he saw me. He said he thought of me the whole of his voyage to the West Indies, Addy."

Eloise brought her hands to flushed cheeks. "And now...he will ask for my hand tomorrow."

"I am relieved you have found happiness. One of us ought to marry for love, and I am not at all surprised it is you," Addy grinned.

"But I always dreamed we would have a double wedding."

"You and Serena shall have a double wedding," Addy replied. "And you must promise that once you have settled into your new home in Bath, or London, you will have me to visit."

"Of course! I would miss you too terribly."

"And I will miss you." Addy and Eloise lay back together on the bed, staring up at the ceiling side by side. "Serena will come to live with us, I think. It will be nice to have her near."

"Both of you must write to me often," Eloise told her.

"I promise we will."

"I wonder which of us will have a child first."

"Make it into a contest," Addy giggled.

"Addy!" But Eloise was laughing too.

Not for the first time this Christmas, the sense that everything was about to change hung heavy in Addy's chest. She hoped it was change for the better, but she didn't let herself hope. She was terrified to.

Early the next morning, she awoke and immediately noticed that it was peaceful outside. Rising, she opened the curtains just a bit to find that the blizzard had ended at last. In its wake, the entire countryside was coated in snow. She caught her breath, relishing how the sun sparkled off the surface of the snow. She would sneak out early today, maybe go for a ride. If it wasn't too cold. But if she stayed in this house a moment longer, she'd burst.

Addy changed and slipped downstairs, out the back door onto the terrace. The air stung her face, but she didn't care. At last, she could walk out of the confines of her aunt and uncle's manor. She could run as far as she wanted. Maybe she would never stop.

Addy started through the garden, wandering through its twisting paths until she suddenly came face to face with Alistair. He caught his breath, now mere inches from her, and her heart began to pound. "Good morning, Lord Dowden."

"Please, call me Alistair," he whispered to her surprise.

"Alistair," she echoed. She loved saying his name. It flowed right off her tongue.

His eyes drifted to her lips, if only for a moment, and she couldn't tear her eyes from his lips either. "I—I hoped I might meet you out here."

"Couldn't bear a moment longer in the house?" she laughed softly.

He laughed too, hoarse. "No, I couldn't."

And then, Alistair drifted closer, leaning down as if to kiss her. Addy couldn't breathe. She prayed he would kiss her. Her head swam as she locked eyes with him, legs going weak.

And then, he drew back, wincing. "I ought to go," he rasped.

"Alistair," she shook her head, nearly reaching for him. "You—" she stopped short then, the words sticking in her throat.

"I ought to go," he said again, breathless.

Addy couldn't move. But her throat had closed. He stepped away then and hurried out of sight around a hedge. She stood frozen, dizzy. What had just happened?

She knew one thing for certain. She needed to go for a ride. It didn't take long to reach the stable, and when she did, she saddled Adonis herself. Before long, she thundered out the stable doors, flying across the snow-covered lawn towards a nearby meadow that surrounded the manor. Her hair streamed out behind her, the frigid air stinging across her face.

But for the first time in days, she felt alive. She rode to forget the moment with Alistair in the garden, pain lancing through her at the memory of his haste to flee her. Eloise had been right. Would he really forego his duty for Addy?

He won't, she told herself savagely. She kept riding until the poor horse needed a rest and walked the rest of the way. It was nearly breakfast when she returned to the house, and she hurried inside to change and make herself presentable. Her hair was a tangled mess, and her lips were chapped from the bitter cold.

Stealing inside, she crept up the back stairs, but as she turned onto the corridor that led to her room, she met Lady Dowden. Lady Dowden fixed her with a cold gaze. "Miss Fawcett."

Addy bowed her head in acknowledgement. She began to hurry on past, but Lady Dowden intercepted her. "Miss Fawcett, forgive me for being forthright, but I must say what weighs upon me. I am not blind. I have seen the way you look at my son. But you must know that he will not be dissuaded. He is a noble man, and nothing will turn him from Miss Ashworth. Do you understand?"

It was as if somebody had struck Addy in the stomach. She didn't move, didn't speak. "Please, excuse me," she said, and tried to pass Lady Dowden. But Lady Dowden again stepped into her path. "I remember well how you plagued my boy. You were and always will be a fractious girl. And I do not wish for my son to have anything to do with you. And if you care for him, even slightly, you will not intervene between him and Miss Ashworth. Have I made myself perfectly clear?"

Addy couldn't speak, couldn't reply.

And with that, Lady Dowden swept on down the wall until she entered her room and shut the door behind her. Addy couldn't breathe, tears welling up in her so fast she couldn't blink them away fast enough. She heard a swift intake of breath and whirled to see Cordelia swiftly shut her door. She'd heard the whole conversation.

On shaky legs, Addy rushed back to her own bedroom and rushed in, heart pounding. She collapsed, sobbing, onto her bed, and couldn't stop for a good long while.

Chapter 21

Alistair was just about to shut his bedroom door when his mother approached, asking him if she might have a word. Reluctantly, Alistair conceded, stepping back to watch Rosalind enter and shut the door quietly behind her. "Where have you been?" she asked him, her voice strained.

"On a little jaunt. Enjoying the break in that storm."

Rosalind stared at him, and he wondered if she believed him. If she wanted to ask who he had been with. But to his relief, she didn't. He did not wish to lie to her, nor would he, but it would be difficult to admit.

"Ah. Well, I must have a word with you about Cordelia. Her parents are growing impatient with you. If you do not act soon, you will forfeit your chance to press your suit. And they have noticed your attentions to Miss Fawcett. You have not even attempted to be subtle."

"Mother." Alistair clenched his teeth. "Please. Perhaps it is unwise to make haste in this matter."

"Unwise?" Her voice trembled. "I am thinking of your future, my boy. Do you not conceive of that?"

"Mother!" Alistair spoke flintily. "I do not wish to rush in this matter. Please endeavour to apprehend that. I beg of you."

"Your father wished it. He set his sights on Cordelia Ashworth for you many years ago. I am only fulfilling his final wish."

"His last wish that he expressed to me concerned my duty to the estate."

"And that encompasses whom you wed!"

"Does it? Because I wonder if Father would wish for me to renunciate my own happiness, my own joy. The estate will be well cared for no matter what."

"It was his last wish!" Rosalind cried, so loudly it startled Alistair. He stared at her, taken aback.

Rosalind closed her eyes tightly. "Forgive me. But if it's the last thing I do, I shall see your father's wishes seen to."

And with that, Rosalind swept out of the room, shutting the door behind her with a slam. Alistair changed and blindly descended the back staircase, making his way to the library where he stood at the window, gazing out at the still wintry garden, caked in snow.

"Alistair?" He jumped and turned to find James leaning against a shelf nearby. "How do you fare?"

"Ah! I am well. Quite well."

"I confess, I heard your...conversation...with your mother." Alistair closed his eyes tightly, swearing under his breath.

"Only because I am the next room over. Forgive me for my intrusion—it was not deliberate."

Alistair shook his head. "It is neither your doing nor your error. Forgive me for the disturbance."

"You are uncertain about Cordelia, no?"

Alistair grimaced and nodded. "If only things were simpler."

"Ah, if only. But they never are, are they?"

"Indeed, they are not."

"And you have feelings for my sister."

Alistair could not speak. He just stared at the ground.

James sighed "My parents anticipate that Lord Badley will ask for her hand on the morrow." After a pause, he continued, stepping forward and setting his hand upon Alistair's shoulder. "And you are in love with Addy. It is evident to all. Including your mother."

"She is right. I would be disregarding my duty if I were to pursue your sister." Alistair winced, wishing he had tempered his tone and words. "Forgive me, but I speak the truth. My father...my father impressed upon me the importance of duty from an early age."

"Duty. And what of your duty to yourself? Would it be fair to wed someone you do not truly love?"

"There is of course the matter of your own parents. Let us not forget that your parents also have designs for Adelaide, which do not include myself."

"Adelaide detests Badley. And I should detest to have a brother such as him. But you and she have been destined this entire time."

"Destined," Alistair nearly rolled his eyes, though his stomach flipped at the mention of that word, one which he scarcely dared to entertain or consider. It was too dangerous to do so. "No, the truth of the matter is that I ought to marry Cordelia, and she ought to do as she pleases, but it cannot concern me for I—" and his voice faltered, if only momentarily. "I am not at liberty to love her. No matter how my feelings may tend, I cannot."

"This is your answer? Your resolution?"

"Indeed, it is."

"But—"

"For heaven's sake, James," Alistair brought his hand down upon the window jamb against which he leaned, the sound as loud as a gunshot. "It will pass. It must."

James clenched his jaw. "It is your choice. Your error to make. I have done my part. But I shall despise watching you choose a path that will bring you nothing but misery."

And with that, James turned on his heel and left the library.

Alistair paced across the library, back and forth, back and forth.

But James' voice rang through his head, and he took a breath, struggling to compose himself again. He had never had a cross word with his old friend. And the urgency behind James' words tightened his chest, like a hand around his lungs.

If he did not act, he would soon lose Adelaide forever to Badley. That is, if she would have him. And yet, if he did not broach her about his true feelings, it would be a chance lost, and she would drift into the arms of another. Someone unafraid of his own feelings for her.

That thought turned his stomach.

He leaned his forehead against the cold windowpane, willing his pulse to slow. But it raced on as he fought to catch his breath.

Chapter 22

At breakfast, Lord and Lady Worthington announced a sleigh ride to celebrate the break in the snowstorm.

"I'm certain you're all going mad in here, though heaven knows I've tried to invent various modes of entertainment," Lady Worthington said to them from her place at the end of the table. "The sleighs will be brought round after our meal, and you are welcome to venture out if it suits you. Of course, it may be too cold, so you are at liberty to determine if you wish to go along."

Excited chatter broke out around the table, and for the first time, Alistair anticipated the day's events. And tomorrow would be Christmas Eve, and the day after would be Christmas. After meeting Adelaide in the garden that morning, he'd been thrown into a panic, realising just how close he'd come to slipping. How he had yearned to kiss her though. Which was bewildering, since he had been telling himself this was just a fancy. It would pass. He prayed it would pass. But with each day that went by, he became increasingly aware of how deep his feelings for Adelaide ran. Just how significantly he cared for her.

Mother would not be pleased to hear of it. She would be disappointed. And Father in heaven would be as well. The thought turned his stomach.

Cordelia bounced, clasping her hands together in the front entryway as a maid settled a cloak over her shoulders. "I love sleigh rides. It seems like ages since we've last been outside, hasn't it, Alistair?"

"Indeed," Alistair nodded, though his secret pricked at him. He had certainly been outside since. With the girl he loved.

He froze at that, stunned. The girl he loved? He loved her?

After a long moment, he knew the answer. He did love Adelaide. But wasn't duty more important?

He intended to follow Cordelia outside to the sleighs, but his mother stopped him. "Alistair, a word?"

He nearly sighed, but he nodded. She led him back into the library, where Lord and Lady Ashford waited. Alistair stopped short at the sight of Cordelia's parents, his stomach beginning to churn again. "Lord Dowden," said Lord Ashford, striding over with his hands behind his back. "Your mother tells me you are eager to ask for Cordelia's hand in marriage."

Alistair stared at his mother. She smiled at him, not an ounce of remorse in her expression. Betrayed anger prickled in him.

Before he could respond, Lord Ashford hurried on, "And she tells me that you hope to propose to her on this sleigh ride." He wagged his finger. "Ah, but it is evident you are a romantic." He chortled loudly. "And I wished to let you know that we are eager for you to press your suit. Cordelia will be delighted."

"Go on now, she is waiting in the sledge," Lady Ashford beamed, hastening forward to kiss him on both cheeks. "She is beside herself, I assure you."

He glanced at his mother again, who motioned for him to hurry on out. Clenching his teeth, he exited, heart hammering. Behind him followed his mother and the Ashworths.

Out on the steps, he watched as Adelaide was helped up into a sleigh. In the sleigh just in front of her sat Cordelia, and the next sledge held James and Serena. Eloise and Captain Crawford occupied the last one.

Cordelia waved to him, beaming, but instead of walking over to her sleigh, he strode over to Adelaide's. Behind him, he heard Lord Badley let out a protesting exclamation, and his mother hissed his name. But he ignored them and climbed up beside Adelaide. "Drive," he commanded the footman. And off the sleigh flew.

Adelaide stared at him, her eyes round. And then she covered her mouth, shaking her head, her eyes glistening, a giddy smile on her face. He settled beside her on the seat, suppressing the urge to put his arm around her and kiss her right then and there. But he restrained himself, gazing into her eyes as they flew across the snow.

"Alistair, I thought—" disbelief coloured her voice, mixed with delight. "I can't believe you did that."

"I don't—I don't know what came over me. Forgive me for stealing you away from Lord Badley."

Adelaide shook her head vigorously. "Please, there is no need for forgiveness. I am in your debt." They burst out laughing together and couldn't stop for a good while. The sleigh carried them on and on, further away from the manor and into the thick forest belonging to Adelaide's aunt and uncle. They stayed warm beneath the thick blankets Alistair settled across their laps, and he didn't even notice the bitter air rushing into his face.

All that mattered was the young woman beside him. Mother would be furious, and he could just imagine Cordelia's mortification. But it didn't matter. His stomach was a mess of knots though, as he tried to anticipate the consequences of his actions. But the wind began to pick up, he realised with a glance up at the treetops. The branches tossed wildly, and thick snow began to fall, so rapidly that he could scarcely comprehend it.

Suddenly, the carriage lurched, as one of the runners struck a root, and the horses began to whinny in fear, racing forward faster. The footman suddenly toppled backwards, knocked off balance by the jolt, and struck his head on the side of the sleigh, collapsing unconscious on the bottom of the sledge.

Alistair didn't think—he just acted.

He leapt forward, snatching the reins, and fought to get the horses under control. At last, they slowed to a stop, but by this point, the wind was roaring. Another blizzard loomed.

"Do you know if your uncle has any cottages or sheds on this property?" he called to Adelaide above the wind.

"Yes! It's further ahead—an old stable. It has scarcely been used since he built his new stable several years ago."

"Can we reach it by sledge?"

"Yes!"

Alistair climbed into the sleigh driver seat and snapped the reins, urging the horses onward. They whinnied nervously as they began to trot ahead in the direction of the old stable. At last, it came into view just as the snow flurries intensified. Alistair jumped down from the seat. "How is he?" he shouted above the roar of the storm.

"It's difficult to tell!"

With great difficulty, they helped the footman inside the stable. The roar quieted the second they crossed the threshold, and Alistair told Adelaide to tend to the unconscious man while he brought the horses in.

The wind stung his face as he pushed outside, using his arm to shield his eyes from the driving snow. With difficulty he freed the horses from the sleigh, making sure to hold onto their reins tightly, though they both reared up.

It took several minutes to calm and steady them before he started back towards the stable. He had to pause and wheel back around, feeling around in the sleigh for the blankets they'd been covered in earlier.

They strained against his grasp, the wind trying to tear them away. He squinted against the whipping sleet, forcing one foot in front of the other until at last they crossed the stable threshold, and he led the horses into a stall.

He hurried back to the door to close it after securing them in the stall. With a groan he shoved the door closed against the swirling snow and sank against it, gasping.

"Alistair!" Adelaide raced over; her face white even in the shadowy stable. "Are you hurt?"

"No, no," he exhaled a breathy laugh. "How is the footman?"

"Still unconscious." They both turned to gaze through the shadows at the still, lifeless form of the footman. Alistair pulled his coat off and wrapped it around Adelaide's shoulders before hurrying over to the footman to check his pulse. It was faint but there. Heaving a sigh of relief, he closed his eyes tightly. The stable smelled of stale hay and manure, but they were safe.

"Alistair."

He opened his eyes, catching his breath. Adelaide stepped towards him, her eyes full of alarm and concern. "You are certain you are well?"

"Just relieved. That we made it to this stable before the brunt of the storm struck."

"As am I."

A shiver went through Alistair as his body slowly registered the freezing temperatures. "We need to build a fire."

Adelaide nodded. "We can burn the hay."

"Let me get an armful of it. You see if there's any loose boards in the vicinity."

Adelaide hurried off, and Alistair strode into one of the empty stalls to gather some hay into his arms. Before long, they'd reunited in the centre of the stable and discarded the hay and boards on the ground. Alistair beckoned Adelaide over so he could fish in his coat pocket for his pipe and matchbox.

He held her gaze for a moment, his face heating as he realised her proximity. He jerked his gaze away and tried to focus on the task at hand—creating a fire. He set apart setting up the sticks in a tent over the hay pile before lighting a match, the flame bright in the dark barn, and lighting a fire. It took a moment to get the hay and boards to catch, as they were fairly damp from all the snow.

The wind whistled past the roof overhead and the stone walls of the stable. The horses whinnied, eyes rolling, and stomped their feet.

"Adelaide, I'll need you to help me carry the footman closer to the fireside. You get his legs and I'll haul him under the arms."

She nodded, curls bouncing about her rosy, chapped cheeks. She nodded at the footman. "Do you think he will be well?"

"I believe so. I can only pray he did not strike his head too harshly."

Adelaide nodded, inhaling and exhaling carefully several times. Alistair was struck by how calm she remained. Most girls would panic in such a situation, but she remained composed and strong, despite the precariousness of their situation.

He tried not to think about the ramifications of this—that they were each on the verge of being betrothed to other people, not each other. And they were unchaperoned. The footman didn't count, as he was unconscious. And regardless, there was his rash decision to leap into Adelaide's sleigh instead of Cordelia's. It was a slight that would not soon be forgotten.

The fire glowed on Adelaide's face, her dark eyes bright and sparkling as they flickered toward his. "I fear that our families will not be pleased. As we are here…"

"Unchaperoned," Alistair finished for her.

She nodded. "Yes. And—and I thought—I thought that your duty meant more to you."

"It doesn't," Alistair whispered, his heart tangled and racing. "It doesn't mean more to me. You—" he couldn't summon the right words. At least, not words that would do justice to how he felt, how deeply he loved her. To use the word *love*…would it be an overstep?

He feared it would be. And what if she did not match his feelings? What if this was nothing more than a jaunt for her? A whim that would pass? And then she would cast him aside and drift elsewhere. But if he had learned anything about her this week, it was that she was far more than the impetuous, hot-headed girl he remembered. She was a woman with beautiful flaws and beautiful strengths, with a sharp intellect and a passion for life that inspired him.

Their eyes met across the fire before he dropped his gaze to the flames, stomach flipping. "Ah, yes." He rose and crossed the stable to pick up the blankets he'd yanked out of the sleigh. "I'll use one of these to cover the footman. The other one we can use."

"We," she echoed, her voice shaking ever so slightly. But he didn't read dismay in her expression. A smile played at his mouth.

"Yes," he managed, just above a whisper.

Her eyes darkened even more, if it were possible, and his mouth went dry. He circled the fire to sit beside her and slowly wrapped the blanket around her shoulders, and then his, so they sat beneath it together, side by side. Her warmth sent his pulse fluttering.

"Adelaide," he finally blurted, after a long, significant pause. "You—you are—"

Her lips parted; her features tugged into an expression of breathless expectation.

"You are an extraordinary woman. I've never met anyone like you in my entire existence. And if we are to part ways—"

"Part ways," she repeated, eyebrows lifting.

"I didn't mean—I meant—I don't know what I would do should we—"

A gasp cut him off. The footman. He slept fitfully across the fire from them, teeth chattering.

"How long do you think this storm will last?" Adelaide whispered.

"I don't know." Alistair listened to the wind scream around the creaking walls of the stable. "I pray this structure holds."

"It's been standing for years. I'm sure it will."

"But when is the last time this country has seen a storm of this measure?"

"Yes, that is true."

The footman groaned hazily.

"He struck his head badly. I worry it may require a physician to look at it."

Adelaide nodded. "What were you saying?"

"I understand the consequence of our circumstances. That we will be under scrutiny for our...ah...want of a chaperone. And I know you and Badley—"

"My *parents* pray for our matrimony. But I am uncertain."

"Uncertain," Alistair repeated, trying to understand her meaning.

"Yes. But I do not wish to operate under any presumptions either."

"Ah." Another heavy silence fell, and they both stared into the fire. Three words sat on the tip of Alistair's tongue, but he couldn't bring himself to say them. He was too terrified. A coward.

"I recall that once, when we were children, you declared you never wished to marry," he said at last, curious about her reply.

"I did say that often. I have said it often recently as well," Adelaide ducked her head. "I have always feared the idea of giving up my autonomy, my independence. I fear that marriage would mean to surrender it."

"I would hope that whoever you should marry would not ask that of you," Alistair whispered.

"It is simply the way of things," Adelaide's voice held a note of sadness in it.

"And what would you wish to do with your freedom?"

"Travel the world. Make a true difference somewhere where it is needed. But also, I fear being lonely."

"Lonely?"

"I don't know…I simply wish it were possible to have one without sacrificing the other. Perhaps that is it."

Alistair nodded. He did wish to marry, but he would not wed someone he did not love. And Cordelia might be a lovely girl, but he could not give his heart to her, share a life with her. It would be a betrayal to himself.

Chapter 23

Another half-hour passed and the storm showed no signs of letting up. Addy was acutely conscious of Alistair's closeness, the way his pupils were blown wide, the heightened flush in his cheeks, and the glances he stole her, as if he couldn't pull his gaze from her. It was strange, frightening, wonderful, all at the same time.

She wished she could just tell him exactly how she felt. But his mother's anger, her indignation, it echoed through the recesses of her mind, haunting her.

And it kept the words stuck in the back of her throat. Furthermore, would it mean surrendering her freedom? Her independence?

She watched the flames leap and pirouette until Alistair cleared his throat. "I recall the second time I came to visit Fairfield. And James and I were engaged in a snowball fight, hurling them at one another. You were so vexed that we would not allow you to join in. When we refused, you became quite cross. And so, you crept up behind us—first me, then James—and shoved a handful of snow down both our shirts."

Addy laughed, covering her face. "Did I?"

"Yes, you did," Alistair chuckled too. "I recall it, vividly."

"I am sure. Who would not?" Addy shivered. "Well, pray forgive me. I simply wished to be included. It was as if you and James were in an order of your own, and I was locked on the outside. I was wild with the desire to have you notice me."

Alistair's eyebrows rose. "You were?"

Addy's face heated. "But every time I tried, I just managed to vex you. Of course, in hindsight, my course of action was terribly flawed."

Alistair grinned. "Well, I certainly noticed you when you shoved ice down the back of my shirt. Or when you—"

"Fired a cherry at you?"

They began to chuckle again. "But then you changed schools, and you never came home with James again, and I confess, I was very melancholy."

"Were you?"

"Indeed. You may laugh at me as you wish now."

"It is no laughing matter," Alistair whispered. "Not at all." He reached out and touched her hand, his thumb brushing softly over her palm.

"Addy. Thank you for telling me. I—I had no idea. We were but children then, and I was foolish. But now...now I'm so grateful that we have met again. My entire perception of you, of everything, has utterly changed."

"It has? How so?"

"I—" Alistair flushed. He cut himself off, lowering his gaze to the fire.

She wished he would just open up, that he would stop holding back so much. But to her surprise, he didn't release her hand.

"You bewilder and amaze me in every way."

"And you surprise me as well," Adelaide smiled softly. Alistair lifted his hand, cupping her cheek in his hand. He drew his thumb across her skin, a breathless laugh escaping his lips. Addy couldn't breathe. He leaned closer to her, his deep blue eyes shadowed in the firelight.

"You don't despise me?"

"No," Addy laughed. "Not at all. You don't despise me either?"

"Never. I never did. I just thought...I was just mortified, I suppose, that you found me a prig."

"And I was afraid you thought me an utter barbarian."

"No, no. In fact, I rather envy you your boldness. Your ability to not care what anyone else thinks."

"I do care, sometimes. I do. I cared what you thought, even then, when we were children."

"And I didn't want to seem a bore to you. I still don't."

"You are not at all, Alistair. You are not."

Alistair leaned closer yet, so that his lips were inches away. His eyes flickered down to her lips, and Addy's pulse thudded wildly in her ears.

Just then, the footman stirred, groaning loudly and pressing a hand to his head.

Both Addy and Alistair drew apart hastily and hurried over to his side. They knelt to check on him.

"What has happened?" the footman murmured hazily.

"Our sleigh struck a root, and you fell and struck your head. A storm began, and we were forced to seek shelter."

"Speaking of the storm, it has begun to let up. At least, that is what it sounds like." Addy glanced up at the roof above their head. Sure enough, the howling had died down, reduced to a faint whistling.

"Good heavens. What of the horses?" the footman sputtered.

"They are safe. Right over there." Alistair pointed to the nearby stall, and the footman sighed in relief.

Alistair walked over to the door and pushed it open. The winds had quieted at last, and the snow now fell in a peaceful flurry. It was dim, despite it being late afternoon, not quite evening.

"We should hurry back. He will need a physician," Alistair's voice cut into her thoughts.

She turned and nodded. "At least the sleight is not buried—at least not deeply."

She and Alistair set about dusting the snow off the seats of the sleigh, before the footman led out the horses, still holding his head. A large knot was visible on his brow.

He insisted upon driving them back to the manor, thanking them for saving him, for helping him out of the storm while he was unconscious. The sleigh ride was silent, filled with meaningful, heated glances that send Addy's heart thundering.

At last, Worthington Manor came into view, and the sleigh drew close to the front steps of the large home. Several footmen hastened down to greet them and help them from the sleigh after asking if they were injured. "Call a physician," Alistair told them, nodding to the footman holding his head, "He struck his head. It may need treatment."

One steward scurried to obey.

The entire rest of the party emerged onto the steps, their expressions tense and fraught. Addy's heart dropped when she saw them, realising what they must be thinking. Cordelia peered out from behind her father, her eyes red, face blotchy.

She and Alistair exchanged glances and proceeded indoors. Both of them hurried upstairs to change out of their snow-soaked clothes. It must have been a good many hours, at the very least. And to be alone, unchaperoned, for so long … in the face of Alistair's slight of Cordelia…it was a grave situation.

And her parents, James, Alistair's mother, and her aunt and uncle gathered in the drawing room to discuss the matter, as Eloise informed her with a worried expression.

It was Eloise who came to fetch her when they at last finished this conference.

Her knees watery, she followed her cousin downstairs and into the drawing room. Alistair, accompanied by James, appeared a few moments later.

"This is a very grave situation," Aunt Agatha began, though Addy wished she would mind her own business. This might be her house, but it wasn't exactly her concern. Of course, that was Aunt Agatha for you. Always putting her nose where it didn't belong.

"A very grave situation indeed," Lady Dowden echoed, glaring at Addy. As if it had been Addy's idea for Alistair to leap into the sleigh and take off with her—alone. To linger in a remote stable alone. It was not by choice, though Addy could not say she regretted it. She enjoyed every moment in Alistair's company, the opportunity to talk to him in the intimacy of the firelight.

Alistair took in a deep breath, and said, "There is only course to be taken in this situation. As it is a delicate one, as we understand. I shall marry Miss Fawcett."

Addy's stomach did a strange somersault, and her heart leapt into her throat, making it feel as if she couldn't even breathe.

She stared at him in disbelief. He wanted to—

But did he want to? His expression was a stony mask, one of resignation and worry.

And all the air left her lungs then. He did not wish to marry her, did he? This was nothing more than another obligation for him to fulfil and attend to. And that made her want to retch.

Of course, she loved him, but for him to consider marriage out of a sense of responsibility? Insufferable.

She dug her nails into her palms, a lump forming in her throat. Lady Dowden stepped forward, shaking her head. "Alistair, no!"

"Mother, it is the only thing to be done."

Something snapped in Adelaide. "I shall not!" she cried.

The earth swept from beneath her feet. She might love him, but that did not mean he returned it. And now, he never would, if he didn't already. They would marry and be miserable. Miserable because he would forever resent her for entrapping him in a marriage never wanted.

"I shall not!"

"Adelaide!" Alistair's eyes went wide as he turned to her, taking a step forward. But she recoiled from him, tears rolling down her cheeks.

"No, no. I cannot." And she ran from the room, heart pounding. She raced out the front door, down the steps, and down the path towards the gardens, and the stables. She needed to find solitude, to be alone with her thoughts. Perhaps she could take refuge in a quiet country house, far from the turmoil, where she could seek peace and attempt to forget Alistair Dowden.

In the stables, she entered Adonis' stall and sank into the hay, tilting her head back against the stall's wall.

Sobs wracked her frame. It wasn't supposed to be like this. She might love Alistair and want to marry him, but not like this. If she were to marry him, it would not be for love. It would be for precisely the same reasons as Badley. Alistair would do it out of a need, an obligation to protect his family name.

And furthermore...she was terrified—paralyzed, overwhelmed. The events of the past few days rolled over her like icy water overhead, and she could scarcely breathe.

Running footsteps caused her to jerk her head up, to see Eloise standing in the stall door, panting.

"Oh, Addy," she sighed, and hurried over, sinking into the hay beside Addy. "I am so sorry that this is happening."

"We did not choose to get caught in that storm. Of course, he went with me instead of Cordelia, but that should not mean we are under any sort of obligation to—to wed."

"Do you say this out of fear of losing your autonomy? Or out of fear that for him, it is merely to be born of duty?"

"Oh, I don't know. I don't know at all. My head is spinning so." Addy pressed her hands to her temples. "There is a reason some baulk against marriage. It is too convoluted, too...everything."

"I think it is the latter?"

"What does it matter if it is? I just—I'm so frightened. And I do love him, but I fear he is going to resent me if we wed out of necessity. It would not be fair to either of us, would it?"

"No, it wouldn't," Eloise agreed.

"Then what am I to do? I cannot go back in there. I cannot. I cannot look in his eyes and see nothing but cold deference, obligation."

"Calm yourself," Eloise whispered. "I've seen the way he looks at you. And there is no mistaking he feels something, that he holds you in high regard. Perhaps he merely wishes to protect your honour?"

Addy nodded, but the tears came anyway. She wanted to badly to believe her cousin, to believe that this was something more than his attempt at dutiful civility. But how could she be sure?

Eloise pulled her into a tight hug as she began to weep.

She calmed at last, resting her head in Eloise's lap as Eloise stroked her hair. Both of them jumped when Gemma appeared in the stall doorway. "Miss Adelaide, they require your presence back in the manor."

Addy sat up, not caring if there was straw in her hair. She exchanged looks with Gemma before clambering to her feet. "Tell them I will change first," she told Gemma in a whisper.

Gemma nodded. "But of course, miss."

And with that, she hurried off, leaving Addy standing numbly in the middle of Adonis' stall. She walked over to the horse, pressing her cheek against his muzzle. What she wouldn't give for a chance to see dear Ares. What she wouldn't give for the comfort of his presence.

"Ready?" Eloise asked when she finally forced herself to turn around.

Addy nodded, clenching her teeth.

Chapter 24

Alistair turned from the window when he heard the familiar creak of the front door. Everyone else in the room stiffened as they listened to the tread of Adelaide's footsteps in the hall, before she came into view in the drawing room doorway, wringing her hands.

"Forgive me," she said tautly, but she did not sit down. Instead, she remained standing, as if she were in a courtroom before a jury.

Alistair took a deep breath, gripping his hands together behind his back so tightly that his joints protested. He looked into Addy's eyes—they were tear-filled, glistening. Her features were twisted in pain, hurt.

He just needed to speak to her—for a moment. To explain himself. To somehow tell her the depth of his love for her; how he could not imagine his life with anyone else, and how, if she would have him, he would have married her yesterday.

"Please, I beg you afford me and Miss Adelaide an opportunity to speak alone," he said to the gathered group. His mother's eyes widened, her mouth going thin as a string.

"Alistair—" she started forward, but he cut her off, his voice like a pistol shot:

"A moment alone, please."

After a long pause, Lord and Lady Worthington exited, followed by Adelaide's parents. Lady Fairfield glared at Addy, in a way that turned Alistair's stomach. Once everyone had gone, he shut the door and turned to Addy.

Stepping forward, he whispered, "Adelaide. I know this is not ideal. But pray set that all aside. I—I love you. I adore you. I cannot be with anyone else but you. And over the past two weeks, I have come to realise this truth. It is your choice, of course, but for my part, I wish to marry you, for I cannot fathom a future without you."

"Alistair!" Addy's face went pale, and then it flushed brightly. "Alistair, you—"

"It is your decision. I will not press my suit, but I am obliged to admit to my true feelings. I will not begrudge you, whatever you decide."

"You—you mean that?" Alistair's eyes welled with tears.

Alistair grasped her hand in his then, stepping even closer, close enough to see the golden touches in her eyes. "Adelaide, I love you. I have never meant anything more with all my heart."

"Oh, Alistair. I love you too. I love you desperately. And I would be honoured to marry you. To be your wife." He could scarcely believe those words had just left her mouth, but she meant them—he could see it in her brown eyes. She meant them with all her heart. He kissed her hand once, then twice.

Addy threw herself into his arms, and he held her close, his heart aching. She smelled of honey and hay, a heavenly scent.

Closing his eyes, he savoured this moment. He had waited so long to hold her, to love her. And now, he could not imagine going back to the way it was before. She was his, and he was hers.

The door opened then, and they broke apart, but only slightly. Her parents entered first, followed by his mother, Eloise and James. Adelaide's aunt and uncle were the last to follow.

"Well?" Adelaide's mother demanded.

"I have decided that I shall marry him," Adelaide said, clutching Alistair's arm.

Adelaide's mother sank onto the couch and began to weep softly. Alistair turned to see the most gutting expression on his mother's face, almost more overwhelming sorrow. Grief. His stomach dropped.

Eloise began to clap. "At last! Now, when shall we begin to plan the wedding?"

James broke out laughing, and soon almost the entire room was full of laughter. That is, except for Alistair's own mother. At last, the party dispersed, with Lady Worthington chattering about the merits of a wedding, even mentioning a triple wedding. Alistair drew his mother aside and asked if he might have a word with her. He half-expected her to turn down his request, but to his surprise, she accepted, and they retired to the library to talk.

Once there, he walked over and took her hands in his. She would not look him in the eyes, tears shining in hers. "Oh, my boy, what have you done?" she choked out.

"I have done what I should. Because I love Miss Fawcett, Mamma. I love her. I did not do this out of malice, or hate, or defiance even. It is born of the deepest affection and adoration of...Adelaide." He loved to say her name. Her name fit perfectly on the tip of his tongue.

Rosalind sighed. "I confess that I have been most unfair in my dealings with you and Miss Fawcett. She is indeed a sweet, good girl. She is not who I imagined for you, I will confess. She is heedless at times and uncivil at others. But it is evident that you do indeed hold her in high regard, and your opinion is one I hold in high regard. So, with that in mind, I give you my blessing."

"Mamma," Alistair whispered, emotion tugging in his chest. "You mean that?"

"I do. I can see that you love her. Deeply. And I want you to be happy. So very much. As did your father. But I told you that I made a vow to your father, as he lay—" here her voice broke, and tears streamed down her cheeks, "—as he lay dying. And I have been so afraid of breaking that promise that I have not given your feelings any consideration."

"And I have not been honest with you either. Nor myself, but I detest myself for not being forthright sooner, and we might have evaded this mess. I too held myself to a promise I made Father. I swore to him that I would always abide by my duty, that I would uphold the name of our family. Even if it meant the sacrifice of my own happiness. But I don't think he would have wanted that. Of course, he would like for our name to remain in good standing. But I am sure he would support my decision to wed Miss Fawcett. He would have liked her very much I think."

To his astonishment, Rosalind nodded. "I think he would have too."

"You think so?" Alistair's heart lodged in his mouth. "Truly?"

"Truly. She suits you very well. Please forgive me for fearing guilt so much that I would have imposed a life of miserable obligation upon you, for the sake of my own peace of mind. Of course, I should derive my peace of mind from knowing you have secured happiness for yourself. That you are well."

She leaned up on tiptoe and kissed his cheek, patting his hand. "Now, why don't you go find that bride of yours? We have a wedding to discuss."

***

The Ashworths left in high dudgeon that very day, just before nightfall. Evidently, according to Lord Ashford, it would present too great a challenge should Cordelia remain under the same roof as the main who jilted her and treated her so ill.

Alistair and Adelaide situated themselves in a quiet, rather dark corner of the drawing room, while James and Serena took a seat before the fire. And in the hall, Eloise and Captain Crawford admired the tree together.

Lord Badley had left hours ago according to James. He had invented the arrival of a letter—no such letter had ever come. But they allowed him to attempt to maintain his dignity, or what was left of it. No one missed him, especially not Alistair.

But Lord Badley was the furthest from his mind right now, standing in front of Adelaide—Addy. His dearest Addy. He jerked his chin upward at the kissing bough of mistletoe hanging over the window, right above their heads.

Addy followed his gaze, her cheeks warming as she caught sight of it. A soft, delighted smile spread across her face, and she looked up at him, her heart fluttering. He reached for her hand, his fingers brushing against hers with a light, tender touch. Slowly, he brought her hand to his lips, pressing a soft, lingering kiss to her knuckles.

The warmth of his gesture filled her chest, and her breath caught in her throat.

When he drew back, she whispered, voice trembling, "You truly love me?"

"I love you, Adelaide Fawcett. With all my heart. Wildly, utterly."

"And I love you. With all my soul. Desperately, completely."

When she leaned up toward him, a sense of rightness flooded over him, and it took all his restraint to keep from wrapping his arms around her.

Christmas Eve dawned bright and sunny, sending the world into a sparkling glory. Alistair woke early, and on the garden path to the stable, he met Adelaide. *His Addy.*

It was almost too dreamlike to believe.

In the stable, with no one around, he caught her by surprise, leaning down to press a swift, fiery kiss to her lips. It was brief, yet charged with an undeniable heat—his lips warm against hers, sending a shiver down her spine. As he pulled away, the playful glint in his eyes matched the racing of her heart, and for a fleeting moment, they both savoured the mischievous thrill of the kiss.

Adelaide, her breath catching, glanced up at him, her cheeks flushed, a spark of something daring in her gaze. Without a word, they turned to saddle their horses, the intensity of the kiss still lingering between them as they fitted the reins over their steeds' heads, slipping the bits into their mouths. Once they were ready, they led their mounts in front of the stable. A footman held the leads as Alistair helped Addy onto her saddle. Today, his hands lingered for a moment too long on her waist, but if the smile twitched at her lips, the blush in her cheeks was anything to go by, she didn't object.

"Thank you," she gave his hand a final squeeze before he stepped away and mounted his own horse. Together they set off on a ride through the nearby meadows and fields, snow flying out behind them. It seemed the worst of the storms had passed, at least for that week. Though according to Adelaide's uncle, the farmer's almanac reported more severe conditions in the upcoming months.

Alistair and Adelaide halted on a crest overlooking the manor. They exchanged smiles, conspiratorial ones, before he dismounted and then lifted her off of Adonis.

"Can you believe that tomorrow is Christmas?"

"I think it is my favourite one yet."

"Truly?" Adelaide laughed before he turned her towards him and kissed her deeply.

"Truly," he said when he drew back, lifting a hand to cup her cheek. She closed her eyes, leaning into his touch. "Now, who do you think will have a conniption on the day of our wedding? Your Aunt Agatha, your mother, or my mother?"

"My best guess is that all three will be beside themselves that day."

They laughed again, before mounting their horses again as the snow fluttered down around them. Then, they returned to the house before anyone missed them.

"Does your mother hold it against me, for coming between you and Miss Ashworth?"

"No. I simply think she was not prepared for her plans to be muddled. But she wishes to see me happy, and she has come to fully embrace the prospect of you becoming my wife."

Addy sighed, relief spreading through her. "That is good to hear. I feared I would forever perturb her, even after we are wed."

"My mother just needed a little time to come to terms with our impending matrimony. But I am certain she is now accepting of it. I beg you to not hold her past coldness towards you against her. Though, I am dismayed that she should have spoken to you thus."

"I do not begrudge her for it," Addy smiled, enjoying Alistair's warm presence at her side in the wintry weather. "I understand holding onto a certain way of things, not being willing to surrender. She is no worse than me when it comes to stubbornness."

Alistair regarded her, admiration warming his blue eyes. "Thank you, Addy, for endeavouring to understand. For being so generous about the whole matter. I hope she has not wounded you too deeply, however."

"No, not at all. I wish to keep looking forward, to not dwell on what has been done."

Alistair pulled her close gently and pressed a soft kiss to her forehead before they returned inside.

Chapter 25

Addy's heart raced as she entered her uncle's quiet study where Lady Dowden waited for her. The older woman turned from the window when she heard the door latch click, and Addy was relieved to see that she was smiling gently.

"Adelaide, thank you for agreeing to speak with me. There are matters from the past few days I need to address, and I am deeply ashamed of my behaviour throughout. I wish to explain myself and make amends where I can. You make my son so very happy, and for that, I can never hold your love for one another against you."

"Oh, there's no need—"

"There is. I was cruel, needlessly so, the other morning. I spoke words I should never have uttered, and I was unjust to you. I confess I viewed you as a threat to my own plans for my son's future, and in doing so, I allowed my fears to cloud my judgment. You see, my actions were born out of a selfish desire to protect my husband's memory. But it is clear now that I was mistaken. My husband, in truth, only ever wished for our son to find happiness, and yet I took it upon myself to impose my own will upon him. It would be folly, however, to force him into a loveless marriage. You are a good woman, of a good family, and your love for him is undeniable. That much is certain."

"I *do* love him, and I understand. My own mother was resistant as well to my courting Alistair. She has come around, but she, too, had her own ideas about what she wished for me—whom she wished me to marry."

"Us mothers do adore our children, but it can come at an expense. And it is something I shall strive to not do again. Ever since my husband's passing, I have struggled to find my place in this world, my duty to uphold the legacy he so painstakingly built."

Addy stepped forward without thinking and grasped Lady Dowden's hand. Tears shone in the older woman's eyes. "I love your son, and I hope we can be friends despite everything."

"Of course," Lady Dowden nodded, using a handkerchief to dab at her eyes. "Thank you, my dear. And I pray you can forgive me."

"I do forgive you," Addy assured her. Lady Dowden's words had been cutting, but she could sympathise with the older woman's struggle.

She stepped forward, embracing her. When she drew back, Lady Dowden smiled softly.

"I think you and my son will suit one another very well. The way he looks at you tells me a great deal."

Addy blushed. They left the study at last, and when they emerged Alistair was waiting for them by a window in the hall, pacing to and fro in the small alcove. His mother kissed him on the cheek and cast Addy a smile before hurrying down the hall towards the drawing room where everyone else visited.

Addy felt as though she were walking on air as she approached Alistair. He kissed her hand. "How did it go?"

"Very well," she told him softly. "We have found common ground. I am eager to have her as a mother."

Alistair grinned and kissed her soundly on the lips. "Ah, excellent. Would you care for a ride together?"

"I would be delighted!"

***

Later that morning on Christmas Eve, Addy placed her hand on the bannister, her heart feeling as though it would burst. At the base of the steps stood Alistair, smiling up at her, and she could hear Serena, James, and Eloise's laughter floating down from the dining room. When she reached the base of the steps, she took Alistair's arm and let him lead her to breakfast. They found the room in an uproar of feverish excitement when they entered together, her arm looped with his. The other two newly engaged couples greeted them merrily, and all six of them chatted about the upcoming nuptials.

At the other end of the table, Aunt Agatha, Mother, Lady Scotfell, and Lady Dowden were talking excitedly about the wedding as well, trying to come to an agreement on where it should take place, who to invite, and what food would be eaten.

Addy exchanged smiles with Serena and Eloise, marvelling that just a fortnight ago, she would have been stunned by this outcome. Her past self wouldn't have believed it.

"Can you believe we are all engaged?" Eloise asked, voice hitching with laughter.

Addy grinned. "Not at all. But I cannot imagine it otherwise now."

"Nor I. I always wished for a winter wedding anyway," Serena nodded.

Addy looked up, meeting Alistair's eyes. He shared a smile meant for her and her alone.

"We ought to have Christmas rose bouquets," Mother was saying. "With sprigs of holly in them. It would be perfect for this time of the year!"

Aunt Agatha agreed. "I will have the church decorated with evergreen and Christmas roses as well."

"They must have wedding gowns as well," added Lady Scotfell. "We must hie to the milliners as soon as possible to get them fitted." The other women agreed eagerly. Addy fought a smile.

After breakfast, everyone retired to the drawing room to sing carols. Addy played and Eloise led them in singing. They started with God Rest Ye Merry Gentlemen and ended with Greensleeves, and the older people looked on, enjoying the concert.

As Addy ran her fingertips over the ivory keys, she gazed up at Alistair and he smiled, a strange, exhilarating expression on his face that sent butterflies soaring through her stomach.

She couldn't breathe.

After carolling finished, most of the party retired for an afternoon rest before the trip into the village that evening for the Christmas Eve service at the church. Addy hung back with Alistair, though Gemma lingered as well to maintain their propriety.

"Addy," Alistair whispered. She started when he reached into his pocket and withdrew a small box. Inside was a hairpin shaped like a gilded falcon. It glistened in the firelight, taking Addy's breath away.

"Alistair, it's beautiful," she whispered.

"Consider this my wedding gift," Alistair whispered.

"Thank you," she said softly, a lump in her throat. "I have something for you as well." She handed him a book—it was a detailed guide to the Italian cities in the Alps. "Mother and Father wish to pay for our trip there. Our honeymoon."

"So, we are to become world travellers together, are we?" Alistair smiled, his voice low and warm. He and Addy sank onto one of the settees together.

"What do you think?" she asked, her eyes sparkling.

"I should love it. An excellent wedding gift indeed." He smiled warmly and kissed her hand softly before stepping back with a glance toward Gemma. Addy grasped his hand, shaking her head gently.

"Do not fret about her," she whispered. "She shall not tell a soul."

That was all he needed to hear. He leaned down slightly and pressed a soft kiss to her cheek before stepping back.

"May I?" he grasped the box, his hand dwarfing it with ease. He took the pin from the cushions and slid it into Addy's curly hair.

"Beautiful," he breathed. The sight of her left him momentarily speechless, stealing the words from his mouth.

Dinner that night was a hearty one. Everyone sat around the table, making merry, laughing, chatting, and planning the future. Addy's heart was so full she couldn't even eat. Instead, she just watched, from the Scotts at the other end of the table to her brother and Serena, smiling into each other's eyes.

Eloise and Captain Crawford were murmuring sweet nothings to each other across from her and when she turned her head, she looked into Lady Dowden's blue eyes, so much like her son's. To her surprise, instead of scowling, Lady Dowden's mouth hinted at a smile, as she nodded in silent greeting.

It was just confirmation of what Alistair had relayed to her last night, regarding his conversation with his mother. That she accepted Addy as her future family. It relieved Addy more than she even realised.

A tremendous sense of peace settled over her, a wonderful feeling. More than ever, she knew that what had scared her the most about this whole matter was the fear of losing him. She feared pain. And yes, she craved autonomy, but she knew that Alistair would never ask her to surrender that. What she really craved was a man who matched her heart, beyond wealth, status and repute.

Alistair asked her if she would like to go for a turn about the garden. Together they ventured out into the snow-covered world, exploring the twists and turns of the hedge maze. Gemma followed along closely behind them until they paused beneath a bower. Twisted branches arched over them, forming a cosy little retreat amid the garden.

"We have a garden at Dowden house," Alistair told her softly. "And a large stable. You can bring Ares, and he will have a stable of his own, of course."

Addy leaned forward to check where her mother and Lady Dowden stood on the terrace, wrapped in blankets, sipping mugs of cocoa.

Alistair glanced towards them as well before leaning forward, dropping his voice to a whisper. "Your mother is eager for grandchildren. She inquired if we anticipated having any right away."

"Did she now? And did she ask my brother that?"

"Yes, but he could not give a reply lest he begin to laugh. I believe Miss Scott was horrified."

"And my mother is mortified of *me*!" Addy rolled her eyes skyward.

She and Alistair started back towards the terrace, where they were greeted by their mothers. Both greeted them blithely. "Where have the two of you been? "We have ever so many matters to discuss for the upcoming wedding," said Addy's mother, her tone brisk with excitement.

"Perhaps we might delay until the morrow?" Addy suggested; her voice steady but laced with weariness. "It grows late, and I am quite in need of rest."

After a brief pause, her mother relented with a gracious nod. "Very well. But we must begin early."

With polite exchanges of goodnights, the household retired for the evening.

True to her word, Mother was astir at the first light of dawn. As soon as Addy rose, she was promptly swept into the drawing room, where a lively assembly awaited. Serena and Eloise were present, along with Lady Scotfell and Aunt Agatha, all engaged in animated conversation. Addy's heart quickened as she surveyed the scene—a veritable flurry of activity centred upon the preparation of delicate nosegays for the wedding.

The date, it seemed, had been firmly settled upon. January the twelfth would mark the occasion.

That afternoon, all the women rode into town by sleigh to visit the local dressmaker's shop for wedding gowns. Addy, Serena, and Eloise chattered happily over the prospect of the kinds of dresses they would like, which was somewhat strange to Addy, given that she had always eschewed things of matrimonial consequence.

But that all fell away as she stood on the little stool in the dressmaker's shop, getting measured and fitted for her dress. It was to be a satin gown, of a shimmery, pearly white, and her mother fussed over her unruly hair. In the mirror, Addy could see Serena and Eloise also get fitted in their dresses, ribbons and lace scattering across the floor as the mothers and dressmakers argued about the merits of silk.

After the measuring and fitting was finished, Addy, Serena, and Eloise walked together through town to shop and explore.

"So Addy, you and Alistair shall live at his family's estate. And I will be at your family's estate I suppose," said Serena cheerily. "And Eloise, you will retire to Bath with your husband?"

"Indeed, but just for a time. William is eager to resign his commission now and join his father's business as a merchant."

"We will have to come visit you then," Addy sighed and grasped her cousin's hand. "Though, we will miss you dearly."

"And I will miss the both of you."

"What do you suppose has become of Cordelia?" Serena wondered aloud.

"I have heard that she is now to be wed to Lord Badley, of all people," Addy chuckled. "At least, that is what the hearsay is."

"Do you suppose they were sweet on each other the entirety of their stay at my parents'?" Eloise wondered.

"I would not be surprised. I rather imagine Cordelia was weary of Alistair—he was quite besotted with Addy, and once or twice I noticed Cordelia and Lord Badley in lively conversation. So, I am hardly surprised if that rumour were to be true."

Addy's head whirled as the next two weeks were filled with planning and preparation, invitation sending and dancing.

She and Alistair went riding every morning as the day of their wedding drew closer, as guests for the ceremony began to arrive. His sister Belinda and her husband and children arrived just two days before the wedding, and Belinda at once darted up to Addy, grasping her hands with a wide smile. "I was wondering who intoxicated my brother so! And of course, it should be the girl who fired a cherry at him."

Addy laughed, blushing. "I confess it was indeed me. And I am rather as surprised as you are."

"Mother wrote me all about your romance with Alistair, and how delighted I am that my dear brother has at last found himself a match. He needs someone exactly like you to draw him out and challenge him, and show him the world is an adventure, not a nightmare."

Addy smiled at her betrothed across the room, who was chatting with Captain Crawford. He returned her glance questioningly, his mouth twitching.

"I've never seen him look at a girl the way he looks at you," Belinda told her, shaking her head.

Addy's heart swelled with joy at that. She could not wait to become Alistair's bride. She'd all but forgotten about her desire to remain unmarried for the rest of her life. She couldn't imagine living a life without Alistair Dowden. That night a dance was held at Worthington Manor amongst the gathered guests—another group of guests would arrive the next morning, and excitement buzzed through the house as everyone took their places in the centre of the ballroom.

Alistair took Addy's hand in his and led her through the complicated steps. As they weaved in and out of the other dancers, eyes locked, Addy knew beyond the shadow of a doubt that everything in her life had led exactly to this moment, right here.

Epilogue

It was a clear, cold day just after Twelfth Night. The small chapel of Worthington was bursting at the seams as everyone invited had to pack themselves in to watch. Alistair and Addy began them.

Addy's heart pounded as a hundred or so misty eyes watched her and Alistair, Eloise and Captain Crawford, and James and Serena get married. Alistair kissed her soundly in the carriage as it pulled away towards the manor, where the wedding breakfast would be held.

Addy sighed, clutching the front of his coat. She could barely breathe, hardly able to believe that this was truly happening. Turning, she saw Alistair's mother dabbing her eyes in the middle of the road, waving her handkerchief in farewell. It would only be farewell for a few moments since everyone would meet back at Worthington Manor.

Looping her arm through Alistair's, she leaned her head against his shoulder, closing her eyes. She knew that he would accept her for who she was, and though they might butt heads, they loved each other. Adored one another. She could not wait to begin her life with him. Her parents had finally come around, and they were even growing fond of Alistair, seeing him as one of their own family.

Before, he had been merely James' friend. Now, he was their son, the man their daughter loved. Even though she told herself she'd get by without their approval, she had to be frank with herself. She wanted him to be liked by her parents, even if he wasn't the suitor they selected for her.

The house filled with chatter and laughter as everyone filtered into the dining hall, taking their seats.

Each newlywed couple sat beside one another, and everyone took turns giving toasts to their respective marriages. Under the table, Addy clasped Alistair's hand, wondering if Eloise and Serena were doing the same with their husbands.

To her surprise, Alistair rose, clinking his glass, and began a speech of his own. "I should like to speak of my dear wife, how blessed I am to have a bride like her on my arm. She challenges me to better myself, she inspires me to live with abandon at times. I am honoured to be Adelaide's husband, and I am eager to see where this life takes us together.

And then, it was Addy's turn. She rose, straightening her back. "And I am grateful for a man like Alistair Dowden. He is practical, kind, good, and noble. And I am delighted to be his wife." Applause erupted around the table, along with exclamations of agreement.

That evening, fireworks were set off, even though they had only just set some off for New Year's. Addy stood on the terrace beside Eloise and Alistair, gasping in awe at the brilliant sparks shimmering across the sky.

Turning, she found Alistair smiling down at her, his eyes flickering to her lips before he bent and kissed her ever so briefly. It was dark enough that they likely wouldn't be noticed. His hand grasped hers, and her heart swelled. Perhaps it was good that Mother and Father forced her to come on this trip after all.

"I have found you a Christmas gift," Alistair told her gently.

"You spoil me," Addy giggled.

Alistair took her hand in his and kissed it. "I am unable to restrain myself," he whispered against her palm.

Addy began to tear into the package and gasped, laughing. "How did you know I love novels?"

"I'm afraid I am to blame for that," Eloise admitted from nearby, where she stood beside her own husband, Captain Crawford.

Addy grinned. "I thought as much."

"And rest assured, I was scarcely surprised to learn of this. I find the heroine in this novel quite similar to you."

"Did you?" Addy shook her head. "You jest!"

"I don't. She does, and you shall agree with me, I am sure of it."

"Perhaps I ought to speculate on that," James commented, stepping up to the edge of the terrace with Serena in tow.

The next morning, she and Alistair walked down to the stables and mounted the horses they'd been riding since their arrival a little less than a month ago. Now, they could go anywhere they liked. They did not need to worry as much about propriety, and Addy was stunned by the sense of freedom that washed over her as she accompanied Alistair across the field. The snow had begun to melt a few days earlier, and the hooves of their horses sent dirt flying.

Somehow, it was even more heady to ride with her husband than it was alone. They raced each other through field after field until they needed to break, sitting on a low wall where they unpacked a lunch the cook had prepared for them.

Addy leaned her head against his shoulder, just as she had the night of their wedding on Aunt Agatha and Uncle Richard's terrace. In just a matter of weeks, her entire life had changed, her perspective altered. And for that, she owed Alistair Dowden the world.

"What are you thinking about, Addy?" Alistair murmured in her ear.

"I'm thinking of how strange it is that we are here, that so much has changed. Just last month, I was rather dreading coming here to see you. I was afraid you remembered how I tormented you so, and how I thought you detested me as well. And now here I am, married to you!"

Alistair chuckled. "I was nervous too about seeing you again. I was worried that you and I would have another battle one way or another. But it seems that Providence had other plans."

"When we met again, what did you first think when you saw me for the first time, on my aunt and uncle's steps?"

"I thought you the most beautiful girl I'd ever seen. But I was certain you still found me a prig."

"A very handsome one. And there is some merit in being so. I for my part can be rather too much tumultuous, much to my mother's dismay."

"Well, I admire that you are unafraid of speaking your mind or being so daring and bold. I envy it, rather. I can be much too careful much of the time."

Addy kissed Alistair's cheek; her heart full. "It just took one Christmas for us to realise that. If only we'd known it sooner."

"Perhaps we would have not been ready sooner," Alistair suggested. "We were both ready at this time to accept that revelation."

Addy conceded to this point, her heart feeling as if it might burst. She slipped her hand into Alistair's, watching the sun pour over the frost-covered landscape. The sight never failed to take her breath away, and she reflected on how so many mornings she'd ventured out alone to take in the fresh air and views. Now, she could take it all in with Alistair, share in the beauty with him, and rest her cheek on his shoulder. He was a warm and comforting presence beside her, sturdy and strong.

For the first time in her life, she was relieved she'd agreed to visit her aunt and uncle this year, instead of trying to find ways to get out of it. Because if she'd never come, she never would have discovered a love like this.

EXTENDED EPILOGUE

1821
The Dowden Manor

Lady Adelaide Dowden carefully lowered herself down so that she could be on eye level with the small boy in front of her. It was her nephew, Alistair's sister's son. In front of the fire, Serena and James sat on a settee, holding their daughter and cooing at her. The child favoured Serena in terms of looks, but in terms of temperament, she was as opinionated and jubilant as James.

Addy rested a hand on her swollen stomach, closing her eyes tightly as she tried to catch her breath. As excited as she was to be carrying her and Alistair's firstborn, she also missed her morning rides on Ares. But such was life.

Alistair wouldn't think of agreeing to let her go on these excursions. But he'd been fussing over her for the past few weeks since they'd learned from the physician of her delicate condition. Ever since then, he'd fretted night and day. It was both endearing and amusing at the same time.

"My dear," he had come to watch her from the doorway. "Is something amiss? Do you feel unwell?"

"Alistair, I am quite well. I just became dizzy for a moment."

"Aunt Addy?" Emily wailed; her voice shrill.

Her mother, Belinda, shook her head, laughing. "Let your aunt have a rest, my dear. Come over and sit beside me?"

Emily stuck out her lower lips in a pout, but she obeyed, leaving Alistair to guide Addy to the nearby armchair and lower her into it.

"Addy, when are Mother and Father going to arrive?" James called from his seat next to Serena. Serena had only just begun to show her pregnancy, and she had been under the weather most of the week. Today, she still appeared pale and quiet, nibbling on a piece of gingerbread to help with the sickly feeling.

"They sent a letter—they hope to arrive this evening."

"Splendid!" James grinned.

In the window stood Eloise and Captain Crawford cooing at their newborn daughter in the captain's arms. She was a beautiful little girl who they named after Eloise's mother, Agatha.

Eloise tickled the baby under her chin, earning a sweet laugh from the child. "She is beautiful, just like her mother," Captain Crawford declared, wrapping his arm about his wife.

Addy called to James, "Ready to resume our task?"

"Very well," James smiled, rising. She directed him, Alistair, and Captain Crawford in placing a wreath upon the mantle, and then another garland higher up above a portrait of Addy and Alistair.

Not for the first time she rested a hand on her belly, wondering if she would give birth to a girl or boy. If it were a boy, they would name him after Alistair's father. And if it were a girl, she'd like to name her Diana, in homage to Addy's independent ideals.

Once they finished hanging the wreaths, Alistair clambered down from the ladder and handed Addy a Christmas rose he'd plucked from one of the boughs. Tucking it into her hair, he kissed her hand, grinning. "A flower, from your beloved prig."

"Oh, Alistair, I don't think you're a prig. Only sometimes now. It's a wonder you tolerate me and my silliness."

"I have a penchant for silly women like you." Alistair drew her into the privacy of the dining room next door, and in the darkness, he kissed her.

"What is this about?" Addy grinned against his lips.

"Imagine a kissing bough hangs above us."

"But there isn't one there, I don't believe. Unless you had one hung?"

"Pretend I did. Perhaps I did."

Addy giggled as he planted more kisses on her face, from her forehead to the bridge of her nose and finally upon her lips. Then they returned to the bright drawing room where Belinda's children ran to and fro.

That night, Christmas Eve, Addy woke suddenly. Alistair stood at the window in the silver moonlight, and when he heard her stir, he turned and smiled. "Good night, my dear."

"Can't sleep?"

He nodded. "I worry about you and the baby night and day. And sometimes at night, I struggle to sleep. What if we are missing something in our preparations?"

"We are not," Addy replied firmly.

Alistair chuckled. "We are hardly changed in some ways, no?"

"You and your fussiness, and me and my madness."

Alistair laughed again, shaking his head, and kissed her brow. "I simply wish to keep you and our child safe throughout this."

"Pray do not fret," Addy whispered. She touched his face softly. "We will be safe. I am strong."

Alistair nodded, chewing on his lip, his eyes dark and pensive. "Indeed, you are."

He held her, wrapping his arms around her and together they gazed out at the Dowden estate, most of it visible from their window. It was the reason Alistair selected this room, so he could see the entirety of his domain. "The vicar and his wife will join us tomorrow, after the morning Christmastide service."

"Good, good," Alistair murmured in her ear. "Now, let us return to bed."

The next morning, Addy's parents arrived. They'd been travelling frequently as of late, and they had visited Spain only last week, and then they had taken a ship around the Mediterranean. Addy's mother held her at arm's length, fixing her with a gentle smile. The tension of the past several years had eased, and in its wake, a new understanding began to form. A stronger connection was growing between them, step by step, as mother and daughter.

Then she kissed her father's cheek, before stepping back to stand beside her husband. "My mother shall be here before long. She is rather tired often these days," Alistair said to them. His expression denoted his concern for his mother. She had been more in need of rest lately, and they had called several physicians to check her. All of them said the same thing. She missed her late husband dreadfully. And as time wore on, the pain also mounted.

Everyone gathered around the Christmas tree, joined a few minutes later by his mother. Together, they carolled, excitedly discussing what the rest of the week would hold.

***

Tears leaked down Addy's face as she stared down into the little face. Her daughter had at last arrived, and it made her heart ache with a pride and joy she scarcely knew to be possible. The door burst open and Alistair strode in, his face shining with exhilaration. "Addy!" he cried, rushing over to the bed where she lay, their infant in her arms. "Is it really—"

"A daughter," she finished, nodding. "Meet Diana."

"Diana," he echoed, awe in his voice. She held out the baby to him and he received her, holding her with a gentleness that warmed her heart. "Our daughter, Diana. She's beautiful. Just like her mother."

Addy flushed as her husband leaned over to press a kiss on her cheek.

But his smile couldn't disguise a hint of sorrow. His mother had passed only a month earlier, and it grieved them both that she'd never been able to meet her granddaughter—her only granddaughter. They both knew though that Rosalind Dowden had gone to be with her beloved husband. Still, it hurt to know she would never meet Diana.

"Diana Rose. Our Christmas Rose," Alistair grinned, his eyes moist. "Now, I imagine she will be somewhat headstrong. Don't you?"

"Oh, but of course. How could she not be, with a father like me?"

"And a mother like me," Addy laughed.

She stared down into her daughter's little face. She bore some resemblance to Alistair, around the eyes. But her mouth was all Addy. So was her expression. "I didn't know it was possible to love this much," she whispered, shaking her head.

Alistair nodded, cupping his daughter's little face. He gave the baby his forefinger, and she gripped it in her fist. "She'd got immense strength," he chuckled.

"She will be an excellent rider, I think," James declared, stepping into the bedroom. Along with him came Serena, their son in her arms. He was a few months older than Diana, and when Diana began to fuss, so did he.

"I believe Eloise and Crawford will arrive soon. Everyone is eager to meet the little girl. And Mother and Father will be here soon as well. I am sure they are anxious to see their granddaughter."

Later yet, after everyone had retired for the night, the house settling, Addy slipped out of bed and stole across the room to peer into the cradle where Diana slept. It was difficult to believe she was the mother to this darling little girl. She started slightly when a hand touched her shoulder. "Addy, how is she?"

"Sleeping," Addy replied. "Very peaceful. Very sweet."

"If Belinda's children are anything to go on, we shall have a time of it with this little one."

"Are you up to the challenge?" Addy smirked.

"Oh yes. Very."

Alistair pressed a kiss into her curly hair, before drawing her back to the bed where they perched, unable to look away from their daughter. She truly was perfect in every sense of the word.

Early the next morning, Addy woke up restless. She rose, tied her hair back, slipped on a cloak, and kissed Alistair on his forehead, and then Diana on the cheek. She tiptoed down the winding corridors, across the garden, until she reached the stables.

There, Ares was saddled for her, and off she rode. It had yet to snow this year, and she didn't mind. She loved the way mist settled over the hills and forests on mornings like this; it was breathtaking to see. She rode on and on until she came to a perfect rise in one of the Dowden farm fields, watching the sun crest above the horizon.

A little over three years ago, she had gotten married. And she had sworn she wouldn't. She'd been so desperate to remain unmatched, to guard herself. And though she still valued independence, she knew it did not need to come at the expense of peace, and joy.

She blew out a breath, watching as a little cloud of frost appeared in the air.

Thundering hoofbeats rose from the field she overlooked on her hill. Squinting down, she recognised that horse, and that coat. Sure enough, the rider advanced up the hill until he was standing just a few feet away. "Lady Dowden," Alistair grinned, dismounting. She hurried into his arms.

"How was Diana when you left her?"

"In good hands. Gemma is attending to her."

"How did you know I would come here?" Addy smirked, giving Alistair a teasing nudge.

"It's your favourite spot on our land." Alistair wrapped an arm around her, and together they watched the sun rise high above the treetops.

***

"Mamma!" Diana called, racing in from the terrace. A glance at her skirts told Addy that her daughter had ventured too far, mired herself in a large puddle, or something or other.

On her heels came little George, named after Alistair's father. George loved to tag along with Diana, curious about all that she did. It was heartwarming, to say the least, even if it mortified Diana to no end. "Mamma, when will cousin Jack and Maria be here?"

"Before long, my dear," Addy said softly.

"With Aunt Eloise and Uncle Will?" Diana added. "Uncle James and Aunt Serena?"

"But of course. They always come for Christmas," Addy smiled, eyes widening as the infant growing inside her gave a kick. Well, she'd certainly inherited that tendency from Addy. The thought made her laugh inwardly.

"And the Malcolms will come as well?"

"Yes, they shall. And so will their daughters. Will you show them about the grounds?"

"Really?" Diana did a little jig right then and there. "I can scarcely wait."

"I can. You all leave me out dreadfully," George grumbled. Diana groaned

"Yes, take your brother along. Please," Addy urged her daughter.

"Fine. May I go wait on the steps?"

"Of course, go on," Addy nodded and turned her attention back to the new wreath she'd begun for this Christmas. She had also had the boxes of ornaments brought out for use this week to decorate the tree.

Diana appeared in the doorway, panting. "Grandmother and Grandfather just drove up."

"Wonderful!" Addy beamed. "Why don't you bring them into the drawing room."

While it wasn't nearly as extravagant as Aunt Worthington's, it was everything Addy wanted it to be. It was cosy and warm in the winter. And she loved the nights she and her husband shared in front of the fire, the scent of spruce and fir strong in her nose on winter nights like these. It brought back memories of that Christmas when everything had changed.

Now, Christmas was her favourite holiday, because of what it had brought her. That night, Addy, Alistair, Serena, Captain Crawford, James, Eloise, Mother and Father, and all the children sat around that fire and told stories. Addy shared her favourite tale of their early days—how she and Alistair had met—and she never tired of telling it.

"You and Papa knew each other when you were children?" Diana giggled, leaning into Addy's arm.

She always loved the story of how her parents fell in love.

"We weren't the best of friends as children," Alistair chuckled. "But that all changed when we met again."

"I remember always trying to keep the peace between them," James spoke up, his hand interlaced with Serena's. "Seems as if I was always trying to break up a silly quarrel between them."

"But you and Papa don't quarrel any more," said George, tilting his head curiously.

"No, not any longer. Sometimes we might disagree, but we've learned a great deal about loving one another, despite our differences."

"Indeed," Alistair agreed. Addy flashed him a soft smile, her heart lifting. She proceeded to talk about their first meeting after years of not seeing each other. She relayed the memory of how on the steps of Aunt Agatha's and Uncle Richard's home, she'd expected Alistair to make some sort of remark about her, one which she would answer in kind.

But instead, it had just been the beginning of something almost too good to be true.

She gazed around the room then, reflecting that she would have never had this if she had clung so tightly to independence that she would surrender love.

Captain Crawford and Eloise sat together on the nearby settee, watching their daughter Agatha roast nuts with the other children over the leaping flames. James and Serena's daughter, Margaret, perched beside James, asking him to tell their love story all over again, earning a grin from him.

Addy's parents shared the other settee, also surveying the cosy scene. And in the corner stood the Christmas Tree, shimmering and beautifully bedecked in an assortment of ribbons and bows and garlands and lace. Addy leaned her head against Alistair's arm. No matter what happened she couldn't wait to face the future with those she loved.

The End

Printed in Dunstable, United Kingdom